DATE DUE

AUG -3 1998	
SEP 2 1 1998	

HORSE OF A
DIFFERENT KILLER

HORSE
OF A
DIFFERENT
KILLER

JODY JAFFE

FAWCETT COLUMBINE • NEW YORK

A Fawcett Columbine Book
Published by Ballantine Books

Copyright © 1995 by Jody Jaffe

All rights reserved under International and Pan-American
Copyright Conventions. Published in the United States by Ballantine Books,
a division of Random House, Inc., New York, and simultaneously
in Canada by Random House of Canada Limited, Toronto.

Jaffe, Jody.
Horse of a different killer / by Jody Jaffe.
p.   cm.
ISBN 0-449-90997-2
I. Title.
PS3560.A3125H67   1995
813'.54—dc20   95-6488
                                                                CIP

Designed by Ann Gold

Manufactured in the United States of America

First Edition: September 1995

10   9   8   7   6   5   4   3   2   1

To the Shepard boys: Charlie, Ben, and Sam.
And in memory of Arthur Isaac, the last bombardier.

ACKNOWLEDGMENTS

Getting your first book published is like winning an Oscar in a way: By the time you get there, you've got fifty-four pages of people to thank. I've whittled mine down considerably, eliminating among others, my first-grade teacher who put my hand-printed sheetful of J's I agonized over for hours underneath the pencil sharpeners to collect pencil droppings.

First to my agent, Rafe Sagalyn, the godfather of this book and the series. Thanks for the idea, the help, and most of all, for selling it to such a good house, Fawcett. To the women of Fawcett, Leona Nevler and especially my editor, Barbara Dicks—better watch out, you're going to give editors a good name. To Barbara's assistant Jennifer Scott, for her cheerful assistance whenever I called, and for always laughing at my jokes.

To my friend Mary Beth Gibson, thank you for the shrewd advice. Also to Jean McMillan of The Mystery Bookstore in Bethesda for advice, encouragement, and two Malice Domestic T-shirts for my sons. Jerry Bledsoe and John Katzenbach took time out from their busy schedules to help out this first-time author—it's much appreciated. To my cybernetic friends Lise McClendon and Lary Crews, thanks for all your help.

On the equine front, Peter Foley deserves a round of applause not only for being the best trainer a timid amateur could have, but for his considerable copyediting and reading skills. Also to Maggie Farance for her knowledge of show horses and her generosity in sharing it. To Dr. Venaye Reese, of the Clemson University live-stock-poultry health department, thanks for telling me about South Carolina equine laws and sending me photocopies of them. And to Brett Reilly and Owen Preston for answering my many horse-shoeing questions.

To Henry Eichel, unofficial low-country historian, thank you for letting me pick your brain. To Alan Dynerman, for his wit, from which this book has greatly benefited. To Vicky Baily, Abbi Bardi, Rachel Carpenter, Len Kruger, and Elise Russo, my faithful writing buddies, for whom I expect to be attending the National Book Awards someday—your encouragement and cogent critiques were invaluable. And to the Politics and Prose coffeehouse for putting up with our raucous meetings. Although my first-grade teacher needs no mention, my writing teachers do: Pam Painter, Anne Bernays, and, especially, Howard Norman.

Since, to me, this book is about the immutable bond between best friends, to my best friend, Anne Boas Sagalyn (who bears no resemblance to Nattie's best friend Gail). Thank you for being my personal medical library, for your encouragement, and most of all, for your friendship.

Finally to my family; to my grandmother Maye P. Steinberg for the red hair, the strong will, and whatever smarts I've got. To my mother Anne Isaac, for among other things, the writing and tenacity genes; my father Philip Jaffe, for the riding genes and sense of wonder; my brother Ricky Jaffe for the legal counsel; my sister-in-law Amy Jaffe for her enthusiasm; and my mother-in-law Jo Shepard for her unbridled optimism. I wish my stepfather Arthur Isaac could have been around to read this. He would have been most proud.

Last and most important, to my boys. My husband, Charlie Shepard, for his relentless belief in me, and to our wonderful sons, Ben and Sam. Thanks for sharing the computer! I love you boys. Now go to bed.

HORSE OF A
DIFFERENT KILLER

PROLOGUE

There might have been a moon outside, but who could tell. It was like the earth was sweating, that's how thick the air was. Not even a sliver of light could pierce the dense blanket of humidity.

Rob Stone looked out the barn doors. He could barely see where the ground stopped and the sky started. His salmon Polo shirt lay close against his skin, moist and hot. He pulled at the front of it, blowing air between his chest and the soggy cotton mesh, trying to cool off. But nothing helped to cut through the dampness for long on these steamy Carolina nights.

The mercury hadn't budged below ninety for nearly two weeks. The horses were sweating so hard they looked like they'd been slicked down with a thick coat of Vaseline. Stone didn't like to run the fans all night. One spark could set the barn crackling, but unending heat like this could make a horse colic. And a bad case of colic, a plain old stomachache to a human, could make a horse twist its insides into a pretzel until they ruptured like a smashed water balloon.

Stone didn't want to chance that. Everything had to be better than perfect for tomorrow. He walked down the aisle, plugged in the fans above each horse's stall, and turned them to the highest speed. As he neared Ruskie's stall, the horse flattened his ears and lunged for him.

"You stupid piece of shit," Stone said. "If you weren't worth a quarter of a million dollars, I'd slam your ass back to Camden."

Ruskie was the most valuable horse in the barn. He was also the meanest. He kicked, he bit, he reared, and he lunged. But he could jump like a jackrabbit. He tucked his front legs up to his ears and made a course of four-foot fences look as effortless as if he were cantering over poles laid flat on the ground.

He was so beautiful that all the little horse-crazy girls at the shows dragged their well-coiffed mothers to Ruskie's stall so they could pet him. Even after they were told to stay away, warned that he would bite them just as soon as he'd look at them, they stood and stared. He was that beautiful.

Part of it was his size. He was huge and ripply with muscles like an Olympic runner's. At seventeen and a half hands high, Ruskie stood bigger than any horse on the A-show circuit. Stone couldn't see over the top of the horse's shoulders and Stone himself was five feet ten.

A pearl-white blaze ran down the center of Ruskie's face. The rest of his coat was a deep chocolate brown, so dark and shiny he looked like glistening hot fudge.

Stone found Ruskie three years ago at the training track in Camden, South Carolina. He'd placed in a few races, but he wasn't fast enough for the trainers to mess with his meanness. Stone got the big horse for two thousand dollars and he knew he had something special. Last year Ruskie was Green Conformation Hunter Champion at the two biggest and most prestigious horse shows in the country—the National Horse Show and the Washington International. This year he was so far ahead in Horse of the Year points that no one could catch up.

The next morning at ten, Lucy Bladstone, wife of L. M. Bladstone of Bladstone Foods, Tobacco and Textiles, was coming with her trainer, Wally Hempstead. She wanted to try Ruskie one last time before she wrote the check. A check for $250,000.

Ruskie had just two things to do for the sale to go through. He had to do what he did naturally: jump brilliantly. And he had to pass the veterinarian's exam.

Stone flipped off the lights and walked into the soupy night air. He could hear twenty-four fans behind him, all whirring at high speed. He went around the side of the barn and stepped quickly upstairs to his apartment. He peeled off his clothes, took a fast shower, and put on a pair of pajamas—blue-and-white-striped Calvin Kleins with knife-blade creases pressed deeply into the legs and arms. Then he opened his drawer and flipped through a pile of neatly folded Polo shirts. He pulled out the deep aquamarine with the magenta signature Polo pony, the shirt that made his tan look tanner and his blue eyes bluer. Next to them, he placed a clean pair of jeans, pressed, like his pajamas, with sharp creases down the center of each leg. Tomorrow, he had to look fabulous, better than ever. He wanted to make Wally Hempstead realize what he was missing.

He turned his air conditioner up to Super Cool, got in bed, and fell asleep. Stone slept light enough that he could usually hear trouble in the barn. If a horse got cast in a stall, he'd hear the horse banging against the walls scrambling to get unstuck. Before the horse could get to all fours, Stone would be there helping him up.

But between the air conditioner and the fans, Stone didn't hear anything that night but a loud whir.

CHAPTER 1

"Watch out, here comes the Shoe Salesman," Jeff Fox said, attempting the impossible for him—a whisper. His desk is next to mine. We allegedly share a computer, but he hogs it, claiming priority because as TV critic he has to pump out daily stories. That means I have to search the newsroom for an available computer, which is just as well. He talks so loud, each time his phone rings I'm forced to listen to every comma in his conversation. Fifteen minutes ago I heard him say this to a caller: "No, ma'am, I don't know Mister Rogers's sexual orientation. No, ma'am, I don't know where you could find that out. And thank you so much for calling."

Being polite to readers is the big push from the new editor, Fred Richards, aka the "Shoe Salesman." That's about how smart he is and how much integrity he has. It was Jeff who discovered the nickname. Richards had been tagged the "Shoe Salesman" by the other editors in the chain that owns our newspaper, *The Charlotte Commercial Appeal.* Jeff had gone looking for a job at our sister paper, *The Miami Morning News,* a scrappy little tabloid that runs headlines like "Fry Him" over stories about convicted child killers. Halfway into his final interview, the executive editor turned to Jeff and said, "So how is it working for the Shoe Salesman?" Jeff didn't get the job, but our newsroom got a great nickname for Richards.

Richards is fixated on what he calls "customer satisfaction." What he really means is advertiser satisfaction. In the four months since he took charge of *The Appeal*, we've already lost our best columnist. Richards pulled one of his columns, a hilarious piece about used-car dealers, saying it was loaded with stereotypes. "We wouldn't run a story about black people and watermelon or money and Jews," Richards argued. Larry, the columnist, tried to explain that used-car dealers weren't a religious group or a race of people, though they may seem like one. Richards remained steadfast. Larry crumpled up his column, threw it in Richards's face, stormed out of the building and into a job with the *Los Angeles Post*. Now he's the number one syndicated humor columnist in the country.

Richards's customer satisfaction mentality does extend down to the readers. Every last one of them. Any reporter who gets caught being rude to a reader is summoned to Richards's office for an interrogation. Then, with the boss standing close enough to invade your personal space, you have to call the offended person, no matter how offensive he or she had been to you, and grovel, apologizing like a Catholic-school girl who got caught with her hand where it wasn't supposed to be, until the boss gives you the okay sign.

"Uh, oh, Nattie," Jeff said, trying even harder to whisper, which was still louder than any normal person talked. "He's heading right toward you and he's got that man-on-a-mission look. You must have really pissed someone off."

Jeff was probably right. It's hard to believe how many people call a newspaper each day. Lonely people who have nothing to do but ask reporters questions like the one about Mister Rogers's sexuality. And it's even worse for me. As fashion writer, my beat taps into the all-important great universal concern: How do I look? People call me constantly, asking what they should wear. I'd like to tell them to worry about something important, like world hunger or the political aspirations of Arnold Schwarzenegger. Instead, I reassure them that their white chiffon from 1974 will do fine for their great-niece's garden wedding.

People don't want to hear the truth, they just want ammunition: "Well, the fashion editor of *The Commercial Appeal* told me it was all right to wear this." I am really only the fashion writer, but readers feel a need to elevate my authority to editor status. They'd knock me down to janitor if they knew how I dress. I've lost count of how many times Richards has talked to me about wearing inappropriate clothes to work—minis, jeans, vintage clothes. In the South, anything outside of khaki, oxford, and Add-a-Beads is inappropriate.

Today I'm actually almost up to code. Quietly flowered blouse, tasteful red skirt to my knees; the only thing wrong with the picture is my blue suede oxfords and lime-green socks, but they're tucked under my desk. So why is Richards marching up to my desk like I'd told the Miss Chitlin Queen of Rocky Mount it's okay to wear white shoes before Memorial Day? What could he want with that kind of look on his face?

"Nattie," Fred said to me, "don't you know something about horses?"

More, I hoped, than he would ever realize. Some days I cut out of work for an hour to ride my horse.

"I know a little bit," I said. "What's up, Fred?"

He pulled up a chair, put his hand down first, and slowly lowered his large rear into it. I wondered if he had hemorrhoids.

"There's a farm outside Charlotte, near Waxhaw," Fred said. "Apparently it's home to some rather expensive show horses. I mean rather expensive. Six digits. Why anyone would pay that much for a horse is beyond me. Anyway, the damnedest thing happened last night. A dead man was found in a stall. He had a bloody crowbar in his hands and was apparently attacking a horse. The horse was barely alive when they found him, broken legs, blood all over the place. By then I guess he was beyond help. So they had to—"

Fred put his index finger to his forehead, cocked his thumb as if it were a gun, and said, "Bang."

"It happened at a place called February Farm? Ever hear of it?"

February Farm. My heart slammed against my ribs and I must have turned paler than normal, which was pretty pasty being a white-skinned red-haired Jew who bubbled and blistered from the sun. February Farm was where I kept my horse.

"Nattie, are you all right? Are you going to be sick?" Fred said.

"Do you know which horse was killed?" I said so quietly Fred had to lean over close to hear me.

"All I heard was that it was an extraordinarily expensive horse that was supposed to be sold today to one of the Bladstones from Camden," Fred said.

Whew. My horse was cheap by horse-show standards and not for sale. Still, a horse was attacked at my barn and I slept through the night without even a tingle down my back? Usually I know when something's wrong at the barn. Though I have had an embarrassing number of false alarms and rushed out in the middle of the night to find a stable full of sleepy-eyed horses startled by my sudden intrusion. I'm a worrier and it's hard to find the line between intuition and worry. I have, however, been right more than I've been wrong. Like when a pretty black foal got its halter caught on a nail. It was three in the morning and I couldn't decide whether I should call the owner. I did, and she didn't believe me at first. I kept telling her that this time I was right. And I was. Except she got there too late. The foal had already hung itself.

Things like that have been happening to me my whole life. I

9

never told anyone, except my best friend's grandmother. The only reason I told her is that she told me first. It was twenty-five years ago. I was eleven, she was peeling carrots, making tzimmes for Rosh Hashanah. "Red-haired Jews and green-eyed colored people," she said, and looked straight at me, like she was looking into me. "You're one and the same. Special. You're not tied to the ground like we are. You know things. God gave you extra to make up for all the bad he let happen to your mothers' mothers."

I didn't know what she was talking about. All I could say back was "Don't make stuffed cabbage." She looked at me funny for a second, then said, "Nattie dear, what will be will be."

Two weeks later she died—no one could have predicted it, she was as healthy as a horse. They found her facedown in a plate of steamed cabbage, her fingers locked around a ball of chopped meat and rice. I knew it before my best friend told me.

I don't know how I know these things. I just do. My father's channeler says I have the most direct connection with horses because I'm karmically linked to equines. Apparently, I was Catherine the Great in a previous life.

All I know is that last night it was too hot to even be alive, let alone receive karma-controlled signals from a horse in distress. I'd stuck my head out the window, trying to suck in whatever bit of coolness I could find. It was dark, moist, and so close, I wondered if I was getting for free what my father just paid five hundred dollars for. He'd spent the weekend with an earth goddess from Cincinnati who went by the name of Celestial Wild-Wombmyn, nee Shirley Moscowitz. Ms. Wild-Wombmyn/Moscowitz promised to re-seize my father's child from within by rebirthing him in an Indian sweat lodge. He could have visited me if he wanted a sweat lodge.

I had to push my bed over to the far wall, so I could sleep with my head stuck out the window. That's the only way I could fall asleep in my apartment. No air-conditioning. It seemed fine when I moved to North Carolina two and a half years ago. I'd come from way upstate New York, where I stayed cold from September to June. I didn't have a clue what a southern summer could be like.

The rent was cheap—two hundred dollars. I couldn't, and still can't, afford anything more, because my horse's board is three hundred and fifty dollars and I've got about 125 years left of student loans that my father took out in my name and forgot to pay. And I'm also paying fifty dollars a month in pasture board for my first horse, who's been retired for more years than he worked and is fast approaching Ripley's Believe It or Not for horse longevity. It sounds crazy, paying more rent for a horse than for myself. I have, however, gotten better over the years about taking care of myself. Still, when it comes to horses, I get lost.

I was one of the horse-crazy girls who grew up to be a horse-crazy woman. I've had horses on the brain since I could remember. When I was little, I thought about them all the time, from when I woke up till I went to sleep, and then in my dreams. I'd see a picture of a horse and kiss it ten times for luck that soon I'd have a horse of my own.

My mother would buy me Barbie dolls, I'd cut off their yellow cottony waves and turn them into butchy-looking women with buzzed-off hair and I'd mix up and layer their clothes so they looked like bag ladies. I don't want dolls, I'd tell my mother. Buy me a horse.

"Such big dreams for such a little pisher," my mother would say. "Where do you get these dreams, from your father? Tell that no-good gonif to send the child support checks instead of filling your head with such nonsense. Who do you know that lives in a row house and has a horse? What do you think we are, Rockefellers?"

So she got me plastic horses instead. Creamy golden palominos with high-arched necks and black stallions upright on their powerful haunches, striking out against imaginary foes with their front legs. I played for hours and hours with my plastic horses.

When my body started changing and my thoughts wandered to the forbidden, it was horses that took me there. With the other horse-crazy girls—and there were plenty of them—we'd play stallions and mares, sometimes with our plastic horses, sometimes with ourselves. You be the mare, I'll be the stallion, one of us would say, and we'd climb on top of each other and pretend to mate.

Black Beauty was the first thing I remember reading and I read it fifteen or twenty times, praying with each page I turned that my next birthday morning I'd wake up to a fat gray pony like Merrylegs in my backyard. It never happened, so I took matters into my own hands. I opened a savings account at Philadelphia Fidelity Savings, Overbrook Park branch, when I was ten. A dime a week. By the time I was seventeen, I had four hundred dollars. That year I went to college, the University of Colorado, and bought my first horse with my savings. Homer. His full name was Homely Homer, because he had the biggest head in the barn. To me, he was the Black Stallion, he was My Friend Flicka, he was National Velvet. I cleaned stalls to pay his board. I skipped my classes to ride and brush him.

Then I dropped out of college altogether. A horse bum. I lived in a dirt-floored cellar for twenty-five dollars a month. My drinking water came from the bottom of the hot-water heater and I had to go outside and up the side entrance of the house to use the bathroom. Homer, meanwhile, lived in a heated barn with automatic waterers and a hot-water wash stall.

I was slinging pancakes on the graveyard shift at IHOP, pulling in a hundred and fifty dollars a week. It was barely enough to support me and Homer. I didn't have the talent to be a professional rider or the right kind of smarts to make it through vet school. Some sane part of me knew I needed a life outside of horses. I knew my strengths—I was a gifted busybody, I'd ask anyone anything, and people always wound up telling me their life stories. And I've always loved to write. It was time to get a degree so I could get a real job.

My mother and father, who hadn't spoken to each other outside a courtroom for ten years, actually came up with a plan. They'd kick in the money to get me back east. My father said he'd handle the college tuition and I had to scrape up the dough to get Homer a ride cross-country.

So I did it. Everything worked according to plan. I got a degree in communication arts and climbed my way up the newspaper ladder to where I am now—fashion writer at *The Charlotte Commercial Appeal.*

I'd never known or cared anything about clothes, but I'd have written about garbage men to get a job on *The Appeal.* It's hard to believe after working here, but pros rank *The Appeal* in the top ten of American newspapers. I think that says more about how bad the other newspapers are than how good *The Appeal* is.

I've been asking the editors to move me off fashion and onto general assignment feature writing for the past year and a half. All I've gotten so far are a lot of "soons" and "when the budget opens up. . . ." It'll do for now. I'm not looking at snow in June and I can run out in the middle of the day to ride my horse without my bosses knowing. They're always in meetings—planning, charting, polling the future wants of newspaper readers. Best of all, my horse, a sweet-natured chestnut mare I show under the name Brenda Starr, lives at the barn of my dreams.

February Farm is horse heaven. The stalls are huge, twelve by twelve, and bedded knee deep in fresh pine shavings. They've got miles of the prettiest trails I've ever ridden on, an Olympic-size ring, and the trainer, Rob Stone, is a miracle worker with horses, albeit socially retarded with people and verbally abusive to his riders. He's done nothing but yell at me for the past two and a half years. However, under his tutelage I've gone from getting fourth and fifth places at local B-rated shows to thirds and even an occasional first and second at the biggest A-rated shows in the Southeast. Whatever else anyone says about him, Rob knows horses. He can turn a two-thousand-dollar plug into a triple-digit star.

Which is what he had done with Ruskie. That must have been the horse Fred was talking about. Ruskie was the most beautiful piece of horseflesh I'd ever seen. He went by the name Russian Caviar at the shows. I knew that Lucy Bladstone was supposed to come today to buy him. But I also knew that Ruskie couldn't make it around a course without his B&B cocktail. That's Bute and Banamine, two painkillers mixed together and shot into the neck or rump muscle to make an overworked, over-shown horse go sound. And when that didn't take the ouches out of him, they'd shoot him up with ten or twenty cc's of Ketofen, a so-far-unrestricted drug that trainers say you can practically show a broken-legged horse on.

Just yesterday Rob had the blacksmith switch Ruskie's shoes from lightweight aluminum to a heavier steel, hoping the extra protection on his feet might help him vet out sound.

"Fred, let me work on this," I said. "I know the horse world. I know the horse that got killed. I have sources that even Henry couldn't have."

Henry was Henry Goode, Mr. Investigative Reporter of *The Commercial Appeal*, the reigning king of news side. While everyone else had to crank out enough stories to make a quota, Henry could work at his leisure on the blockbuster of his choice. He did, I must admit, earn that privilege. He won *The Commercial Appeal* its first gold medal Pulitzer for Public Service by breaking the Jim and Tammy Bakker story and toppling PTL, a multimillion-dollar

Christian televangelistic empire that had a theme park resort outside of Charlotte.

"No can do, Nattie," Fred said. "This is strictly a news side story. Maybe you can do a color piece, say a fifteen-inch sidebar on what the people wear on the horse show circuit. I've already told Henry about it. He's hot to trot. Ha, get it, hot to trot? When you get a chance, why don't you tell him what you know."

"Color piece my ass," I whispered under my breath. Once again the features department was getting the shaft. Whenever a really meaty story came our way, one of the news side editors yanked it their way. Not this time. I smiled at Fred and said, "I'll go talk to Henry."

Funny thing about Henry, he bore a striking resemblance to Ruskie. He was big, gorgeous, and, from what I'd heard, would fight to the end like poor Ruskie had apparently done. Henry towered above everyone else. He was six-four or better. He had a J. Crew kind of face with those perfect boarding-school bones: broad cheeks that swept out and upward at just the right pitch, a nose that half my ninth-grade class paid Dr. Diamond five thousand dollars for, and eyes clear and crystalline blue as the ocean his family's summer home no doubt looked out over somewhere on Cape Cod.

He was incredibly handsome in a high-octane super-Wasp way.

"Hey, Henry," I said, "I hear you're working the horse beat now."

Henry looked up at me and smiled. I forgot to mention his smile. Perfect teeth, of course, neatly aligned like the queen's soldiers. And whiter than a peppermint Chiclet.

"Nattie, I was just on my way over to talk to you. Let's talk horses. Tell me what you know about February Farm."

CHAPTER 2

Henry Goode was famous for getting people to spill their guts without realizing their stomachs had been slit halfway to their chins and back. He spoke in a calm, reassuringly clinical manner that made you feel like you were talking to Dr. Kildare—and that everything would be okay afterward even if you had inoperable brain cancer. People ended up telling him astonishing things, like when he got Jim Bakker's boyhood friend talking. Before the guy knew it, he was going on and on about Bakker as a young Bible-college student and how he wouldn't wear underwear on his dates with Tammy. That way he could feel it better when he rubbed up against her. Then Henry got the head of First Carolina yakking about his bank's business dealings with South African companies that supported apartheid. When it hit the paper, the bank head publicly announced he'd severed all connections to those companies and privately vowed he would never talk to another newspaper reporter again.

So where was Henry's magic touch now? Asking me straight out what I knew? Maybe I'd been staring at him too much and he thought I'd be dying to spill my guts to *the* Henry Goode. What he didn't factor in was this: I may be a sucker for tall blonds with good bones, in fact my life story could be called Natalie Gold: In Search of the Goyisha God, but I know where to draw the line when it comes to doing stupid things for a guy. The line is work and in the twelve years I've been a reporter, I've yet to cross it.

16

I wasn't about to write a color piece on the latest equestrian fashions, not when there was a bloody corpse and a dead $250,000 horse twenty minutes from my desk. Any story coming out of February Farm was going to have two names on the byline: Henry Goode *and* Natalie Gold.

"Let's talk on the way," I said, and started walking toward the door.

"The way where?" Henry had gotten out of his chair and without much effort had caught up with me. His legs were a good twelve inches longer than mine. Walking next to him I felt like a Shetland pony trying to keep pace with a steeplechase horse.

"February Farm," I said. "Where else? Knowing the Waxhaw sheriff's department, I'll bet you anything the dead guy's still in the stall with a swarm of flies buzzing around his head."

We walked down four flights of escalators before we reached the lobby. As we were going down, I saw my friend, Kathy Powell, the popular music critic, coming up—a smiling blur of purple and red. She was blurry because we were moving fast, with Henry's daddy-longlegs legs and my urgency to beat the medical examiner to the barn. She was smiling because just yesterday we'd made a list of all the cute guys in the newsroom and rated them on how we thought each would be in bed. Henry scored the highest. "I saw him dance at a party," Kathy had said. "He was something else. The music was reggae, early Bob Marley, and he had Wendy—remember when they were going out?—pressed up against a wall, writhing in and out to the beat. I thought she was going to come right there. If not her, me."

So he can dance. Like I said, I don't cross the stupid-tricks-for-a-cute-guy line when it comes to work. I can compartmentalize.

"Look at this lobby," I said to Henry, "any crazed Christian could come in and gun you down."

"I don't think that's likely," he said.

After breaking the Jim and Tammy Bakker story, the paper

17

shipped Henry out of town because of the death threats from offended evangelicals who thought Henry was Satan's errand boy. The publisher hired an armed guard. That lasted a week. Now, there was no security in the lobby. Any lunatic could come in and usually did. Last week a man came wandering into the newsroom with architectural drawings of a parking lot that stored cars like a dry cleaner stores hanging clothes. You bring the parking lot attendant your ticket, he presses a button, and your car comes down a ratcheted track in its number-coded compartment. He thought it would be the ideal parking lot for *The Commercial Appeal* and not wanting to be rude to a member of the reading public, Fred, the Shoe Salesman/editor, met with him for almost an hour before pawning him off to the business editor.

"Let's take your car," I said to Henry. It had to be better than mine, an old diesel Rabbit with no air-conditioning. We walked across the parking lot, a plain, flat concrete affair with faded yellow lines. I followed him to his car; sure enough it was a new and shiny silver Accord. I wondered how he was going to fold himself up into it.

He unlocked my side first. I sat down on a water pistol and released enough water to make it look as if I'd had a urinary accident.

"Sorry about that," Henry said. "I keep telling Chet to take his toys out of the car. He's eight, and preadolescence seems to have arrived early, so his answer to any of my requests is a sneer. But he's a great kid. Want to see his picture?"

Before I got to the downswing on my nod "Yes," Henry pulled his wallet from his pants and flipped open to a portrait of two little blond boys. They looked like miniature Henrys.

"Gorgeous kids," I said. Standard answer to kiddy pix. But this time I meant it. Henry, as clichéd as it sounds, beamed beacon bright.

I'd heard that Henry was a single father, absolutely devoted to his sons. The story was that Henry's then-wife, a labor organizer he met in college (he—Harvard; she—Radcliffe), was drafted by the new Teamsters to clean up the old Teamsters in Newark. Apparently Henry refused to go because he didn't want his kids breathing New Jersey air, which is something like the equivalent of smoking fifteen packs of Luckies every hour. So they worked out joint custody, where Henry gets the kids during the school year and the now-ex-wife gets them summers and holidays as long as she takes them someplace other than Newark.

I handed Henry the orange plastic water pistol. He slipped it into his shirt pocket and walked around to his side of the car. For someone almost as tall as Lurch, he fit himself in quite agilely.

"Okay, we're in the car," he said, "now tell me about February Farm and how a horse that doesn't race could be worth $250,000?"

"Start driving fast," I said. "The Union County sheriffs may be slow, but they're not dead. Take Providence Road all the way. After it becomes Route 16, just keep driving until you stop seeing brick colonials."

I talked as we watched the city of Charlotte, the Queen City of the Carolinas, pass by. One new redbrick subdivision with tons of azaleas after another. We rarely passed a building over twenty or thirty years old. Any signs of heritage or history had been bulldozed to make way for shiny glass skyscrapers with names like NationsBank Towers (dubbed the Taj McColl after the megabank's Napoleonic leader, Hugh McColl). What Charlotte lacked in architectural glory it made up for in the splendor of its trees. Tall, graceful, arching halfway to heaven; they're considered the jewels in the Queen City's crown and the pride of its residents. When Hurricane Hugo veered 250 miles inland and crashed through Charlotte, the city mourned its felled trees with such grief, you would have thought a busload of kids had been killed.

The biggest and most majestic trees live on the many Queens Roads, a labyrinth of streets all with the same name that runs through Myers Park, one of Charlotte's oldest and toniest neighborhoods. No one has ever explained why five or six streets bear the same name. The only thing I can figure is that Queens Road is the high-dollar, old-money address in town, so the developers just kept naming more and more streets Queens Road to cash in. Because there are so many streets by the same name, it's easy to get lost in the Queens Road maze, which isn't such a bad thing if you're not in a hurry. Willow oaks as tall as office buildings line the roads, their top branches interlocking, making canopies of feathery green so you feel like you're driving through a fairy tunnel.

As we drove, I told Henry a little about the horse show world, how $250,000 isn't much money to people who pay cash for two-million-dollar weekend getaways in Virginia hunt country, people whose last names are in every home in America: Dodge, Maytag, Johnson, Bladstone, Du Pont.

"You've got to see it to believe it," I said. "Imagine a gaggle of little ten-year-old girls driving their custom Honda motor-trikes across the horse show grounds while their grooms get their $100,000 ponies ready. They get a leg up on their ponies, canter around the course, get yelled at by their mothers and trainers if they don't get to the fence right, say five inches too close or six inches too far away. Then if they don't get a blue ribbon they throw a major tantrum and Daddy buys them a new, more expensive pony.

"And here's the worst part—nobody ever smiles. You've got a sport that's supposed to be fun and nobody's smiling."

"So why do it?" Henry said.

"I ask myself the same thing all the time. Horses make me feel centered. I know I'm sounding like my father, who's a certified new age flake, but it's true. If I go a week without riding, I feel like I'm losing my footing. Tense would be a kind way to describe me, bitchy would be accurate. When I jump a course of fences with my horse and I get it right, nothing feels better. Then at shows when Rob starts yelling at me, I have to admit it, I'm not doing too much smiling myself."

"Who's Rob?"

We'd turned into the entrance of February Farm, where two huge maples arched across the white crushed-stone driveway.

"That's him," I said, and pointed to a man in a turquoise Polo shirt and crisply pressed jeans. He was sitting next to the front door of the barn, hunched into a navy-blue director's chair with the letters *FF* stenciled in hunter green. He had a paper towel over his mouth, a bucket by his feet, and his eyes were redder than the barn. Just as Henry looked where I was pointing, Rob vomited in the bucket—a hunter-green bucket bearing the FF monogram in navy blue.

"Rob's my trainer," I said as I looked the other way. "He runs the barn for Cameron Clarke."

"Clarke, meaning Clarke crackers?" Henry said.

"You're getting the gist of things now," I said. Every vending machine on earth offers an assortment of Clarke crackers. Cheez'n Wheat, P'NutterButters, Mallowtallows, and so on. The Clarkes were old Charlotte money with half the art museum named after them. All the daughters' daughters were named either Maryclarke, Sarahclarke, Kimclarke, or just plain Clarke.

Henry pulled up by the barn, next to a Union County sheriff's car. One of the officers was outside, ostensibly examining the scene but mostly eating mulberries from a gnarled old tree that looked like the hand of an arthritic giant making a grab for heaven. Since cops come in twos, I figured his partner must be inside, with the corpses.

When Rob glanced up and saw what I had sitting next to me, he kicked the bucket behind the chair and with, I must say, great grace under such circumstances, wiped his mouth clean. Henry and I got out of the car. Rob perked up and actually said hello to me, but he was looking at Henry. In the two and a half years that I'd trained with Rob, we had never had a normal conversation. He'd never said, "Hi, Nattie, how are you," or anything resembling civilized chitchat. Usually I'd be on my horse, warming up for a lesson, he'd walk into the ring, looking immaculate regardless of the weather or mud. Then he would mumble, "How's she going?"—meaning my horse. I'd start talking about how she was going too fast or too slow and he'd interrupt and say, "Just trot." Then we'd get to jumping and if I screwed up really badly, he'd stick his hand on his hip and scream, "Honey, do you think you're driving a Mack truck up there?"

I don't normally care about approval from authority figures; in fact, it's usually just the opposite, but I've always craved it from trainers. They reduce me to tail-wagging, tongue-flapping puppy behavior. And today was no exception.

"Hey, Rob, this is Henry Goode. He works at *The Appeal* with me."

Rob smiled. Even with red eyes and green pallor, he was still pretty damn handsome. Another blond with good bones. But he was so manicured, with every hair in place and so carefully, and artificially, highlighted that he looked like a freshly clipped topiary tree.

If Henry noticed he was being stared at, assessed by Rob, he gave no indication.

"God, you wouldn't believe what happened this morning," Rob said. "It's been the worst day of my life and it should have been the best. First I woke up to . . ."

Rob was being downright talkative for Rob. He must not have

had the what-I-wouldn't-do-for-a-cute-guy line to cross. He was starting to green up again, and I wondered which system had more power over the human body: hormones or gastrointestinal.

"It was Wally," Rob said. "I found him dead in Ruskie's stall. He'd been trying to kill Ruskie."

CHAPTER 3

I left Henry with Rob. Part present to Rob, part present to me. Without Henry I could make my way past the Union County deputy sheriff who was, in fact, milling around the barn.

As I walked inside, I heard the first cop—the mulberry eater—walk up to Rob and Henry. "Mind if I take a look up in the hayloft?" he said to Rob.

"I'd rather you didn't," Rob said. "All the hay is stacked in piles and I don't really want things messed up."

"Look, fella," the cop said, "I could come back with a warrant and be real messy, or I can look now, neatly. It's your call."

"Suit yourself," Rob said. I recognized the sharp snarl in his voice—it's the same tone he takes with me after I pull my horse away from a fence for the third time because it scares me. "It's at least a hundred and eighty degrees up there. Go ahead if you insist. The steps are over there on the left."

I slipped around the back to Ruskie's stall. They were both there. Ruskie and Wally. Both of them bloodier than a package of chopped meat. I felt my stomach lurch and all conscious brain activity fall to my toes. I grabbed the side of the stall as I blacked out. It lasted only a few seconds, but when I came to, I saw Henry standing next to me.

"Nice try, Gold," he said. "Next time tell me where you're going. Rob told me some interesting things."

"I'll just bet he did," I said. "I'm sure he's dying to tell you more later, in private."

Henry laughed and put a hand on my shoulder. "No thanks. Are you okay?"

"I'm woozy, but let's look at this guy before that deputy finds out we're in here."

I took a deep breath and steadied myself, the same way I do before I jump my horse over a big fence. "Throw your heart over first and then go catch it," a trainer once told me. That's what I did as I bent down to examine Wally.

He was puffed out all over, swollen and black and blue from where Ruskie had kicked the shit out of him.

"He took some beating," Henry said. "I didn't realize horses could be so violent."

"You didn't know Ruskie," I said. "Wally picked the wrong horse to tangle with."

I couldn't hold back the tears. Ruskie was lying there with his brains oozing out of his head, his beautiful long legs bent and broken and bloody. If Wally hadn't been dead, I would have punched him in the face.

"I hope he rots in hell," I said, wiping my eyes with the back of my hand and no doubt smearing mascara across my face.

"You're crying over a horse?" Henry said.

"Yes, I am. Do you mind?" I turned back to Wally. He was slumped against the side of the stall with his head falling sideways at an angle possible only by dead people or sleeping babies in car seats. His body was covered with hoof imprints.

"Hey, what in God's name are y'all doing in there? A man's dead and we cayn't have people tearing things up."

I looked up to see the cop staring down at me. He was a man of about thirty-five with dark curly hair and deep olive Mediterranean skin, not exactly back-country-Carolina coloring.

"Oh, hi," I said, trying to act like I was just out at the barn to see my horse. "I own the horse across the aisle. That chestnut with the white blaze."

"Do what?" the cop said.

"That horse, the one sticking her head out of the stall. She's mine. I brought my friend to see her, he used to ride as a kid and he's thinking about starting again. Then Rob told me about poor Ruskie and I just wanted to see what happened. Can you believe someone could be so cruel?"

"Looks like that man got what was coming to him. You better get out of that stall before the medical examiner gets here. He fancies himself Quincy and doesn't like evidence being rustled around even if it was a horse who committed the crime."

I took hold of Henry and pulled him out of the stall. "Well, I hope they get Ruskie and the dead guy out of here soon. Much longer, and you'll need a gas mask it'll smell so much. Come on, Henry, let's see if you're not too tall to ride Brenda."

I opened the door to my horse's stall and motioned for Henry to follow me. After seeing what Ruskie had done to Wally, Henry wasn't keen on coming in.

"Come on, I let my friends' kids ride her. She won't do anything but nuzzle you."

Brenda put her nose to Henry's face and started blowing air. That's how horses check out people. He raised his hand to her neck and stroked her.

"See, you're a natural," I said.

"So who owns Ruskie, and does he or she need money badly enough to have the horse killed?" Henry said. "That's it, isn't it? Insurance, if I'm not mistaken?"

Henry was up on current events. Killing horses used to be horse showing's dirty little secret until July 27, 1994, when the U.S. Attorney handed down twenty-three indictments against some of the industry's most well-known pros.

"You got it," I said. "Disgusting as it may be, killing a horse isn't against the law. It's really up to the insurance agency to prove fraud. Even if the cops figure out why Wally was swinging a crowbar at Ruskie, they won't be that interested. But I'll tell you something it doesn't sound like the deputy knows yet: Ruskie didn't kill Wally. Wally was murdered by someone who wanted it to look like Ruskie killed him."

"And just how do you know that?" Henry said.

"Shh," I said, "don't say anything. Look."

The cop was walking, or, more aptly, ambling down the aisle toward the front door. He stopped by my horse's stall and looked in.

"It's already starting to smell," he said. "I'm gonna wait outside till the M.E. comes. If you can think of any reason this fella might've been hammering away on that big horse, call me, would you? Name's Odom, Detective Tony Odom. Here's my number."

He wrote it down on the back of a dry cleaner's tag.

"I'll think about it and call you if I can come up with anything," I said.

"You do that now, hear?" He looked my way a few seconds longer than needed. I was the one who broke the stare.

"Sure will," I said. "Watch out you don't get sunstroke in this heat."

He turned to walk away and then stopped. He pointed at Henry's shirt and said, "Hey, you got a license to carry a concealed weapon?"

Henry blanched for a second and then slapped at his shirt pocket, remembering his son's water pistol. Odom laughed and finally walked away.

At the front of the barn he stopped by the double sliding doors. Both sides of the walls were lined with color eight-by-tens, framed and matted. Some were of Melissa Mayfield, whose father developed half of Charlotte before his company went belly-up. Rob started training her as an eight-year-old on ponies and took her all the way up to the National Horse Show. She won large junior hunter champion three years straight. But most of the pictures were of Ruskie, either jumping fences or wearing the tricolor champion ribbon.

Odom was looking at the photos and I wondered if he recognized the rider atop Ruskie. It was Wally Hempstead.

I turned to Henry. "I think we should get out of here before that detective gets more curious."

"I don't think he gives a damn about the horse," Henry said. "He was trying to figure out who I was and what my connection to you is. I think he's interested in you. Maybe he wants to find out if it's true what they say about Yankee women."

"And exactly what is that?" I asked.

"Some other time, let's head back," Henry said. "The smell's getting a little thick in here for me, too."

Rob was still sitting out front, looking green enough to clash with his turquoise shirt. Tony Odom had walked out by the paddock. He was stroking Allie, formally known as All Dressed Up—a gorgeous blood bay gelding that belonged to my best friend, Gail—but watching me and Henry get in the car.

I waved bye to him, feeling a little uncomfortable. I wasn't wearing a bra, not that I needed one. I didn't have much to jiggle, even at a flat-out gallop. But I wondered if Odom could tell and add that to his preconceptions about Yankee women.

Henry walked past Rob and laid a hand on his shoulder. "Thanks for your help, Rob. I hope you feel better. If there's anything else you can think of about Wally and why he'd do this, call me at *The Appeal*."

Boy, talk about working a source.

We got back in Henry's Honda and blasted the air-conditioning.

As we headed down the driveway, the tires of Henry's car crunched the crushed stone.

"Spill it, Nattie. If that deputy thinks the horse killed Wally, why is it that you think Wally was murdered?"

"I don't think," I said, "I know."

"Okay, then, how do you know?" Henry said.

"Let's get something settled first," I said. "I have the contacts, I know the horse world. So are we working on this together?"

"Sure, you can tell me if everyone is color coordinated." Henry was smiling, so I knew he was joking. But I wasn't laughing.

"Look, I covered nuclear energy at the last paper I worked on, so cut it out, okay?" I said.

"Natalie Gold, known far and wide in the newsroom for her razor tongue, can dish it out, but she can't take it. Is that it?"

"Okay, okay. I admit, I'm sensitive on the subject. This sounds corny, I know, but I take journalism seriously and I don't want people thinking I'm an air brain because I cover fashion."

"Believe me, Nattie, no one would ever mistake you for an air brain. Now, would you please tell me how you know that's a homicide in there?"

"The hoofprints. They were wrong," I said. "First of all, they were down, like an upside-down *U*. A horse can't kick that way."

Henry gave me a what-do-you-mean look.

"Pull over and get out of the car. I'll show you," I said.

Henry pulled into someone's driveway, and if that someone was watching out his or her window, he or she would have seen the following peculiarity: a short woman with long red hair backing up to a blond giant and kicking him.

"Pretend I'm a horse," I said.

I pulled my knee up and kicked back against his thigh.

"Now grab my foot and look at the bottom of my shoe. My

29

heel is pointing up toward you. If I were a horse, that would be the top of the U. All the marks on Wally were going the other way."

"Interesting, but maybe the horse trampled the guy," Henry said.

Henry knows doodly-squat about horses and in two seconds flat he's figuring out where a body would have to be to receive those kinds of hoof imprints.

"I thought about that, too," I said. "But Wally was sitting up when we saw him. He could have dragged himself over to the side and propped himself up, trying to get away from Ruskie. He could have, but I doubt it. Even if it did happen that way, the shoe imprints were still wrong. Someone else, someone human, was slamming him with a horseshoe attached to something."

"Really, how can you be so sure?" Henry said. "Is Ruskie sending you post-mortem messages from horse heaven?"

I'd told Henry a little about my strange connection to horses and I was beginning to regret it. He must have picked up on the look on my face.

"Nattie, I'm only kidding. I'm sorry if I've offended you. Please, tell me how you know."

This guy had manners and sensitivity. Him, I could take to meet my mother.

"Ruskie wasn't wearing the kind of horseshoe that smashed into Wally," I said.

Henry looked at me with a combination of surprise and awe. "Nattie, that's absolutely brilliant. How do you know that?"

I didn't want to tell him it was luck, that I just happened to be at the barn yesterday when the blacksmith changed Ruskie's shoes. I liked being thought of as brilliant.

"The hoofprints all over Wally were flat and wide. So whoever killed him knows the horse show world and what the horses wear on their feet. What they didn't know is that Ruskie just got new shoes yesterday. New steel shoes at least an inch narrower than the aluminum plates he used to wear."

"Plates?" Henry said.

"That's what they're called. Maybe because they're about as big as dinner plates. They're horseshoes made out of aluminum. Practically all the top horses wear them because they're lightweight."

"Lightweight? What's the significance?" Henry said. "And why the sudden change to steel shoes?"

I filled him in on horse shows. I told him that Ruskie competed in the hunter divisions. Originally, hunter classes tested a horse's suitability for the hunt field.

"You know," I said, "that alleged sport where people in pink coats chase a pack of yapping hounds who are chasing a fox that's scared out of its wits because it's about to be ripped to shreds. And by the way, never call them dogs. That's the height of hunter illiteracy. Didn't you learn this stuff in boarding school when you dated the Miss Porter's girls?"

"I stuck to the young ladies from Madeira. Now, go on," Henry said.

The irony of this conversation was not lost on either of us: me, the Jew from row-house Philadelphia, telling him, the Wasp from the rolling hills of Connecticut, about fox hunting.

"Anyway," I said, "one of the things a horse is judged on is how much ground he can cover with the least amount of effort. That way he can go longer and farther in the hunt field. The more a horse bends its front knees when it trots or canters—that's called knee action—the more the energy's going up and down instead of long and forward. So you want the horse to be what they call a daisy cutter, trotting far and long with almost no knee action. Too complicated?"

"No," Henry said, "go on. I'm trying to correlate it to basketball."

I finished telling him about good movers and how one way to make a horse a better mover is to lighten up his shoes. The more weight you put on a horse's foot, the higher he lifts it.

"And that's why all the top horses and the wannabes wear lightweight aluminum plates," I said. "The problem is plates don't offer much protection against rocks or even hard-packed dirt. If you pound a horse enough around a show ring, you're asking for soundness problems. Rob had campaigned Ruskie hard this past year, going for Horse of the Year points. Ruskie's feet were starting to crumble and it was taking more and more drugs to keep him sound. So Rob switched him to steel shoes, I guess thinking it might mean the difference between passing and failing the vet.

"Besides, you never put aluminum shoes on the hind. There's no point to it. Judges care how straight the front legs are, not the back. Ruskie's hind shoes were steel and he had trailers on the back."

I lost Henry with that one.

"Trailers?" he said. "Is that like lifts for short men?"

"Not even close," I said. "It's more like orthopedic Mary Janes for a gangly legged girl. If you've got a horse whose back legs are too close together, he'll bang his back ankles together when he does anything more than stand still. To stop that, you put trailers on the hind shoes, little tails on the heels of the shoe which extend outward a couple of inches. It cocks his feet out just enough to stop him from hitting himself. Believe me, trailers would leave a very distinctive mark, something like the cursive letter U. And I didn't see anything like that anywhere on Wally. Soooooooooo, that's how I know the hoofprints on Wally have nothing to do with Ruskie."

"Excellent," Henry said. "And not another crack from me about your sartorial beat, ever again. I promise."

CHAPTER 4

E thics. Tricky business for print journalists. Emphasis on the word *print*. As far as I can tell, broadcast journalists don't seem to do much head-scratching on the subject.

Every newspaper reporter or editor I know loves to pontificate on the what-ifs of journalistic ethics even more than they like to complain about the boss. Questions like, when is deception in pursuit of a story acceptable? Years back, the *Chicago Sun-Times* did a blockbuster on building inspector kickbacks. A bunch of reporters opened a bar to see who and how much had to be paid off to get the right licences to open the place. No one knew the bar owners were reporters until the paper splashed it across the front page. That spawned a huge controversy in the newspaper business: Was it ethical to lie? The upshot was no, in varying degrees.

Different papers have different guidelines. Because Fred Richards is so crazed about offending readers in any possible way, the rules are rigid: Identify yourself immediately as an *Appeal* reporter when working on a story.

I had clearly stretched, if not broken, that rule with the Union County detective. On the way back to town, Henry and I debated whether we should call Odom and tell him why we were really there.

Henry was a good boy who played by the rules. He wanted to call as soon as we returned to the newsroom.

"I bet you park your car right between the yellow lines," I said.

"I do," he said. "And I'll bet you straddle both spaces or, worse, park on the curb by the entrance."

"Okay, I admit it. I don't take a ruler out and make sure I'm six inches inside each line. And sometimes, yes, if I'm in a big hurry I will park by the door if all I have to do is run in and buy a box of Tampax."

I watched Henry's face redden. It's funny how menstruation talk shuts a man right up. "Look," I said, "if this Quincy wannabe is so good, he'll figure it out. Let's give it a day, see what we can dig up, and then you can call Odom. Deal?"

"Let me think about it. I'll let you know when we get back to town."

Henry was a ruminator, that was for sure. There weren't going to be any quick moves or fast decisions on this story. But I could live with that. How often does a fashion writer get a chance to crack a murder?

"Just tell me one thing," Henry said. "Why the violence? If you're going to kill a horse for insurance money, it seems to me it should look as if it were a natural death. Four broken legs isn't natural."

It had puzzled me, too, and that's one of the reasons I wanted to go into Ruskie's stall. Unfortunately, Odom interrupted me before I had a chance to look through the bloody straw.

"I'll bet someone finds an extension cord with two alligator clips in that stall," I said. "It's gruesome, but it works. You turn the horse into a giant filament. One clip goes on the ear, the other up his rear. Plug him into an outlet and there's enough juice running through him to barbecue his insides. He falls over dead, the vet writes it up as colic. But if the horse isn't insured against colic, then the killer slams a leg or two to make it look like the horse was flailing around in his stall and broke his leg."

"Are horses that stupid?" Henry said.

"Not stupid exactly," I said. "Dumb to our ways is more like

34

it. Horses are supposed to live outside, in the open. They're graz-
ers. What do they know from four walls? If a horse lies down too
close to the wall, he can get wedged in. He doesn't have enough
room to roll over into a stand—that's what happens when a horse
gets cast in its stall—he panics and starts smashing all around. For
such big creatures they're surprisingly fragile. Leg bones can snap
just from the percussion of running. And a stomachache can kill a
horse."

"I can see why people insure them," Henry said.

"Mine's not. Even if I could afford it, which I can't, I wouldn't.
Insurance salesmen give me the heebie-jeebies. They sell paranoia
and I worry enough without some guy in a shiny suit telling me all
the things that could go wrong."

"Now, that's a real head-in-the-sand approach," Henry said.
"If something happens to your horse, can you afford to replace
her?"

"Nothing's going to happen," I said with more snap in my
voice than needed.

Henry shut up after that, and I watched the scenery speed by
Route 16. I was hungry and thought about asking him to stop at
the Circle K for a package of Chee·tos. But I didn't want to interrupt his internal debate of whether or not to tell the deputy. Plus,
I'd let my father corral me into trying his latest miracle cure-all,
the Fit for Life diet, which meant nothing in my mouth before
noon except fruit. The Fit for Lifers, an ascetic band of vegetari-
ans who eat nothing but uncooked plant products, contend the
human body stays in the "elimination process" until noon and
can't digest anything before that without dire consequences—
everything from gas to cancer. Fruit doesn't count because it goes
right through you.

About halfway into Charlotte, just before the strip malls started
springing up, the temperature gauge on Henry's new Honda jumped
into the red zone and his hood started rattling like a pressure cooker.

Henry pulled over to the side of the road. Steam was hissing out every available crack in the car's front end.

"Shit," Henry said. "I'm going to walk back to that gas station and call Triple A."

It was hotter inside the car than outside. So I got out and fried under the Carolina sun until Henry got back. Together we waited for the tow truck and exchanged the stories of our lives.

By the time we pulled into the parking lot with Henry's rehy-drated Honda, I knew enough about Henry to write a primer on prep schools, tennis, and sailing lessons. And he, I suppose, knew enough about me to understand a Woody Allen movie. Also by then I couldn't control my stomach—which was grumbling louder than a whiny eight-year-old—any more than my words.

"So what's it going to be?" I said. "Just a day of digging before we call Detective Tony-Bob?"

"I'm still thinking," Henry said.

Holy Manoli, I'd underestimated the depths to his rumina-tions—this guy must've been a cow in his last life. I rolled my eyes and muttered.

"Are you always this impatient?" Henry said. "Calm down. We'll work out a mutually agreeable plan. I'm inclined to call him, but if it's so important to you, I'll give you a day. One day."

Yes! I wanted to jump up and kiss him. But I didn't.

CHAPTER 5

Whoever designed the newsroom at *The Charlotte Commercial Appeal* must have had a sense of humor. He or she made it so that the interior walls of all the offices are glass. You can always see who is meeting with whom, and if you're a good enough lip-reader, you can follow their conversations. Even if you can't read lips, you can usually get the gist of things by watching who's furrowing his or her brow the most.

We walked into a lot of brow-furrowing behind the glass walls of Fred's corner office. Fred's forehead was just about knitted shut. Next to him was the features editor, my boss, Candace Fitzgerald, an automaton who was hired after scoring virtually no feeling points on her management psychological exam. She was in one of her power outfits chosen and purchased by her personal shopper: a mega-shoulder-padded power suit in victory red accessorized with an aggressive band of gold that collared her neck and made her look even more like a pale-faced and overbred Doberman pinscher.

Next to her was Henry's boss, the city editor, Ken Grant. He was a wizard with words but so patronizing to women, the older females in our newsroom signed a petition and forced him to go for sensitivity training. He'd probably been or fancied himself the dashing sort thirty years ago, when he covered the Vietnam War for ABC and won an Emmy. By the time he wound up at *The Commercial Appeal,* he was one of those half-bald men who wraps the same gray hair around his shiny pate a million times. Add that to a face dragged earthward by gravity and booze, and you don't have the most attractive puss around. He must have held some allure to very young women under five feet four inches, because he was methodically working his way through all the short female copy kids and interns above the age of consent. And there were plenty of them around. Being only five-five himself, Ken never hired anyone he had to look up to.

The trio saw us walk into the newsroom and started motioning wildly for us to come in Fred's glass office.

"Don't Candace and Fred look cute together?" I whispered to Henry as we walked through Fred's glass doors. "They could mate and breed perfect little team players."

Henry smiled and so did I. Were we ever wearing the wrong expressions for this meeting.

"Sit down, you two," Fred barked. "I just got a call from the Union County medical examiner and he's as mad as a fly's nest, I mean bee's nest. Or is it hornet's nest? Whatever, you know what I mean. What is this about you rummaging through the stall where a man was killed? And you didn't even identify yourself as *Appeal* reporters. You know the rules."

Fred's face was turning an unattractive shade of fuchsia.

Being the winner of a Pulitzer, Henry carries more weight around this place than I do. So I, for once, shut up. It was the right choice. Henry isn't one to let his emotions take the reins. He spoke in his usual calm, authoritative way.

"I didn't think there was much to the story when we got there—maybe a watch item in the Carolinas column," Henry said. "So that's why we never identified ourselves and . . ."

By the end of the conversation, Fred was complimenting me on my analytical abilities after Henry told him my horseshoe/murder theory.

"Here," Fred said, handing Henry a pink I'll Get Back to You slip. "This is the medical examiner's phone number. Call him, explain what happened. And, Nattie, call that Union County detective that was there while you're at it. We don't want anyone's feathers ruffled. Union County is a key penetration area. We can't afford to lose even one reader."

Candace's marble face cracked a smile at Fred. To me she hissed, "I'll see you later, in my office." Ken didn't say anything; he was busy scoping out the new crop of summer interns walking around the newsroom.

Henry and I left, to our respective telephones.

I picked through my purse and found the dry cleaner's tag with Odom's number on it. He answered on the first ring.

"Hi, this is Nattie Gold, you know, the woman who was at the barn this morning."

"Oh," he said, "you mean Natalie Gold, the reporter who came with Henry Goode, the reporter?"

There was an edge to his voice, but I couldn't tell what kind of edge. Was he playing around or pissed off?

"Sorry," I said. "I was going to call you tomorrow and tell you who I was. How'd you know?"

"Your picture's in the paper every Sunday—though I'd have figured on you being taller than you are. What do you think we are here, idiots?"

I do have a column that runs Sunday with a one-inch square mug shot of me smiling out. And I do get recognized when I go places—shopping mainly. Once I was trying on a dress in a fitting room, wearing only a torn pair of panty hose and five extra pounds, when the saleslady flung back the curtain and chortled, "Aren't you the fashion editor for *The Appeal*?"

"Fashion writer," I said, and smiled as graciously as I could.

But it's usually only women who recognize me.

"I didn't see you as the type who follows fashion coverage," I said to Odom. "What do you mean, you thought I'd be taller? How can you tell from a mug shot?"

"You have a tall head," he said.

I'm not usually left speechless, but a tall head? I paused a moment, gathering my thoughts. This was getting too personal.

"Look, I should have identified myself right off, I'm sorry. Like I said, I was going to call and tell you. Now that I have you on the phone, let me tell you something else. I don't think Ruskie killed Wally, the hoofprints were going every way but right. Besides, Ruskie doesn't even wear the kind of shoe that was plastered all over Wally. Someone set it up to make it look like Wally was trampled. But I think he was murdered."

"I know that," Odom said. "Hold on a minute, I gotta turn this down."

I heard opera blasting in the background. Madame Butterfly's final aria, if I wasn't mistaken. I listened as a pair of boots clunked across the room and cut her off just before she plunged the knife deep into her aching heart. Women can be such fools, why'd she ever listen to that schmuck anyway?

"Opera?" I said. "At the Union County sheriff's office?"

"My mama's Italian," he said.

"Oh, that explains everything," I said. This guy was certainly an anomaly, but I didn't feel like discussing his eccentricities just then. I knew Candace was about to pull me in her office and read me the riot act for overstepping my beat.

"You know Wally was murdered?" I said.

"Yes, darlin', I do," he said. "And since we're baring our souls to one another, I'll tell you something else. That Rob Stone fella, the one that was having such a hard time with his stomach this morning? He's gonna have a harder time this afternoon. He's down here now, being booked for murder. We found a section of one of those rails you jump your horses over, this one was blue and

green, just like everything else at February Farm. Except this particular one had a bloody horseshoe nailed to it. Found it in the
hayloft, next to a pair of bloody sneakers—size nine. Stone's size."

"Rob? No, no way," I said. It was a possibility I hadn't even
considered. Rob can be unpleasant, in fact he's a pain in the ass
most times. But a murderer?

"Well, I'll tell you what," Odom said. "Mr. Stone had best find
himself a damn good lawyer, because I'll bet you dollars to dough-
nuts that club comes back from the lab with his prints smeared all
over it. That means premeditated murder. In North Carolina, that
means meeting your maker."

CHAPTER 6

As soon as I hung up from Odom, which took some doing—he wanted to talk about tie widths and Giorgio Armani—I called the barn. Gail answered. She worked for Rob—cleaning stalls, wiping down tack, saddling up horses, occasionally riding, if he let her. She was always complaining about what a pain Rob was. And he was.

He wouldn't get on a horse if it didn't look good enough to walk into a show ring. Its coat had to sparkle and its hooves had to be slicked down with hoof dressing. His saddle had to be kept spotless, his bits gleaming and his bridles soaped with just the right amount of water so his hands didn't slip on the reins. His saddle pads had to be washed each time they touched a horse's back. The water buckets had to be scrubbed every day and the stalls picked out morning, noon, and night. An errant mound of horse manure could send him into a rage. And if he saw a horse rolling after a bath, forget it.

"Nattie, I heard you were already here," Gail said. "You wouldn't believe what's happened. They've strung that yellow crime tape all over the place. I can't even get to the aisle to sweep it down. I guess it doesn't matter because Rob's not here to scream at me. Old man Clarke's wandering around looking worried. The last thing he wants is another scandal. He'd have my head if he knew I was talking to you. You know how much he hates *The Appeal* after what happened with Lally."

I sure did. I almost had to move my horse from his barn when Clarke found out I was a reporter. Rob finally calmed the old geezer down. He convinced him I was no threat because I covered only parties and fashion. Clarke still blames *The Appeal* for what he regards as his family's bitter fall from grace. It's really a southern spin on the old shoot-the-messenger story. About five years back, Lally, his eldest daughter, ran off with four million dollars in embezzled cracker money. Daddy sicced the police on her and they found her months later, go-go dancing in a bar on Route 17 in Teterboro, New Jersey. This was way before the Shoe Salesman's customer-satisfaction reign at the paper. *The Appeal* ran a long series called "The War Between the Clarkes," in which Lally said she ran away with the money to get back at her father because he sexually abused her as a child. She claimed she had just recovered those memories and there were worse ones bubbling up, ones that involved ritualistic satanic worship. The editors splashed it across page one, above the fold and on Sunday, when circulation doubles to half a million. Then Geraldo Rivera featured her on a show called "Demon Dads."

Daddy Clarke denied everything and Lally eventually recanted after he dropped the embezzlement charges. But after that the Clarke family hunkered down to near-monastic living and I've yet to see one of them at any of the society parties my editor forces me to cover.

"Gail, you don't think Rob did it, do you?"

"Maybe. It's possible," Gail said. "You know as well as I do Ruskie could never pass the vet. Did you know Wally owned half the horse? He and Rob bought Ruskie together when they were an item. So Rob sure as hell had a good motive to kill him. Maybe Rob didn't want to split the insurance money with Wally. Maybe Rob never got over Wally dumping him. You know he broke Rob's heart into eighteen pieces. I'm not saying Rob was ever really normal, but he got worse after Wally left."

My left shoulder was scrunched up against the phone, which was pressed to my ear. My fingers were flying across the keyboard, clicking and clacking with Gail's every word.

"Even if he did it, you know, kill Wally, I say so what? Good riddance to bad rubbish. I don't care if he was the top trainer in South Carolina, he was scum. You've seen him beat on horses at the shows and that's nothing compared to what he did to them at home. And he was really nasty to Rob, too, parading around his new boyfriends when he and Rob were still living together. Then he dumped Rob altogether, leaving him with a pile of Visa bills and a Jack Russell that won't eat anything except boiled lamb and refuses to pee outside like a regular dog. And who'd he leave him for? Lucy Bladstone of all people."

"Yeah, well, maybe she really is a man," I said, and we laughed. Lucy Bladstone has a set of shoulders that could stop a train. The joke on the show circuit is that L. M. Bladstone found a big surprise between Lucy's legs when they finally did it, but by that time he was either too drunk or so in love, he sent her/him off to Trinidad, Colorado, to be fixed.

"I don't know, Gail, I just can't or maybe I don't want to believe Rob killed Wally. If nothing else, he wouldn't do it because he wouldn't want to get his clothes dirty."

Rob's the neatest person I've ever met. He can walk through a ring, knee-deep in mud, and come out the other end spotless. I drive up to the barn and my clothes are already stained before I get out.

"Hey, by the way," I said, "I looked for you yesterday to go trail riding and ended up riding in the ring with Rob yelling at me. I thought we could go to La Paz for Mexican afterward. I called you, but you weren't home."

"Sorry, I took the day off," Gail said. "I was feeling kind of depressed because Allie's been such a pig about his lead changes. Rob can ride him and he goes perfect. But me, I get on him and . . . Oops, I gotta go. The old man's heading to the office and I don't want him to see me on the phone. Call me tonight, okay? I've got more to tell you. Also, I bought a book for your mother, you know, to help her out. Call, I'll tell you about it."

Gail and I clicked the day we met two and a half years ago. I was unloading Brenda from the van. She'd just arrived from upstate New York and I was as worried as a new mother that fifteen hours in a van would traumatize her into a colic.

"Get that girl a cream soda before she faints," I heard someone say behind me. I turned around; there was a tall woman standing by the barn door. Her hair hung halfway down her back and maybe twenty years and twenty pounds ago, people mistook her for Joni Mitchell.

"Welcome to Shangri-la," she said. "You must be the new boarder and this must be Brenda Starr. Bring her on in, we're putting her next to the black stallion with one eye."

"What?" I said.

"A joke, it's a joke. One-eyed black stallion, black-haired man with an eye patch, Brenda Starr's mystery man. . . . Get it?"

We were best friends before the week was out.

We ride together, go out for dinner a couple times a week, shop T. J. Maxx for cheap clothes, and talk on the phone at least once a day. Most of all, we share a passion for horses.

The problem is Gail doesn't have much else in her life other than that and I worry about her. She can go on for hours about Allie and his lead changes, as if whether a horse's inside leg leads the canter stride is essential to life. Unfortunately for Gail, it is. I could understand it more if Gail took Allie to horse shows or planned to sell him. A horse that can't do flying changes—switch his leading front leg in midair as he changes directions around a course—is worthless on the A show circuit, no matter how high he tucks his legs over a fence. If he canters around the ring on the wrong lead, with his outside leg striking the ground first, and won't switch automatically, the rider has to bring him down to a trot and then ask him to canter on the correct lead. By that point you can kiss any hope of a ribbon good-bye.

Gail is obsessed with Allie's lead changes. I love her like a sister and Lord knows, she's certainly been there for me every time I've needed her, but she's a living lesson to me that I'd chosen the right path in not becoming a full-time horse person. Over the years, I've noticed that people who make a living with horses either start out or end up so idiosyncratic, they can get along only with big, dumb creatures that don't talk back.

"I don't have to call you later," I said to Gail. "I'm coming to the barn tonight to ride, I'll see you then. What book?"

"*We Don't Die.* . . . I gotta go." She hung up.

My eyes teared up. "Yeah, if only it were true," I mumbled to no one. David, my stepfather, died six months ago and it still hurt plenty to think about him. I was as close to him as any daughter could be to her real father. It had been Gail who broke the horrible news. Rob was giving me a lesson and she walked up to him and whispered something. "Nattie," he'd said. "I'll take Brenda, Gail needs to speak to you."

I sobbed in her arms. She drove me home, put me in the shower, got me dressed, packed my bags, and drove me to Greensboro, where my mother and David lived. She stayed with me the whole week, using one of her two weeks of vacation to clean my mother's house for the funeral guests, help with the arrangements, but mostly to stay by my side.

That's a best friend.

I wiped my eyes, took a deep breath, and walked across the newsroom to Henry's desk. I recognized the position, in fact we could have been salt and pepper shakers. His head was tilted left to his shoulder, with the phone wedged against his ear. His fingers were flying across the keyboard, taking notes. I looked at the green letters on the black screen, saw Rob's name and Wally's name, some numbers, the word *cocaine* a few times. He hung up a few minutes later.

"That was the medical examiner," Henry said. "I'm sure you know by now about Rob. You were right about the wire. They found it and the clamp under the horse."

"Was Mr. Quincy or whatever his name is still mad about us being in the stall?" I asked.

"He cooled down. He told me his mother had been a PTL Platinum Partner, which meant she turned practically all her social security check over to Bakker's ministry every month. He kept telling her Bakker was a scoundrel, that a minister shouldn't be driving a Rolls, no matter how old the car is. But his mother kept sending in the checks. Then the ministry went under and now his mother has money to live on. So he was actually thanking me."

"Was he appreciative enough to tell you anything about Wally and why the cops are so sure it was Rob who killed him?"

"As a matter of fact, yes." Henry said. "Rob's prints were all over a bloody pole they found in the hayloft, right next to . . ."

"Let me guess," I said, "right next to a pair of sneakers caked in Wally's blood. Rob's sneakers, right?"

"You've got it," Henry said. "I hope Rob's got the money for a good lawyer."

"Funny, that's exactly what Odom said."

Odom had been right about the prints. Could he be right about Rob? Rob had a motive—a couple of them, in fact—and no alibi. He'd told Henry he'd heard nothing unusual the night before and everything seemed fine at the barn until he found Wally dead in Ruskie's stall. I could see why Odom was so sure Rob did it. Still, something inside me—call it woman's intuition if you still can in the nineties—some part of me was screaming, or praying, it wasn't Rob who killed Wally.

"Another thing," Henry said. "It seems Wally was a big-time cokehead. His septum was almost eaten through."

"Well," I said, "he's not the first druggie on the horse show circuit and he sure won't be the last. Rumor has it that Lucy Bladstone's been caught with coke four, five times by the Camden police. The Bladstones own the town, so it's no big surprise she's never been busted."

"This is sounding more interesting all the time," Henry said. He's the only person I know that sounds out all four syllables in in-ter-es-ting. "I think we should go to Camden. It's almost five now, I've got to pick up the boys at six. What are you doing tomorrow morning?"

"Going with you to Camden if I get my Sunday column finished."

I found an empty desk in Sports, far from the snooping eye of Candace, and banged out a twenty-inch testimonial to shoulder pads, the great equalizers. "If I were to get implants, the only place they'd be is on my shoulders. Shoulder pads, God's gift to women with real hips . . ."

At six-thirty I was almost out the door, when Candace caught me.

"In my office, now," she said.

I followed her in and before I had a chance to sit down, she was spitting fire. She was not at all happy that I'd spent half the day tracking down a murderer.

"You know as well as I do we're understaffed back here. We haven't filled a vacancy in two years. That leaves me precious few warm bodies to turn out the features pages, and I won't have one of them traipsing off for a story that's going to run somewhere else. So if you want to play investigative reporter, you'll do it after you finish your column and any feature you're assigned. Got it? Now, if you'll excuse me, I've got readership surveys to read."

What was the point in arguing? It would just give me an ulcer. At least I had insides to chew up. If they cut Candace open, they'd find red and green wires.

By six thirty-five, I was out the door and on my way to the barn. The traffic was its usual nightmare. Thanks to mild winters and a firm kibosh on unions, the city of Charlotte had been on a roll for the past fifteen years, with new businesses moving down all the time. IBM, Gold Bond, BMW—just to mention a few of the biggies. Like other boomtowns, Charlotte had done little to ease the traffic pains. Route 16, once a country two-laner, ran through the heart of the city's southeast development. So traveling down it anytime near rush hour was bumper-to-bumper L.A. hell.

What should have been a twenty-minute trip took me an hour. An hour inside an un-air-conditioned car in the middle of one of the worst heat waves in North Carolina history without even the breeze of fifty miles an hour to cool me down. Time to trade in.

I was wetter than an overworked horse when I drove up to the barn. Gail was out front, sweeping.

"Nattie, come here. I've been thinking about something since you called."

She pulled me down the aisle, an immaculate strip of black macadam free from even one wisp of hay. Someone must have posted bail or bond—whichever it is that springs you from jail— for Rob.

Like I said, I loved Gail like a sister, if I'd had one, and she was a wonderful friend to me, but when she told a story, she dragged it out forever. Every night when she called me to tell me what Allie had done that day, it took her thirty minutes to get to the point. And then there wasn't usually much more of one other than that he might have bucked or tripped or rubbed his head against her in a cute way.

She led me into the office, which, mercifully, was air-conditioned. "Something's been eating at me since this whole Wally-Ruskie thing started," she said. "I couldn't stop thinking about it when I was riding Allie after you called. Oh, my God! You wouldn't believe what he did. Three flying changes to the left without bucking. Finally! I've only been working on that for almost three years. And then he—"

"Gail," I said, "that's great about Allie's lead changes. I hope that means you'll finally take him off the farm to a show now you've got that nailed. But listen, I've got something to tell you, you can't tell Old Man Clarke. I'm doing a story about the murder. So tell me what it is about Wally and Ruskie, and anything else you can think of."

"Well, I was thinking about Ruskie and then I started thinking about Yankee Doodle, Keith Rollings's horse. Remember him?"

"How could I forget?" I said. "Last fall I showed against him all the time. And lost. His horse was a machine."

"You're right," Gail said. "Was a machine. When's the last time you saw him at a show? Then I remembered seeing a full-page ad in *The Chronicle* with Yankee Doodle's picture in it. It was taken at Tri-Color. I could tell because you could see the Tri-Color flags in the background. That's where I'd love to take Allie, I know he'd canter around that course because it's exactly what he likes—"

"Gail, what kind of ad was it?" I asked. "A for-sale ad?"

"Nope," she said. "It was an in-loving-memory ad, with Yankee Doodle's dates of birth and death underneath. He died, I think, in March. He was almost twenty, can you believe he was that old? I remember because he was born the year I graduated art school."

"So horses die all the time, especially old ones," I said.

"Yeah, I know that. Then it came to me," Gail said. "Right after Allie's second lead change. Maybe that's the key to him, maybe I should be thinking about other things, so I'm not so nervous."

"What, Gail, what came to you?"

"Right of Way," she said.

"Right of way, what right of way?" I said. "What are you talking about?"

"Oh, I forgot," she said, "you weren't here then. It just seems like you've been here forever. Right of Way, that was Melissa Mayfield's horse who won large junior hunter champion three years in a row at the National Horse Show. He was a big blood bay, like Allie. When I brought Allie here, Melissa started crying because he reminded her of Waysie, that was Right of Way's barn name. Of course, she cried anytime any bay walked into the barn."

"Did she cry because her horse had died?" I asked.

"Bingo," Gail said. "You've got it. It happened almost three years ago, just before you came here, when Wally was living with Rob, co-training with him. Waysie died right out of the blue, the week before he was supposed to start the indoor shows. No one could figure out what the hell happened; the vet thought maybe a cerebral hemorrhage. The funny thing is, that horse had never been sick a day in its life. Not a touch of colic, not a cold, not even a lame step. Nothing."

"That's horrible," I said.

"Yeah, Melissa was a wreck for a long time afterward. There's more," Gail said. "Here's what came to me. I can name at least four more horses, expensive, very fancy horses, that died in the last two or three years. Died suddenly, with no explanation. All of them trained by Wally."

This time Gail had a point.

CHAPTER 7

I can think of one good thing about living in Upstate New York. In the summer, it stays lighter longer. But you pay for it mightily six months later, when the sun sets hours before you even get hungry for dinner.

Had this been a night in New York, I could have ridden without worry. Here, however, in the southernmost part of North Carolina, I had to move quickly. I brushed Brenda and picked out her hooves. It wasn't a bang-up job of horsemanship, and Rob would have screamed bloody murder if he'd seen me lead my dusty horse to the mounting block. But Rob was upstairs in shock. "When he got back," Gail said, "he didn't even say anything about the mud the cops tracked all over."

I was trying to beat the sun to the horizon. It's not the smartest idea to ride the trails alone, and it's even stupider to do it at dusk. If anything happens, it's just you and the trees and the owls. Gail had more work to do and there wasn't anyone else around. It was too hot to ride in a sandy ring and Brenda is a pretty reasonable horse. She's not much of a spooker and she's never run away with me.

"If I'm not back in an hour," I called to Gail, "send out the posse. Okay?"

I went deep into the woods, where it was dark and cool. The last light of the day was dancing through the leaves and a small wind was blowing. It had been hot enough to melt the pine tree sap and the air was thick with it. I took a deep breath. I'd been seeing smells since I was a kid, and this one came in sharp and narrow, with a wide green backflip.

Brenda stretched out her neck as she walked, relaxed and steady. I envied her calm. I couldn't stop thinking about Rob and Wally and all those dead horses. But this is why I ride: Soon, I settled into her rhythm, my body moved with her body and my mind emptied. It was like turning on a faucet and all the stuff rushes out: Wally, Rob, Ruskie, Candace, Henry, Waysie, Yankee Doodle. . . . Out, gone, forgotten. Just me and my horse in glory land. I was under the spell.

I rode farther into the green, every once in a while seeing patches of red and purple sunset through the breaks in the leaves. When the sky darkened to an unbroken wash of dark lilac, I turned Brenda around and looped the reins to her, holding on at the buckle that joins the two strips of leather. I let her have the bit. She knows these trails better than I and can always get us home. Going out, her pace had been a slow amble, like that Union County detective who listens to opera because his mother is Italian. Coming back was a different story; she geared up to a New York walk: alert, fast, and ready to argue with anyone who stood in her way.

It was twilight when we got back, a velvety-gray sky dotted with the yellow twinkle of lightning bugs. Gail was standing by the barn door, rake in hand and a worried look on her face.

"Come on, Nattie," she said, "don't do that again. I was about to call the police to go looking for you. The only reason I didn't is because I know your horse would rather die than let something happen to you."

"Don't be such a worrier," I said. "You're worse than my mother. Nothing's going to happen to me out there. Not on Brenda."

"I hope you're right," Gail said. She raked the dirt in front of the barn where Brenda had walked. First she raked diagonally to the left, then crisscrossed over it, to the right. It seemed like a lot of useless effort to me, especially since it ended up looking like a flock of chickens had been line dancing. But Gail raked it that way every night, adding another twenty minutes to her long and underpaid day. Once, before I knew her well enough to suggest therapy, I asked if Rob made her do it that way. "Nope," she'd said. "I just do it for myself. It gives me a sense of accomplishment." A few days later, I gave her the name of the shrink all my newspaper friends use.

"Guess what?" Gail said as she raked to the right. "I called Melissa Mayfield, she's home for summer break. I thought you might want to talk to her about Wally and Waysie and all that stuff for your story. I asked her to meet us at La Paz. I used to baby-sit her all the time at the horse shows and when her parents went off to Europe or Hawaii. Rob and I sort of raised her. She was real excited that I called and said she'd get there first to get us a table."

I jumped off Brenda, who between the sweat and dirt was a sticky mess. "Gail, you must be reading minds. I was going to ask you to introduce me to Melissa. This is great. Wait till I tell Henry."

"Henry? New boyfriend? What happened to John? I wish I could find someone that cute."

I took off my hard hat, a black velvet bubble of Styrofoam that was supposed to keep me from becoming a vegetable in case of a fall. After riding for an hour in ninety-plus degrees with my head cooking inside it, that's exactly what I felt like—a vegetable, an overboiled bowl of broccoli.

"I'm gonna die if this heat doesn't break soon," I said. "Henry's the other reporter on the story. We're colleagues, that's all. John and I are still going out, but who knows how much longer. You're right about his looks, that's what got him the job reading news on Channel 9. The problem is, he's a lot cuter than he is smart. Not to mention, he's nearly mute. The thing about looks is, after the first night, what does it matter anyway? You can look at a guy for only so long. Last Friday I couldn't take it anymore and I kept saying to him, 'Talk to me, talk to me. About anything other than Nielsens or sweeps. Tell me what you're thinking.' Know what he said? I couldn't believe it. He said, without the least bit of irony, 'What you see is what you get.' "

Gail handed me a halter to slip over Brenda's head. "At least," she said, "he's someone to go out with on Friday nights."

Oh, God, what was I thinking. Me going on and on about John, my fifth or sixth boyfriend since I'd moved to Charlotte, when the last time Gail had a man in her life was three years ago. And he walked out on her.

"I'm sorry, Gail. I should've thought about what I was saying. You know that's not something that comes naturally to me. But speaking of men, I gave Jeff your number—remember I told you about him; he's my desk mate, the TV critic at the paper? Don't give me that look."

Gail was scrunching up her face, like she'd just seen a dead rat.

"He's calling you tonight," I said. "He's inviting you to his house for a homemade dinner, says he's Julia Child with a penis. There's a scary thought. Anyway, he's calling you. Stop wincing, he's a great guy, even if he talks loud and hogs the computer. He's a bit of a lothario, but just consider him dating practice. Unless, of course, your hormones start raging and you want to take it beyond practice. I'd bet you'd be in for quite a ride. The way he tells it, he's unstoppable in the sack. So you'd better say yes when he calls, I don't want to hear any sick horse stories, that you can't go because Allie had a funny look in his eyes. I'm tired of you sitting home every night, rereading old issues of *Practical Horseman*."

Now Gail was rolling her eyes. "What's the Jewish word you call yourself? Something that starts with a *Y. Yintoo* or *yessee* or something like that? Well, stop being one. I can take care of myself."

"It's *yenta*, you dumb shiksa," I said, and poked her arm with my sweaty hand. "I'm not going to stop until we're double dating. Got it?"

"I'll go on one condition," Gail said. "You name your next horse Yenta."

"That'll go over real big in South Carolina, where I couldn't walk in half the country clubs. I like it, though, a horse named Yenta. Nothing like a little in-your-face-the-Jew-is-here to crack a congenital case of Camden lockjaw. It's a deal."

I led Brenda to the wash stall and Gail followed me. "Why don't you go ahead to the restaurant? It'll take me at least another twenty minutes to get the grime off Brenda and my tack."

"That's okay," Gail said. "I'll stick around, make sure everything's closed up."

Sometimes I wondered if Gail trusted me alone at the barn. I'm not as neat as she is, but I can leave the place presentable enough.

"Suit yourself," I said. "Hand me that bottle of Vetrolin, would you? Brenda deserves a good washdown tonight."

I don't know who likes the liniment wash more, me or Brenda. The smell, the color, the tingle afterward; everything about it says horses to me. Vetrolin looks like liquid emeralds and turns a bucket of clear water into a milky mint-green soup that smells like a Swedish sauna gone mad.

"I wish this stuff weren't so expensive," I said, and tossed the bottle toward a nearby trash can, missing the mark by six inches.

"Well," Gail said as she picked up the bottle and dropped it in the can, "you know what Doc Loc says about it anyway—fancy alcohol, he calls it, says we'd do just as well to wash the horses down in the fifty-nine-cents-a-bottle stuff from the drugstore."

"Yeah, look where Doc Loc is now," I said.

Little red dots started popping up on Gail's cheeks—fury splotches, she called them. "He's still the best horse vet I've ever seen," she said with an edge in her voice that could slice hard cheese. "He was set up and railroaded. As if the Coggins test means anything anyway. When's the last time you ever heard of a horse coming down with swamp fever?"

Doc Loc was a great guy, no doubt about it. Kind as the day is long. And he did get shafted. Gail idolized him. She worked for him years back, riding out on calls with him, holding horses, helping him give shots, helping him worm, she even helped stitch up a few. He'd been the vet everyone used until the state pulled his license for falsifying a Coggins test.

Doc Lockton—Doc Loc to his regulars—was notorious for his views on the Coggins test. Any chance he'd get, he'd tell you what a useless waste of money it was. "Just something to make the labs rich," he'd say. "And then killing good horses for nothing." The Coggins test sampled blood for equine infectious anemia, better known as swamp fever, a mosquito-transmitted disease as fatal to horses as AIDS is to humans. No one has found a vaccine, but Leroy Coggins, a vet at Cornell, developed a test for it. Nowadays you can hardly put your horse in a horse trailer without a Coggins test, let alone take him anywhere.

God forbid your horse tests positive. Even if it's never shown a symptom in its life, it has to be destroyed or freeze-branded with a two-inch-high number coded specifically to each state. The freeze brand permanently turns the horse's hair white, so everyone can see you've got a swamp-fevered horse. Then it has to be quarantined away from any other horses.

I'd heard that Doc Loc wrote out a Coggins for a horse before the results came back from the lab; that he figured the horse would test negative—which it did—because it tested clean every year. The owner begged Doc Loc to do it, saying he had to get to one more A-rated show to qualify for Devon, a big horse show near Philadelphia. He did it and got busted. Lost his vet license for five years. And the horse never made it to Devon anyway.

"Can't say I've ever known a horse with swamp fever," I said. "You're right about Doc Loc being a good vet. He knew right off that Brenda had cracked her coffin bone and needed a few months' rest. The vets I'd taken her to in New York State kept telling me to rub her legs with Mineral Ice and wrap her because she'd strained her tendons."

The red spots on Gail's cheeks disappeared. I put Brenda in her stall and gave her a flake of hay. Gail followed behind, sweeping up the stray strands of alfalfa behind me.

"To La Paz," I said. "I'll clean my tack another time."

Gail flipped off the lights and we walked to our cars. I saw Rob's silhouette, framed by the four-board wood fencing of the paddock. Moon Pie, the Jack Russell terrier Wally had left behind, was jumping up and down, trying to get Rob to pet him. Rob's back was to us, so I couldn't see what he was doing. But I could hear him. He was crying.

CHAPTER 8

D‌o people breed for long legs and narrow hips? Is that where these women come from? I see them all the time, towering above me at the horse shows. Legs like marble columns, hips no wider than a willow branch, not a dimple of fat rippling beneath their skintight britches, looking like Greek goddesses whose bodies defy gravity.

Melissa Mayfield was one of these perfect creatures. I could tell before she stood up to greet us, because sitting down she was almost eye level to me.

Her hair was as straight and shiny as strands of yellow glass. She wore it pulled back with a teal grosgrain ribbon, the exact color of the piping on her shirt, espadrilles, and straw shoulder bag.

"Gail, it's been a month of moons since I've seen you," Melissa said as she jumped up and wrapped her long, slim arms around my friend. She stood a head taller than Gail, who stood a head taller than me.

"I can't believe you're in college, Melissa," Gail said. "I can't believe you're not still riding small ponies. Say hello to my friend Nattie, she boards at February Farm. She's got a beautiful chestnut mare by Sir Thompson—remember that champion hunter stud of Diana Dodge's? Nattie's mare looks exactly like him. If only Allie wasn't a gelding . . ."

Melissa extended her hand my way. I noticed her nails, elongated ovals of pale coral with tiny half-moons of white at the base. She had a firm handshake, must be a business major.

"How do you do, ma'am?" she said. Southerners have a quirky verbal tick of ending every sentence in an upward swing. Statements, rhetorical fragments, complete thoughts—they all come with a question mark at the end when you're below the Mason-Dixon line.

"I'll be fine," I said, "if you stop calling me ma'am. It makes me feel like your grandmother."

"Don't mind Nattie," Gail said. "She's from New Jersey."

Being a newspaper reporter, I'm a stickler for accuracy. "Actually it's Philadelphia," I said. "I lived in New Jersey only for my last year of high school."

"Whatever or wherever," Gail said, "you're still a pain in the ass. Let's eat."

We looked at the menu, six laminated pages of one Mexican concoction after the next. I never can remember the difference between a burrito and an enchilada, much less anything else. Usually I ask the waiter or waitress to explain it. But it was a lost cause with this guy. He was so moony-eyed over Melissa, he could hardly remember what a taco was. Being so God-given pretty, you'd think Melissa would have gotten used to it after a lifetime of stares. But her cheeks flushed just the palest shade of magenta, perfectly, I must say, offsetting the teal.

I ordered a combination plate, alleviating the need to make a decision. Melissa ordered a salad and Gail ordered something called a chimichanga.

"Make sure it doesn't have any tomatoes," Gail said. "Okay?"

Gail won't eat anything red. Tomatoes, cherries, strawberries, raspberries, even apples. Says she can't stand the sight of red on her plate. Her sister won't eat anything blue. And her mother hardly eats anything other than green, specifically the green olives at the bottom of her extra dry, no-vermouth martinis. From what Gail tells me, she followed pretty closely in her mother's footsteps until Doc Loc, himself a recovered alcoholic, dragged her to an AA meeting. As for her food peculiarities, who was I to judge? I can't stand chocolate or anything that feels slimy on my tongue.

We chitchatted until the food came. Pleasant talk, mostly about Allie, and then, where Melissa's old riding buddies were now. Some had turned pro, riding horses for this trainer or that. The rest, like Melissa, had gone off to fancy private colleges.

Throughout the conversation, Melissa never said a cross or unkind word about anyone or anything. It was becoming clear that she must have been one of those girls who intimidated the shit out of me in high school and, truth be told, still made me wobble a bit. She was as sweet as she was pretty, and from what Gail told me, also very smart. I didn't, however, detect a lot of spunk there, but southern women can fool you. What you see isn't ever what you get. That's why they're called steel magnolias.

Over dessert—sopapillas with wine sauce (for me, not Gail) and vanilla ice cream—Gail told Melissa that Wally had been found dead in a stall, next to a horse he'd been trying to kill. That's what it took to get a look at what lay beneath her honeysuckle southern veneer.

"I guess there is a God after all," Melissa said. You could see her jaw muscles working, ropy and taut against the back of her face.

I pulled my reporter's pad from my purse and fished around for something to write with. "I don't know if Gail mentioned it," I said as I speared a blue fine-point Rollamatic, the best kind of pen to take notes with because it flows fast and smooth, "but I'm doing a story about this whole Wally mess. Mind if I ask you a few questions?"

"No, ma'am, I don't mind at all," she said. "But I can't understand why. Wally wasn't worth the paper it'd be printed on. He wasn't worth it alive and he surely isn't worth it dead. Besides, what would you be interested in him for? Don't you write about fashion?"

This is exactly why I'm so sensitive on the subject. It happens all the time. I'll be reporting a story on birth defects or ovarian cancer or whatever disease of the week my editor gets a wild hare about, and I have to justify my journalistic credentials to whomever I'm interviewing.

"I only do fashion half time," I explained as I've explained countless times before. "The other half is general assignment. Now, about Wally, why such hard feelings?"

"He killed my horse," Melissa said.

My hand fell off the edge of the table and I heard Gail gasp.

"Of course, I can't prove anything," Melissa said. "But Waysie died the week after Daddy declared bankruptcy. And it was Waysie's insurance money that rescued Daddy's company."

"My God, Melissa, how do you know that?" Gail said. "And how come you're telling us?"

I wanted to kick Gail.

"Mother told me," Melissa said. "I don't care who knows. I don't care what happens to him. His new little wife can come visit him in jail.

"Oh, you didn't know?" Melissa said, looking at Gail, who looked astonished. "Last Christmas Eve, Daddy came home and told Mother he was leaving. He said he was moving in with his secretary, who happened to be just seven years older than me and pregnant. Then he wrote me a letter, rather, he dictated it to his 'secretary,' I saw her initials at the bottom. He said I would have to go to a state school because he could no longer afford what he called the 'exorbitant tuition' at Hollins. He said he has to make sure he has enough money for his new child's college education as well as mine. Write whatever you want, Nattie."

No sweeter words can a journalist hear. My hand was moving so fast it was cramping. I don't usually tape interviews, but I wished I had a recorder now—in case I needed the tape in court later.

"Did your father admit he had your horse killed and that Wally did it?" I asked.

"Not to me," Melissa said. "To Mother. He said it was the only way to save the business. The only reason he ever told her was because Wally kept calling and coming by the house asking for Daddy. Finally, Mother asked Wally to please stop bothering us so. I was there when she told him and I saw Wally smile; the same twisted and mean smile he'd get on his face when he'd beat up on a horse that misbehaved. Then he said, 'Tell your husband if I don't see fifty thousand dollars tonight, he's going to jail tomorrow for insurance fraud.' Daddy admitted the whole thing to Mother, saying it had been Wally's idea. Wally told him he could make it so no one would ever know Waysie had been killed. No one, of course, but Wally."

Blackmail. Murder. Deceit. Gail had been right about Wally, he was scum. And I had to agree with Melissa. There must be a God after all.

"The police think Rob killed Wally," I said. "They arrested him this afternoon."

Melissa blanched and her eyes glassed up with tears. "Oh, Lord," she said. "Poor Rob. Even from his grave Wally's still tormenting him. Rob didn't do it. He couldn't have. I know he can be unpleasant at times, but that's because he cares so much about the horses and wants everything to be perfect. He wouldn't hurt anyone. I know he wouldn't. Please believe me. Gail, tell her about Rob, tell her what a decent man he is."

"Take it easy, Melissa. I think you're right," I said, mostly because I did, but also to calm her down. She looked like she was about to explode in waterworks. "Do you know where your father was last night?"

"I have no idea," Melissa said.

Anger can wipe away sadness quicker than a horse can spook, and that's exactly what I was hoping for. At the mention of her father, Melissa steeled herself back into the fury that had been brewing for three years.

"I haven't spoken to him since Christmas Eve and I have no intention of ever doing so again," she said.

"What about you?" I asked. "What were you doing last night?"

"I wasn't killing Wally, if that's what you mean," Melissa said. "I was shopping at Montaldo's with Mother. Are people from New Jersey always this direct?"

"Philadelphia," I said, "I'm from Philadelphia."

The bill came and I reached for it. The hell with the contingency budget. If *The Appeal* couldn't pop for this meal, it was time to go to work for the *National Enquirer*.

We walked to our cars. Melissa must have cashed in before Daddy's little indiscretion, because she stopped in front of a big black BMW, vanity tags "Waysie."

"Whatever I can do to help Rob, I will," Melissa said. "He's a lovely person, underneath. Call me if you have any questions. Even your New Jersey questions."

"Philadelphia," I yelled as she pulled away.

As I drove home, I thought about Melissa. It's funny how her face softened when she talked about Rob. I think Gail was on the money when she said Melissa thought of her and Rob as a second set of parents. Judging by this evening, I'd have bet that Melissa would have preferred Rob and Gail be the first set.

I got home around eleven-thirty. The place was still hot enough to hallucinate in, which I may have appreciated twenty years ago, when I was willing to smoke moldy banana peels for a buzz. I opened the windows, crawled in bed, and called Henry again. I'd called him from La Paz, twice, but each time his five-year-old son, Hank, answered.

"May I speak to your father?" I said.

"No," Hank said, and hung up.

I called back and Hank answered again. "If you hang up," I said quickly, "I'll personally write a letter to Santa Claus and tell him you weren't a good boy this year."

"I don't believe in Santa," he said. Click.

I figured I'd try one more time. If the kid was still awake at eleven-thirty, I was going to buy Henry a child-rearing book.

Henry answered. Hallelujah. I told him everything. Melissa, Waysie, Wally, Daddy Mayfield, Yankee Doodle, four other dead horses—the whole stinking mess. I was so excited, I must have been talking as loud as Jeff, my desk mate at *The Appeal*. Because before long, Mrs. Flock from next door was tapping on the wall. "Sorry," I called out, and finished my conversation in a whisper.

"Henry, can you believe it? Tell me, is this great stuff or what?"

"It's interesting," Henry said, his voice as calm and collected as it had been earlier today in Fred's office. Then it was reassuring, now it was infuriating.

"Jesus, Henry, can't you be a little more enthusiastic?" I said. "The daughter of Charlotte's biggest developer tells me Daddy committed insurance fraud—maybe even murder—and it's *interesting*?"

"It's more than interesting if it's true," Henry said. "Does she have any proof? Anyone other than her mother who can corroborate the story? And why would she tell a reporter now, years after it happened? She could just be an angry daughter trying to hurt her father. Or she could be emotionally unstable. Or she could be telling what she believes is the truth. It could be any number of possibilities."

"It could be. But it isn't," I said. "I saw her when she talked about Wally. A hate that deep comes from something big. He killed her horse and that horse had been her life. She still can't even mention Waysie's name without crying. She's been living with this hell for almost three years, keeping it to herself, probably thinking it was her job to hold the family together. Henry, what she's telling isn't *her* truth, it's *the* truth. Believe me on this one. I know it as sure as I know my name."

"About names," Henry said, "can we use hers? Did she talk on the record?"

"You bet your ass she did." I knew the rules at *The Appeal* as well as Henry. No anonymous sources without a dispensation from the publisher, which meant no anonymous sources. "Every damn thing she said we can quote, with her name, age, blood type. Whatever we want. We're on to something here, Henry. At the very least, Melissa's father is guilty of insurance fraud, at the most, murder. Now, if you can just get off your high horse . . ."

"Okay, okay, you're right," Henry said. "I was a little harsh and too skeptical. It's been a while since I've worked with another reporter on a story. This is a good start. Let's figure out what we need to do next. Then I'll do a records check on Melissa's father. . . ."

I heard a little voice screaming "Daddy" from his end of the phone.

"I've got to go," Henry said. "I'm sorry if I seemed like a wet blanket. That was a great job you did reporting. See you at nine-thirty tomorrow. My car, in the parking lot."

CHAPTER 9

Anyone looking for charm on the back country roads in South Carolina won't find it on the way to Camden.

What you will find are scruffy pines, sandy lowlands, plenty of tar-paper shacks perched on cinder block, and a Bojangles chicken franchise in every town over 15,000, which there aren't many of. Mostly, it's little gatherings of beaten-down homes, with railroad tracks jutting through the middle like a bumpy spine on a skinny kid.

Somewhere between Lancaster (where there is a Bojangles) and Elgin (where there's nothing but a redbrick Baptist church and the Catfish Stomp in December), Henry started waxing academic on the South.

"It's the legacy of poverty," Henry said, explaining the social topography of the Palmetto State (named, I wondered, after the tree or the titian-colored roaches bigger than my index finger that bombard themselves into people during rutting season).

Henry's first job out of Harvard was covering South Carolina for *The Appeal*. He was as familiar with that state as I had, I'm sorry to say, become with Seventh Avenue. He could talk low-country scandals, tobacco allotments, and Strom Thurmond's child brides with the best of the South Carolina pols. While I could chat up a discourse on the eclectic eccentricities of Geoffrey Beene or the unstructured structure of Calvin Klein.

"You had a very stratified society before the Civil War,"

Henry continued. No problem guessing Henry's major at Harvard. History. "Very rich and very poor. Then the war devastated the South. Where was the money going to come from to build and maintain quaint villages in the middle of nowhere? They didn't have that kind of economic development. The rich people stayed together in bigger enclaves. Like Charleston, Beaufort, even Camden."

Camden proper was lovely. Lots of grand old homes and beautiful, well-tended gardens. That was because back in the early 1900s, Camden was a Palm Beach of sorts, with lots of rich Yankees and their horses wintering down here. While most of the big, fancy hotels are history, the migratory practice isn't. Till this day, lots of big-bucked northerners pack up their clothes and barns and head to Camden or Southern Pines until the snow melts.

I'd driven to Camden many times, for horse shows or day trips to the tack shops. But I'd gone the seventy miles with my horse friends and we didn't exactly talk about the economic woes of the region. I found Henry's explanations fascinating and his enthusiasm for the subject contagious.

I was, however, concerned when I saw the heat gauge on Henry's car start creeping up on the Heath-Springs-to-Camden shortcut, a thirty-mile stretch of sand and pine with nothing but a few empty ramblers and Mr. K's Social Klub. The needle miraculously slipped back down to the blue zone and we made it into Camden with no problem.

Any question about this town's financial and emotional heart can be readily answered by a drive down DeKalb Street, the main thoroughfare. The first thing that smacks you in the face is a two-story-high mural of a pink-coated huntsman jumping his mount over the hedgerow of an antebellum mansion. Even the McDonald's on the corner of DeKalb and Fair is equinely themed. Eat a Big Mac and you'll be staring at life-size paintings of horses and hurdles.

Between the steeplechasers, the polo players, the fox hunters, and the show riders, horses make for Camden's second largest industry. Drive a little farther down DeKalb and off to the side and you'll get a hint at the first. The grand old homes of Camden proper turn into clapboard huts. Poor black men and women sit out front, trying to catch a breeze. Mill workers. Camden has at least five big mills. Du Pont. Hermitage. Kendall. Veratech. They spin everything from nylon fibers to polyester cheesecloth.

I took Henry on a quick horse-driving tour, past the two training tracks in town, Springdale and the Camden Training Center. Then we went down Firetower Road, horse show row and home of Lucy Bladstone. I'd suggested earlier we call first.

"It's much easier to hang up on someone than it is to close a door in your face," Henry said. "Let's knock and see what she does."

"On Lucy the Terrible's door? I've never seen that woman smile, and you should hear her scream at her grooms and trainers."

"All the more reason to surprise her," Henry said.

"All right, you won the Pulitzer, not I," I said. "Let's go."

CHAPTER 10

I hadn't seen the Bladstone place before. What I expected was a mansion along the Charlotte moneyed lines, an elaborate two- or three-story antebellum deal with fluted white columns, a sweeping horseshoe driveway, and rolling hills graciously land-scaped by colossal magnolias and commanding oaks. What we saw was anything but. Crammed amid a spindly forest of half-dead pines was a rectangle of redbrick, squat and undistinguished, with a grid of wind-out casement windows that looked as if they hadn't seen a coat of paint since 1953, when the house was prob-ably built.

"Sure she lives here?" Henry asked.

"It's the address in the phone book," I said. "I guess this is how the rich stay rich."

Fifteen or twenty dogs were running around, and even those weren't what I'd expected. They were mutts. Brown ones, black ones, yellow ones. Nothing even close to a Jack Russell or Welsh corgi, the official horsey breeds of dog.

I didn't get out of the car because dogs scare me, especially big, growling ones like the black shepherd mix that was snarling by my door.

"You first," I said to Henry.

"Let's think about this for a minute," he said.

While we were thinking, Lucy Bladstone opened her front door and squinted her eyes our way. She had a wide triangle of frizzy black hair and a pointy nose ("Looks like she could open a can with it," Gail said whenever she saw her). Around her eyes she penciled thick black lines, making her look even more like the Wicked Witch of the West.

Usually rich men wear beautiful women on their arms for jewelry. In Lucy's case, no one could figure what L. M. Bladstone, heir to the biggest food, tobacco, and textile conglomerate in the country, saw in her, except maybe her marksmanship. Apparently she could shoot an apple off your head, if you were stupid or drunk enough to let her. From what I'd heard, L.M. was both. Add that to his alleged gun problem—he supposedly likes to squeeze the trigger at inappropriate times just to hear it pop—and I guess Lucy looked pretty good to L.M.

"Ranger," she yelled at the black snarler, "get over here."

Then she motioned for us to come out.

Henry and I cut a path through the rest of the canines, who seemed more interested in sniffing our crotches than killing us.

Lucy was smiling. Before I got to the door, she said to me, "You look familiar? Don't I know you?"

It took me a second to figure out what she was saying because she talked so fast I thought I was back in the North.

"Sort of," I said. "I ride a chestnut mare, Brenda Starr."

"Good jumper, lots of chrome?" Lucy asked.

"Chrome?" Henry said.

"It means lots of white on her," I said. "Long white stockings, big white blaze. That's Brenda."

"Cute mare," Lucy said. "What can I do for you? Are you lost or looking for someone's farm?"

"Actually, yours," I said. "I'm a reporter for *The Charlotte Commercial Appeal.* My name's Natalie Gold and this is Henry Goode. He's also a reporter."

"Oh, God," Lucy said, "all that crap with Wally and Ruskie. That's what you're here about, isn't it? Jesus H., I can't believe that son of a bitch went and got himself killed. Well, I suppose it's inevitable, a story in the newspaper, TV cameras, the whole friggin' nine yards. It's too damn hot to talk out here. So come on in, I'll have Dorothy make us some tea."

Lucy the Terrible was turning out to be Lucy the Tolerable. Henry looked at me, and if it was anyone else, someone who registered emotion on his face, I'd have sworn he gave me an ironic so-this-is-Lucy-the-Terrible? look. We followed behind as Lucy walked to her door. Henry would have had to be dead not to notice her body. She was wearing dove-gray stretch britches that clung to her like Saran Wrap. She may have had the shoulders of a fullback and the face of Margaret Hamilton, but she had the butt of a centerfold, two perfect cantaloupes perched atop a shapely set of gams.

"None of them bite, but a couple of them might hump you," Lucy said to us, and we stepped into her living room.

I don't know what was more overwhelming. The sight or the smell. There were at least as many dogs inside as out, sprawled across the sofas and chairs.

"They're all strays," she said. "People keep dropping them at my house because they know I'll keep them. I'm a sucker for lost dogs. L.M. can't stand them, but I told him if he wants to take them to the shelter, go ahead. 'Their blood'll be on your hands, not mine,' I said to him. 'Because you know what happens to ninety-nine percent of those dogs. And even the dogs they keep, you know what . . .' "

I nodded in agreement because Lucy didn't leave many spaces in the conversation for another person. As I was nodding and listening to Lucy's tirade about animal shelter brutality, I looked around at the furniture. My stepfather had been in the business, so I have a working knowledge of it from spending so much time at the furniture market with him in High Point. I could tell the stuff in Lucy's house had been top of the line, once. Baker probably. Tapestry and brocades from the triple A swatches, stretched across sofa frames that would last three generations, which is important to old money. I suppose the frames were still serviceable, but everything else was shot to shit. Every time a dog moved, feathers clouded up through holes in the cushions. Heavy silk fringe that I can only guess had one time been ivory looped off the sofa skirt seams, onto the floor, and into a couple of dogs' mouths who were using it in a tug-of-war. What had once been gold braid piping on an overstuffed chair was frayed into a blur of dingy brown.

As I was looking around, trying not to look startled, an old black woman in a starched white uniform walked in. She saw the look on my face and rolled her eyes, pale green eyes, translucent as a shooter marble. I couldn't take my eyes off her eyes. I felt like I was looking into a secret, private place, as if she'd left her underwear drawer open—on purpose.

"I keep telling her to get rid of these nasty, stinkin', filthy dogs, but she won't listen to anyone," the woman said. "They won't even do their business outside. Imagine that, grown dogs peein' and doing whatever on Mr. Bladstone's grandfather's rugs. If I had anything to say about it, I'd—"

"Don't mind Dorothy," Lucy said, interrupting the woman mid-sentence. "She's been with us so long, she thinks she owns the place. You know she raised L.M., she feels like she owns him, too. Dorothy, be a dear and get us some tea. Also, bring some of that lemon poppy-seed bread Sully made. It's in the freezer."

The old woman was still grumbling as she walked back into the kitchen.

"You know Sully, don't you?" Lucy said to me. "Cute little blond girl who braids? She does the best tails I've ever seen."

I knew her all right. She was the most expensive braider on the circuit. Thirty bucks for a mane and twenty for a tail. I used her once, she was nice enough, downright friendly for a horse person. She loved to gossip about anything. It didn't matter if it was true or not.

A few months back she told me she'd worked for Doc Loc after Gail had. Then she went on and on about how Gail and Doc Loc had something going other than the veterinary business. Gail thought that was hysterical, given the fact that Doc Loc has more than thirty years on her.

"Don't listen to anything that kid says," Gail said, laughing hard enough to bring on a coughing fit and hard enough to say she was going to swear off cigarettes. "She's a mutant. Just look at her eyes, they're the lightest shade of blue I've ever seen on a human. Her father must have been a Siberian husky. I hear she barks at the moon at night."

Gail was right about her eyes, they were paler than an Icelandic sunset.

I never used Sully after she handed me the bill. Fifty-five bucks for a horse hairdo—three times what I pay for mine. But I saw her at all the shows, usually at four in the morning, standing sleepy-eyed horses under a spotlight while she wove their manes and tails into intricate braids.

You can turn a plug into an elegant-looking hunter with a set of braids. It's all part of the ritual charade that one of these six-digit show horses might actually ever set foot in a hunt field. Braiding makes sense when you're galloping through the woods and your horse's mane and tail could get tangled in the trees. But in a show ring? The closest you come to a branch of anything is a brush box, a jump made from two panels of wooden slats stuffed with pine boughs. It's a sanitized simulation of what horses jump in the hunt field. Because it's an uncomplicated hurdle, one that horses jump unquestionably, it's usually the first fence in a course of eight unless you get an overly creative course designer who thinks it's amusing to start horses over difficult obstacles like ox-ers—wide, spread fences.

Sully braided Lucy's horses practically every time they stepped out of the stall. Every show she went to—the big ones, the small ones, the unrecognized ones, even the ones where no one else's horses were even brushed—Lucy's horses were do'ed and dolled to the nines. What was fifty bucks a head and tail to the woman who was married to the man who kept America in chicken noodle soup and filtered menthol lights?

"Rob braids for us," I said. "He doesn't think anyone can do as good a job as he can. You know how he gets about things."

"Who doesn't know how Rob gets?" Lucy said. She laughed and her eyes squeezed shut so all that was left were two dark lines of black, making her look like she had equal signs below her eyebrows. "It's no surprise to anyone that he killed Wally."

"It is to me," I said. "I don't think he did it."

"Oh, really? Then you didn't know him well enough. Here, sit down," Lucy said as she pushed a few of the dogs off the sofa. She squeezed herself into the overstuffed chair, next to a dead ringer of Old Yeller.

"Is that Mama's sweet, sweet little boy?" she cooed to the dog in baby talk. "Mr. Muffsky-wufsky?"

I don't know what it is with Wasps and their dogs. Here's a breed of stiff-upper-lippers who would rather die than emote. Yet around a dog they become mush. I'd seen it in college, with my roommate. She was as pedigreed as they come. Her father had been ambassador to Romania; her mother was a newspaper heiress. They never kissed or hugged or screamed or shouted. Everything was so level, I thought they were dead. When my roommate got married, her father made a long, pedantic toast. Not once did he mention his daughter's name or talk about what she'd been like as a little girl or anything more personal than the "heritage that will be passed along and the service these two young people will contribute to society." But when any of them got near their golden retriever, Sally Sue, watch out and grab a shovel. They babbled like babies.

"You know, if Wally weren't dead, I'd kill that son of a bitch myself I'm so mad about what he did to Ruskie. He knew I wanted that horse. But he's dead and there's nothing I can do now. What can I tell you other than that?" Lucy said. She was stroking Old Yeller's stomach and his back leg was jack-hammering back and forth.

Henry took out his reporter's pad and a tape recorder.

"Have any objections to our using this?" Henry asked.

"Should I?" Lucy said.

"None that I can think of," Henry said. "It's as much for your protection as ours. This way, you'll know we're getting exactly what you say."

Lucy flashed a smile Henry's way. "All right, then," she said, "shoot."

And that's what he did, right between the eyes.

"Let's start with you," Henry said. "Where did you grow—"

"Me?" Lucy said, slicing off Henry's sentence. "What does any of that have to do with Rob killing Wally?"

"Well," Henry said, "there are plenty of murders in Charlotte, and we don't write about them all. What intrigues me about Wally is the world he lived and died in. It's a world very few people know about, yet it's centered in the Carolinas. Everybody I talk to says you're one of the most important people in this world, the horse show world. That's why we're knocking on your door first. We'll be interviewing lots of other people, asking them the same questions . . ."

By the time he finished schmoozing her, talking so smooth and calm, she looked loose enough to tell him what positions she likes best, if he'd have asked. But Henry stuck to the pertinent facts and it seemed once Lucy got started, she liked nothing better than to talk, especially about herself. I didn't think she'd ever come up for air.

"Bayonne, ever hear of it?" she began. "That's where I grew up."

Bayonne? Well, knock me over with a feather. I knew Bayonne, it's a tough North Jersey town sandwiched between Newark, Staten Island, and Brooklyn. The only fox hunting up there is looking for sexy babes. I'd assumed Lucy had grown up in L.M.'s world, a child of privilege whose mother scrambled to find the best and most photo-opportunistic disease to fund-raise for, while her father made sure the hired help kept the four-board fencing creosoted, before creosote was banned.

So much for assumptions. I was wrong about her house and I was wrong about her. The only thing Lucy had in common with old Wasp money was her oochy-goochy muffie-wuffie doggie talk.

As it turns out, Lucy's mother and father were the hired help.

"My mother worked the graveyard shift at the HoJo's on the Jersey Turnpike, Exit 14B," Lucy said. "She worked there thirty-fours years. When she left to move down here, they gave her a little gold HoJo pin. She still wears it, can you believe it? I buy her jewelry from Cartier and she still wears her HoJo pin.

"My father, he worked for the state highway department, fixing potholes in the summer, spreading sand in the winter. I got a scholarship to Jersey City State Teachers College and I took it because the last thing I wanted to do was wind up at the HoJo's with my mother. The next to the last thing I ever wanted to be was a teacher. But I figured something else would pop up."

Which it did. The first week of classes, Lucy saw a sign for the school's gun club. She'd grown up stealing her brother's toy guns to play with, because her mother would buy her only dolls.

"I was born to shoot," Lucy said. "The first time I held a real gun, I put the bullet smack in the middle of the target."

It was one championship after another, and soon Lucy was the reigning queen of college shooters. Winter of her sophomore year, Lucy and three of her friends went to the Newark civic center to see the Great Union Circus.

"Tiny Tim was the ringmaster," Lucy said. "Remember him? That creep with the long, stringy hair who played the ukulele and sang 'Tiptoe Through the Tulips'? That's where he wound up after marrying Miss Vicki on Johnny Carson. Anyhow, he introduced the first act, 'Ladies and gentlemen, Miss Annie Oakley.' The lights went down and a record started playing Ethel Merman singing 'Anything You Can Do.' Out into the spotlight she comes and tries to shoot beer bottles off a wooden horse. The horse wound up with more holes in it than the West Side Highway.

"So my friend turned to me and said, 'Lucy, you could do better than that asleep.' And you know what? She was right. I hated school, anyway. The idea of being a teacher made me sick. After the show I found the manager and out-Annie-Oakleyed their pathetic little Annie Oakley. I had them bring in a real horse and set two bottles on him. Before the horse could even think about spooking, I shot both bottles off his butt. They hired me on the spot."

Lucy toured with the circus for two and a half years. It was there, she said, she learned to ride from the troupe's equestrienne, a woman who went by the name of La Donna Mobilay, billed by the circus as "The Genuine Italian Contessa from Venice." Never mind that Venice is an island and probably doesn't have a horse on it.

"Her real name was Alma Darnell," Lucy said. "She was from Toxey, Alabama, never even met an Italian before! She got that name when she started traveling with the circus and liked it better than Alma, so that's what everyone called her, La Donna. She introduced me to L.M. Fifteen years ago this coming October. Good old La Donna."

Lucy got off the chair and Old Yeller sprawled himself back across the space where he'd been to start with. She walked over to the bookshelf, found a silver-framed eight-by-ten wedged between two Dick Francis mysteries.

"That's La Donna and me," she said.

Henry turned the picture so I could see it. Lucy must have been about twenty-five. Her face was smooth as an unlined piece of parchment paper. Before all the years of unprotected sun and too much coke, Lucy had been pretty. Her hair was in long braids and she was wearing a fringed suede skirt, matching vest, and moccasins. Next to her stood a severe-looking blonde with chiseled bones and arctic blue eyes, a regular poster girl for Hitler's Aryan nation. She was a study in black—body suit, riding boots, leather gloves—except for a shimmer of silver at her heels where she wore the longest, meanest pair of rawled spurs I'd ever seen.

"La Donna could make any horse do anything," Lucy said.

I'll bet, considering the lethal-looking whip in her hands, the weapons attached to her boots, and the don't-fuck-with-me look etched into her face.

Lucy pushed Old Yeller back into his corner of the chair, sat back down, and continued to talk with no encouragement from either Henry or me. She'd met L.M. during the Great Union Circus's run in Columbia, South Carolina's state capital twenty minutes west of Camden. L.M.'s girlfriend at the time, a show rider by the name of Ceezie Leads, got tickets for his birthday.

"You know Ceezie, dontcha?" Lucy asked me.

I wanted to say, "You mean Sleazie Leads?" That's how I knew of her. She'd been fined and booted from the shows umpteen times for pumping her horses full of Ace, a tranquilizer that makes even the most wild-eyed maniac lope around a course as if he were in no hurry to do anything but please his owner.

"Well, they went to the circus," Lucy said, "and Ceezie couldn't take her eyes off La Donna's big chestnut. Talk about daisy cutters. This horse floated around the ring."

Apparently L.M. was equally transfixed. With Lucy and her guns. Ceezie dragged L.M. behind the big top after the show, searching for La Donna so she could buy the horse. While the two women were hammering out a deal, Lucy walked up and La Donna made introductions.

"L.M. called me that night when he got back to Camden," Lucy said. "And then every night after the show, we went out. Dinner, movies, target practice.

"For the next six months, he flew into wherever I was playing. And then we got married. Romantic, huh?"

"Sounds like magic," I said, and wondered where it had gone. Probably the way it does most times people get married, out the window. In Lucy and L.M.'s case, however, it seemed to have landed even farther afield considering her intimate alliances with Wally, and from what Gail told me, every other trainer before him. How stupid could L.M. be? Didn't he see the two-carat chunk of diamond in Wally's left ear that Lucy bought? Or was it true that L.M. was an inbred drunk with an IQ firmly fixed in double-digit land?

"Whatever happened to La Donna?" I said. It had nothing to do with the story, but that look in La Donna's eyes made me want to know where she was, just to make sure it wasn't anywhere near me.

Lucy clearly liked playing to a male audience better. She smiled at Henry while she answered me.

"I introduced her to a friend of L.M.'s, one of the Kleenex guys," Lucy said. "She up and married him, moved to Wisconsin, and is freezing her ass off there. She rides hunters now and I see her at the indoor shows."

Lucy kept yakking about herself and L.M. Their courtship, their wedding, their honeymoon, their summers in Camden, their winters in Palm Beach. She made it sound as if they were joined at the hip and happy about it. Finally, I found a break in a sentence and steered her toward our story.

"How long had you been training with Wally?" I said. "And how did that get started?"

"A couple years now," Lucy said. "I'd been through a string of trainers. Don, Jack, Stewart, Lyle, Joey, Johnny—you know them all. None of them could do anything with Lady. She bucked around the courses, missed the distances, swapped leads before the fence. I had one of the fanciest horses in America and I couldn't get her around a course.

"Then I ran into Wally at Upperville. You know how it always rains at that show? Well, Lady hates mud. Wally and I got to talking at Sally's party—Sally Lymon, you know her, don't you? The Lymons of Middleburg? Billy Hawkins used to ride for them, before he got the bug. Anyway, Wally said he'd take Lady in second year green. And Lord, if that horse didn't go the best she's ever gone. She won the division and then I took her amateur and I won every class."

I knew Henry didn't understand the horse talk, especially the part about Billy getting the bug—AIDS. But I didn't want Lucy to stop and I figured I'd translate for him later, in the car.

"I made Wally an offer he couldn't refuse and he moved to my barn the next week," Lucy said. "He was a hell of a trainer,

I've got to say that for him. But what I had to put up with from that lunatic in Charlotte. It was sick. Rob would call fifty times a day, and if I answered, he'd hang up. I'd see his car, a little black Camry—not a speck of dirt on it—I'd see it parked down the road. Him sitting there, staring up toward the barn. Like I said, it was sick."

Lucy buried her face in the yellow dog's fur. "Isn't that right, Mr. Muffsky-Wufsky? It was just sick. I'd hear Rob screaming out the other end of the phone. Wally would hold it out from his ear, put his hand over the mouthpiece, and whisper, 'That asshole's going to be the death of me.' Wally didn't know how right he was."

I didn't want to go into my Rob-is-innocent shtick again. As a reporter, I'm supposed to be objective, a journalistic charade every bit as silly as pretending show ring horses are competing as field hunters. Besides, what was the point? Lucy and probably all of Camden thought the sheriff arrested the right man.

"When was the last time you saw Wally?" I asked.

"About a week ago," she said. "He said something about going antiquing in Virginia, but he promised he'd meet me at Rob's yesterday to watch Ruskie get vetted."

Dorothy finally came back in with a silver pitcher of iced tea.

"God, Dorothy, what took you so long?" Lucy said. "What about the lemon poppy-seed bread? Didn't I tell you to bring that in, too?"

"I ain't touching that bread ever again," Dorothy said. "I took it out of the Frigidaire and it near killed me. A shooting pain right upside my head and down my back. No, ma'am, you want that bread, you'll have to be getting it yourself. There's tears in that bread and I got enough inside of me to last a life."

"Don't start that low-country voodoo talk with me again,

Dorothy, just go get the bread. Close your eyes if you have to, or light a few candles and say some prayers or whatever it is you do. Just bring the damn bread in. And hurry up this time."

Dorothy walked out of the room talking to herself, loud enough for me to hear at least half her words. Something about Mrs. B. choking on that bread. To hide my smile, I took a sip of the tea she'd poured us. It was sweet enough to make my teeth ache and remind me how overdue I was at the dentist.

Lucy talked more about Wally and his way with horses. Even when she said something nice about him, she had an edge to her voice. Was she trying to make us believe there had never been anything but horses between them and he'd soured that by killing Ruskie? Or had the magic gone out of that relationship, too?

One thing nagged at me. Why was Wally traipsing around the Virginia countryside looking at junk during peak show season? Most pros wait until after the indoor shows are over in mid-November to take a break. Upperville was coming up and the shows don't get much bigger or fancier than that.

I said, "So if Wally's gone, who'll you be training with for Upperville and Deep Run?"

Lucy gave me an odd don't-you-know? look, as if I'd just asked if Rodney Jenkins, the most famous horseman in America, has red hair. He does, and he's almost as famous for that as he is for careening a jumper around a course faster than anyone.

"No one," she snapped. "That's why I wanted to buy Ruskie this week."

I felt the hair on my arms stand on end and I knew what was coming next. Another dead horse.

"Lady died three weeks ago," Lucy said. "It was the night before a little schooling show at Max Bonham's old place. I'd turned her out in the paddock so she wouldn't be high the

83

next day. It wasn't supposed to storm that night. But, Jesus, did it. Thunder and lightning, I woke up in the middle of the night. It was crashing like nobody's business. I wanted to bring her in, but L.M. wouldn't let me go out. Said it was too dangerous. And the phone lines were out, so I couldn't call Thomas—my farm manager—or Wally. I heard one hit the house. It blew out our television set. Then a few seconds later I heard another one a little farther away. That must have been the one that got her."

I looked at Lucy. Her eyes were watery, but the rest of her face was hard, hard and cracked like a piece of shattered safety glass. Her throat was squeezing shut back and forth, like she was trying to grab back the tears.

"I'm sorry, Lucy," I said. "I had a horse die once, and I still cry about him."

"I'll get over it," she said, dismissing any further talk of Lady. "That's it, what else can I tell you?"

Just then Dorothy came back in the room, carrying a tray at arm's length. On it were neatly sliced pieces of lemon poppy-seed bread. I took a piece. It was delicious, tart and sweet, with tiny balls of crunch.

"One more thing," I said between bites. "What were you doing the day Wally died? Did you hear from him or anything?"

"I already told you," she said. She didn't look at Henry this time. And she didn't smile. "He was in Virginia, near Middleburg. And no, he didn't call. I was with L.M., at the gun club. Call them, it's Camden Rod and Gun, if you don't believe me. Anything else?"

"I don't think so," I said. "But thanks."

Henry was packing up the tape recorder. He handed her his card and said, "If there's anything else you can think of about Wally and who wanted him dead, give me a call."

Lucy let out a loud and dramatic, "Ha!"

"That's a good one," she said. "Half of Camden wanted him dead. Just ask anyone who bought a horse from him."

CHAPTER 11

Henry was hungry and wanted something authentic. So I took him to the Shrimp Boat on the wrong side of town. I ordered fried chicken gizzards and Henry looked at me like I was nuts.

"Pippicks, haven't you ever seen anyone eat a pippick before?" I said.

Henry was still looking at me like I'd picked up a dead opossum on the road and taken a bite out of it. I guess I was going to have to give him Jew lessons along with horse lessons.

"Chicken soup," I said. "You can't make it without gizzards. In Yiddish, they're called pippicks. That's what my grandmother called them. We fought over who got to eat the most pippicks after she made a pot of soup. When I moved down here and saw them by the plateful, that was almost enough to make me forget about the white stuff they call bread. Try them, they're delicious."

"I'll have an order of shrimp," Henry said to the man behind the counter.

Over lunch, Henry and I charted our course. We figured we'd stop by Keith Rollings's place to find out how his horse, Yankee Doodle, died. And also, his connection with Wally.

"I've got to pick the boys up by six," Henry said. "But if we get back to Charlotte in time, I think I'll go down to the courthouse and do some record checks on Melissa's father, see if I can find any kind of paper trail."

"I'll call around to my horse show friends," I said, biting deep into a fibrous lump of gizzard. "Ask them what they know about Wally, and whom he might've pissed off big-time in the past few months."

Fried gizzards taste great going down, but it takes only a few minutes for the assault to register. By the time I got to Henry's car, an Alka-Seltzer chaser would have suited me fine. Instead, I stifled a few burps and silently chanted my personalized Transcendental Meditation mantra, a twenty-first birthday present from my father which in the past fifteen years I've used only in times of extreme indigestion or equally uncomfortable situations.

"Hello, Nattie, are you there?" Henry was tapping me on my shoulder. "How do we get to Rollings's farm? I asked you once and you didn't answer."

"Sorry," I said. "The gizzards are a little hard going down. Just get back to DeKalb, take a left, and keep going till you see four-board fencing around acres and acres of what looks like indoor-outdoor carpeting."

I knew exactly where Keith lived. I passed his farm every time I went to a show at the Tri-Color showgrounds, a few miles east of Camden. His place was next to the DuPonts and every bit as colossal. Big magnolia trees, sweeping acres of bright green pasture, and a mansion for Scarlett to die for, whom he happened to have married. Her name had been Bryce Whitfield Hastings before the nuptials. She was southern aristocracy, descended from two of the oldest families in South Carolina. I'd met her a couple of times, once a few weeks ago at a symphony party I was covering, the other at a horse show. She was so well bred, so gracious, so mannered, so smiley, so sweet, I felt like I'd been sucking on a pack of Equal after I talked to her. She must have used the word *darling*—

as in "Isn't this just"—fifteen times a paragraph. And that was in between "Don't you just love" whatever it was in her field of vision.

The way I figured it, they deserved each other. They could bump into one another every few months in their big house and talk about how darling everything was. Which I'm sure it was, given Rollings's money. The house must have had well over thirty rooms, judging by the sheer bulk of the building and all its windows. I can't imagine what they did with them all. It was just Keith, Bryce Whit, and their two-year-old daughter, Hastings.

"Now, this," said Henry as we drove under the feathery arch of oaks leading to Keith's house, "is more what I expected. How'd he make his money?"

"Make?" I said. "Keith Rollings doesn't make money. He has money. I'd bet he's never seen a paycheck in his life. Rollings Paper. If you've ever driven through Brunswick, Georgia, you've smelled his family's money. They've stunk up the town so bad, none of them live in the same state anymore. Keith's job is riding in the amateur division on the A-show circuit. Or should I say 'shamateur division,' because that's what it is, a sham. He's got his own personal trainer who finds him the horses, trains them, rides them everyday to keep them tuned up so Keith's groom can give Keith a leg up at the shows and Keith can canter around the courses and win every class he goes in on his $250,000 horses."

"Jealous?"

"You bet, and angry," I said. "I'm one of the few amateur riders who actually works for a living. But that's life in the show world. Anyhow, I do all right. I get thirds—I'm always right behind Lucy and Keith."

Henry banged the fox-head door knocker. No answer. I

peeked in the sidelight windows and saw a bunch of heavy, dark furniture and gilded framed portraits of dour old men. We drove around back to the barns, where the wood was so shiny white, it hurt my eyes.

Some southerners have yet to acknowledge the outcome of the Civil War, and Rollings was clearly one of them: Right at the entrance of his barn stood a black-faced jockey statue glimmering like Al Jolson in black greasepaint. Next to him were rows of green window boxes full of crimson geraniums. There wasn't a spent blossom in the bunch, a weed in the grass, a wisp of straw out of place.

"Hello," I called out. A fiftyish black guy in green overalls turned the corner. He was carrying a can of white paint in one hand, a paintbrush in the other. He said his name was Lawrence, that he was the barn manager.

Henry and I introduced ourselves, told him we were working on a story about Wally and asked if we could talk to Keith or his trainer, Jack Thompson.

"You could if they were here," he said. "I'm sure they'd have plenty to say. Not a piece of it good. But they're in Ocala, looking at horses. They'll be back late tonight. You say Wally Hempstead is dead? Well, Lord have mercy, I wouldn't want to be on the receiving end of his judgment day. That was one nasty white boy."

"So we keep hearing," I said. "I heard he trained Keith for a while, even found him Yankee Doodle. Is that right? God, Keith must've been a basket case when that horse died. How'd it happen, anyway?"

Lawrence put down the can of paint, pulled a worn handkerchief from his pocket, and wiped the sweat from his forehead. "You're right about that," he said. "When that horse passed, it tore Mr. Rollings up one side and down the other. I've never

seen a man cry for an animal like that in all my days. I was
the one who found the horse in the stall, just as cold and stiff
as a run-down squirrel. Never did find out what caused it,
neither."

"Had Wally been around the barn before it happened?" I
asked.

Lawrence paused and looked at me hard.

"Look, Miss Reporter," he said, "I know what you're getting
at. I can't be answering that question or any more. Come back and
talk to Mr. Rollings or Mr. Thompson. The last thing I want is for
it to get back to them that I was talking about their business. Jobs
ain't easy to come by here, not where you're not breathing cotton
dust all day. I'm sorry, but that's the way it is. I wish I could help
you, but I can't."

He bent down and picked up the paint can and started to walk
away.

"No, wait," I said. "Wait one second. Please. Look, no one has
to know you've been talking to us. They arrested Rob Stone for
Wally's murder and I'd hate to see him go to jail or get the chair
for something he didn't do."

"They arrested Mr. Stone?" Lawrence said. "Maybe them police ain't as dumb as you think. Those two boys used to come here,
bringing horses to show Mr. Rollings. They'd fight so bad between
them, I thought one of them would end up dead. I just had it figured the other way around. I thought Mr. Hempstead would be
doing the killing. One time I saw him come at Mr. Stone with a
pitchfork, press it right up against his neck and near about draw
blood. Like I said, that was one crazy white boy. And that's all I'm
going to say."

A reporter can beg only so much. I thanked him for his time
and handed him my card. "If you think there's anything else I
should know, give me a call, okay?"

90

"I said all there's to say," Lawrence said. "Now, I got to be going. Mr. Rollings wants his barn painted by the time he comes back."

We got back into the car and drove back to Charlotte with no auto incidents. But Henry was clearly agitated.

"My God, Nattie, how can you be involved with these people. Black jockey statues?"

I'd been dreading this. He was right. He and I both knew it.

"I'm not defending anything," I said, "but I do have to say, of all the barns I've been to, that was a first. Rollings's is a throwback. But you're right, overall. Horse showing is a rich white person's sport. I can't say I much fit in, being a Jew and not a rich one at that. When I first started showing in college, it was very small, very local, against people like me, people who loved horses. I don't know what happened, I just kept wanting to get better and better, moving up higher and higher, until I found myself competing at the top. Sometimes I think I had more fun at the bottom."

"Enough, already," I said. The gizzards were starting to back up again. "This is too much philosophizing, it makes my head hurt. Tell me more about your kids."

Henry was only too willing to oblige. He regaled me with Chet and Hank stories all the way back to Charlotte. I don't usually like listening to darling-children stories, but it was fun to see Henry so animated.

Back at *The Appeal*, I listened to my voice mail first thing. A few of the retailers were mad at me for writing that only anorexic women could wear this season's hottest rage—fanny sashes—and not look like wide ends. Then the chair of the Designer House Committee, Mrs. Harden Oakley III, called to express her displeasure about my reporting skills. I'd covered their preshow party and she wasn't happy with my description of the buffet table. "Those were not tin cans of caviar as you wrote. Anyone knows those are called tins of caviar. Please call me immediately so we can correct this."

A "We Were Wrong" about caviar? Fred, the editor/shoe salesman would make me do it, too. Anytime you got something wrong in the paper, you had to write, in triplicate, an explanation of how the error occurred and how you planned for such an occurrence to never happen again. Then you had to personally give a copy to each of the three top editors and go over it again. At the end of your evaluation year, your supervising editor counted up the number of "We Were Wrongs" and subtracted ten dollars from your weekly raise for each one.

I wasn't calling Mrs. Designer House the Third too fast. Maybe she'd get a fixation about something else—say, the mismatched tartan taffeta in the sunroom—and forget about caviar tins.

Gail left three messages, ecstatic and shrieking about the lead changes she made Allie do. Then the manager from Montaldo's returned my call to say that her store was closed Tuesday night, the night of Wally's murder, for inventory. So Melissa had been lying about her shopping trip to Montaldo's. Interesting. She seemed pretty convincing last night at dinner. I gave a silent thank-you to my old editor, a wonderfully crazy guy by the name of Stuart Rimowitz, who left *The Appeal* in disgust at the way the reporters were treated—and also because the *L.A. Times* offered him a job he couldn't refuse. Whenever he edited a story, he'd ask if you'd double-checked all your facts and quotes, no matter how sure you were they were right. Then he'd say in his thick New York accent, "Remember, if ya' motha' sez she loves ya', check it out."

Finally there was a message from Rob. No name, no hello, just "Call me."

Which I did.

"Hi, Rob, it's Nattie," I said. "How're you doing? I mean, are you okay?"

"You were supposed to be here at three to school your mare," Rob said. "If you're still planning on going to Tri-Color this weekend, be here at six-thirty, otherwise, find yourself another trainer."

I didn't even get a chance to tell him where I had been before he hung up. Knowing Rob, that would have made him madder. I'd assumed going to the show with him this weekend was off. I thought he'd have more on his mind than whether I could get my horse to canter over a course of three-foot-six-inch fences. Once again I'd assumed wrong.

It was three-thirty. I figured I'd work the phones a couple of hours, then leave for the barn. I called all around North and South Carolina, tapping into everyone I knew from the circuit. Grooms, trainers, blacksmiths, horse show mothers, riders, veterinarians—you name them, I called them. Most everyone was only too happy to talk about Wally, and none of them had much good to say. He'd lied, cheated, and drugged his way through the horse world. There was, however, one thing everyone agreed on. Wally had been a gifted rider.

"He could make a school horse look like a million dollars, but if he lost his temper, get away from him quick," a friend of mine from Southern Pines said. She'd groomed for him at the big shows. "One time I saw him slap a horse so hard upside the head in the schooling ring at Devon, he made the horse bleed. I guess the steward didn't see it, and no one reported it, because not ten minutes later he took that horse in the ring and laid down the most fabulous trip. He ended up working hunter champion. That was Wally."

A trainer I knew in Greensboro had known Wally most of her life. She'd come up through junior division with him, competing against him at the big shows in Georgia, where they were from. Her name had been Lark Lowery until she married a trainer by the name of Donnie Starke, making her Lark Starke.

"He had so much God-given talent," Lark said, "he could have been another George Morris. But Wally's family didn't have the money to really campaign him, to send him indoors. His father was just a policeman. Maybe that's why, but whatever it was, Wally had more nastiness inside him than anyone I know on the circuit."

That was saying a mouthful. Trainers aren't known for their gentle ways. George Morris, for instance, the man whom Lark compared Wally to, set the standard for hunter riders—and razor-tongued trainers. He wrote the Bible on the subject—*Hunter Seat Equitation*—and writes a monthly column in *Practical Horseman* magazine, where he critiques pictures of riders jumping their horses. He never misses an opportunity to point out the extra pounds on the rider's rear. He also goes around the country teaching clinics that people can't wait to attend, after they lose fifteen pounds. Morris is famous for shredding and shaming chubby equestriennes.

By the time five-thirty rolled around, I must have talked to ten people and left messages for another ten. The red light on my phone was blinking, which meant calls had come in while I was talking. Probably Mrs. Oakley and her caviar problem. Reluctantly, I played back the messages, in case any were from my riding contacts.

A trainer from Hilton Head called back, as did an amateur rider from Tryon who'd trained with Wally. I'd met her by the in gate at the last Tri-Color show. She'd been in tears and Wally had been screaming at her. She left a long and rambling message about how she couldn't possibly talk to me about Wally.

I saw Henry walking my way. He had a big smile on his face and was motioning to a stack of papers in his hand, so I wasn't really paying much attention to the last message. I thought I misunderstood or maybe heard Jeff, my desk mate, roaring into his phone. But some part of me heard it right, because the hairs on my arm were standing straight up again.

I pushed the replay button. "Four dead horses. Could be five. Back off or die."

I must have gasped or looked like I'd seen a ghost, because before I knew it, both Henry and Jeff were by my side, asking me what was wrong.

My hand was trembling as I passed the phone to Henry.

"Listen to this," I said.

Henry put the receiver against his ear and I pressed the playback button again.

"That's a good voice disguise," Henry said. "I can't tell if it's a man or a woman. It looks like we're hitting on something that's making someone very nervous. The trick is to figure out what and whom. Then we'll have one hell of a story."

"Great," I said, "someone wants to kill me or my horse. Probably both. And all you can think about is the story."

Jeff had gotten the gist of what was happening and put his hand on my shoulder. He faced Henry and said, "Back off, Bob Woodward, can't you see she's upset? What've you got inside of you, icicles?"

Henry's cheeks flushed. "Jeff, this is between Nattie and myself, if you don't mind."

Jeff puffed up like a rooster, and I didn't know what was going to happen next. There's so much tension between the features and news departments at *The Appeal*, I thought Jeff was going to slug Henry right there and claim a smashed-up Henry as a victory trophy for Features. Mercifully, Jeff's phone rang.

"What a hothead," Henry said. "Is everyone back here this excitable?"

"Henry, he did have a point. Someone just threatened my life, for Christ sakes."

"All right, I understand your concern. Just realize it happens all the time. People feel protected by the anonymity of the telephone and will say anything. I suppose it's scary the first time."

"Just the same, I'm calling the police. I want someone with a gun to know that a wacko is after me in case he or she feels protected by the anonymity of a dark parking lot I may be walking through, or an empty apartment I may be walking into."

"Nattie, you're overreacting. If you call the police, it will blow the story. You report a death threat and it will go over the scanner. Reporters listen to scanners all the time and it'll alert them that you're working on a good story. They'll call their police sources and before tomorrow morning WBTV, WSOC, and even the *Waxhaw Gazette* will run a story about your death threat, Wally's murder, Rob's arrest, the Bladstones, and so forth. Anything we write after that will be old news. Also, what can the police do anyway? I mean, if you get a pattern of calls, it might make sense. But one call?"

"One call's enough for me," I said.

Henry stood up and started to walk back to his desk. He said, "I don't like working on a story with another reporter to begin with, and now this. I don't know why I agreed to this. Features and news, they don't mix."

"You agreed because you didn't know Jack shit about horses or the show world. You agreed because you knew I had sources you could never have. You agreed and I'm just as good a reporter as you are, even if I do work in lingerie. That is what you trench coats call our department, isn't it?"

"I haven't ever used that term," Henry said. "However, you do seem to be very emotional back here."

I took a deep breath. I wasn't going to let him get the better of me, or any more than he'd already gotten. "How about a compromise? I won't call the police or 911 or whatever it is you're afraid of. Odom gave me his home phone number. He told me yesterday that today is his day off, but I could call him anytime. We'll call him together, tell him what happened, and beg him not to broadcast it over his scanner or take out a billboard saying I've received a death threat. Okay?"

Henry nodded like a little boy who'd lost a fight and picked up a phone at a nearby desk. I made the conference call from mine.

"Well, Lordy loo, it must be my lucky day. A joint call from Lois Lane and Clark Kent. I hear you've been all over Camden asking questions. Find out anything interesting? My friends at the Kershaw County sheriff's office tell me Mrs. L. M. Bladstone can talk your ear off. Is that so?"

"Something like that," I said. "I think I've got a problem here. Or what might be one. But this is unofficial. I mean no police reports or anything like that."

"I'm officially not working today. You don't sound as perky as you usually do," Odom said. "Something must be really wrong. What's up?"

I played him the message and heard him exhale loudly at the end of it.

"Damn, I hate it when people who have no business in it get involved in police matters. What's it gonna take to stop y'all, a bullet in the head? That was a real live dead person in that big horse's stall. This ain't no television show."

Odom had lots of questions and I was eyeing the clock. I could still make it to the barn in time for Rob if I left in the next five minutes.

"Listen, Detective Odom, I appreciate your concern, in fact I'm happy to hear someone tell me this is more than routine," I said, and glared at Henry. "But I've got someplace to be. Can we continue this later?"

"Call me Tony," he said. Henry rolled his eyes. "That's what everyone but my mama calls me. She calls me Antonio. So you've got someplace to be more important than trying to find out who wants you dead? That's fine by me. When would it be convenient to *ree*-sume our conversation?"

I hesitated to tell him where I had to be. There was no sense in lying. "I know it sounds trivial, but if I'm not out at the barn and on my horse by six-thirty, Rob will kill me. I didn't mean kill me. I mean . . ."

"You horse people are crazier than a June bug in heat. Tell you what. I don't live but three miles from February Farm. I'll just stop by and we can continue then. Does seven-thirty suit you?"

"Perfect," I said. "And thanks."

"My pleasure, I'm here to serve the public," Tony said, and hung up.

Henry had a grumpy look on his face.

"I'll see you tomorrow," I said to Henry as I gathered up my notebooks filled with quotes from the phone calls and interviews. "If I'm alive."

Jeff was still on the phone, bellowing about ratings. I hugged his shoulder and mouthed "Thanks."

"Don't show him your notes," Henry called after me. I didn't turn around or respond. The next thing I knew, Henry was by my side, looking even grumpier.

"I said don't show him your notes, didn't you hear me?"

"Of course I heard you, the whole damn newsroom heard you. What do you think I am, an idiot? I know not to show a cop my notes. Now, if you don't mind, I'm in a hurry. Good-bye."

I pushed past him, remembering I'd forgotten to ask him why

he'd been smiling and motioning to a stack of papers. Must be something he found earlier this afternoon from digging through the court and city records. I was too mad and too late to turn around. It would have to wait.

CHAPTER 12

Oxers. I hate them. Big, wide, spread fences that leave little room for error. I don't know if Rob was mad at me or mad at the world, but he built a course of the biggest, meanest oxers I'd ever seen.

"Okay, jump the course," he said as he set the last pole of a triple oxer close to four feet high with a four-foot spread in place. My first car, an orange Volkswagen, was smaller than that. "Keep your pace up and don't let her die around the corners, that's where you always lose your rhythm. And if you pull up in front of any of them, take your mare into the barn, because I'm not going to stand here and watch you ruin her."

I do have a bad habit of pulling my horse away from a fence when I'm scared. Scared that I've gotten her to a spot that's too far from the jump or too close. It may look simple, jumping a horse around a course of fences. It looks that way only when the rider's good. A talented rider can see a distance halfway across the ring, meaning she knows how fast or slow to make her horse canter so the horse will get to exactly the right spot to jump the fence. That's especially important with oxers, because if your horse jumps from too far back, you can land right in the middle since it's so wide. I've gotten Brenda to long enough spots where she's had to paddle through the air to get over. Lots of horses would have stopped dead in front of them. Quitters, they're called. But Brenda is an honest horse—she never refuses a fence—and game enough to take off from wherever I ask her. She's also an athletic enough jumper to pull us out of disastrous pilot-error situations.

I swallowed hard and squeezed her with my legs. She cantered around the course and I knew we'd hit a lick. I felt like I was flying as she sailed over the fences. I leaned forward and pressed my hands into her neck as she leapt into the air, my legs hugged at her sides, and I could feel her stretch out and over. Again and again until she jumped eight fences. Perfectly. Even the triple oxer/orange Volkswagen. When we finished, I was breathing hard and patting Brenda's neck as I brought her down to a walk. Rob was smiling.

"I don't know why you can't do that at a horse show," he said. "She's not ever gonna go any better than that. Put her up for the night. Be sure and wrap her legs."

Rob headed to his apartment and I started back to the barn when Brenda spooked so hard I almost fell off. Out of the shadows near the far end of the ring came Tony Odom walking my way.

"Sorry about that," he said. "How is it that a horse isn't afraid of those big fences and then gets in a fuss by a person walking nearby? Go figure it. Anyway, you sure make it look like poetry, jumping that little horse over those giant fences."

I reached down and wrapped my arms around Brenda's neck. I inhaled deeply, trying to fill myself with the briny smell of horse sweat. I closed my eyes and saw it, a swirl of brownish-red with sharp edges and a fat golden middle. I fell in love with that smell the first time my father took me to a stable.

"It's Brenda," I said. "She takes care of me. She must have been my mother in a previous life. Usually I make lots of mistakes. It was a lucky night."

"Your mother? I thought animals don't reincarnate," Tony said.

"What do you know about reincarnation?"

"A few things here and there. I took some Eastern religion classes in college."

He was smiling and I noticed his eyes, dark brown eyes, set deep into his face.

"And," he said, "I don't know if I'd call it a lucky night when someone tells you they want you dead."

In my panic about jumping a course of oxers and then the flush of happiness about doing it right, I'd forgotten about the phone call.

"Oh, God," I said. "Back to reality. Maybe Henry was right, that it's nothing to worry about."

"And maybe Henry's wrong, and if that's so, he can write you a real nice obituary. I'm not wanting to scare you for no reason, other than to make sure y'all take this seriously. I don't want to see how you look as a corpse. Okay?"

"Okay. I'm all yours after I wash Brenda and wrap her legs. But I don't think I should talk about it here, not with Rob upstairs."

"Fine by me, let's talk about something else."

He walked with me as I led Brenda into the wash stall and asked how I got started riding.

"You look like you've been riding your whole life. Your mama must have been a rider, and she got you started before you could walk, right?"

"Wrong," I said. Then I told him a little about my childhood, at least the part about the plastic horses my mother bought me and my dreams for a real horse.

He ran his hand down Brenda's neck. "She seems like a fine animal. I'm glad your dreams came true."

"Thanks, me, too," I said. "So what were your dreams as a little boy? A big gun and a shiny badge?"

"Not hardly. Well, maybe for a few years. My daddy was a sheriff and that's what I thought I wanted to be. Until I learned to read. Then my mama said she couldn't get my nose out of a book. From then on I was going to be the next William Faulkner. I've read every one of his books two, three times."

"I have to admire anyone who can get through one of his sentences one time."

Tony laughed, a slow, easy laugh. "You just have to learn how to slow down, take your time, and appreciate Mr. Faulkner. He's there for you, every beautiful word. You Yankees, y'all talk fast, think fast, even read fast."

"Well, at least we can get a complete thought out before the sun sets," I said. "Speaking of sunsets, that's what it's doing now and I've gotta get her finished."

I put the hose in a bucket, squirted shampoo in, and turned the faucet on full blast. The water exploded out and shot a cloud of bubbles into my face.

"Ahhhhh," I screamed. I couldn't see anything but white froth.

"Hold on there a minute, Nattie." Tony put his hands on my shoulders and turned me toward him. Then with the softest touch I'd ever felt in a man, he wiped my eyes clear. I opened my eyes and his face was close to mine.

"Nattie." I turned and saw Gail standing by the edge of the stall.

"How you doing tonight, Gail?" Tony said.

Gail ignored him and glared at me. "Nattie, Rob'll blow a gasket if he sees him here."

"You two know each other?" I said.

"He came by the day after Wally was killed, asking more questions than you do," Gail said.

"We'll be out of here in five minutes," I said. "I'll call you later tonight and explain everything. Besides, we've got to finish planning for Tri-Color. This show could be your and Allie's debut now that you've nailed his lead changes. Rob said there's room on the trailer and I know we have an extra stall at the show grounds.

What do you say, Gail, this show's as good as any to unveil your masterpiece."

I reached over to put my arm around Gail's shoulder, to give her a friendly hug. She spun away, and when she turned around she looked as if she'd dipped her face in puddles of hot-pink paint. Her fury splotches were erupting like Mt. Vesuvius.

"I'll take Allie to a show when I'm good and ready," she said. "And not one second before. So stop pestering me about it once and for all."

Then she stormed out of the wash stall.

"Boy, must be a full moon coming tonight," I said. "First Jeff, my desk mate, then Henry, then me, now Gail—all of us getting mad enough to kill. Whew. I don't know what's up. I've never seen Gail that way."

"Dead bodies set everyone on edge," Tony said. "Or you've been mining in a contaminated area."

"Mining? Mining what? What are you talking about?"

"Whatever it is that set Gail off," Tony said. "Going to a horse show, wasn't it? Must be something about that that makes her madder than a baby bull being weaned. And I don't guess she appreciates my presence much, neither. Let's get out of here before she charges me with her horns. Come on, I'll give you a hand."

I washed Brenda's back and Tony held her while I wrapped her legs. Together we walked her to her stall. Before we left, I knocked on the glass door of the office and waved good-bye to Gail. She was talking on the phone, pretending not to see me.

"Where to?" I said. Any place in Charlotte was a good fifteen miles away and there was nothing open in Waxhaw, the nearest town, this time of night.

"Like I said, I don't live three miles from here."

"I don't know, Tony, I don't want to blur any lines. Who knows what would've happened in the wash stall if Gail hadn't come in. I've got to keep my head straight for this. It's a big and important story and it could be my way out of fashion writing."

"Nothing happened in the wash stall and nothing's gonna happen at my place. You were feeling vulnerable because someone threatened your life, so it's as natural as apple pie that you'd want to lean on someone. Leaning's as far as it'll go."

I didn't know which I hoped for more—that he was telling the truth, or that he was lying. But I knew one thing for sure. It was hot, I was thirsty, and someone seemed to want me dead.

"If you can't trust a man of the law," I said, "who can you trust? Lead the way, I'll follow."

What I would have given for air-conditioning in my car. I could practically see the heat waves rippling. Except this time I wasn't sure where the heat was coming from. The night air or me. As I drove, I stuck my head as far out the window as I could, trying to cool off. Tony turned onto a dirt road that cut through a stand of long-needled pine trees. I held my hand up and let my fingers brush against the feathery spikes. At the end of the path was a small white clapboard house with green shutters, a front porch, and a wooden swing.

"Where's Lassie and Timmy?" I said as I got out.

"I don't know about Lassie, but I've got a Rin Tin Tin. Here, boy, c'mere and meet Miss Nattie Gold, *re*-porter *ex*-traordinaire for *The Charlotte Commercial Appeal*."

An old, decrepit German shepherd creaked his way from around the back of the house. He could barely walk, he limped so bad. But his tail wagged wildly, as if that was the last part of his body he could make pay any attention to his commands. He rested his head up against Tony's leg.

"That's a good boy," Tony said. "He's an old po-lice dog. His sniffer still works like a pup's, but nothing else does. Huh, old fella?

"Have a seat on the porch. I'll get us some lemonade or something."

I sat on the steps and Rin Tin Tin followed me. He eased his body down, pressed up against me, and flopped his head in my lap. I stroked his fur and he drooled on my jeans. I could feel a hot patch of moist denim spreading across my thighs, but it seemed cruel to move him since he'd settled in so quickly and was snoring louder than my old boyfriend, John.

"Y'all are fast friends, I see," Tony said. He was carrying two frosted glasses of something that looked very cool. The glands in the back sides of my mouth swelled up. "He's a good one to have. He'd risk his life for yours if you'd ask him. God bless it, it's a hot one tonight."

"Want to know exactly how hot?"

"Is this a joke or a bet?" Tony said. He sat himself on the next step down from me and Rin Tin Tin.

"A bet's fine by me. I'll win."

"Them's fighting words, Miss Nattie. If you lose—which you most certainly will because how could a Yankee city girl know anything about nature?—you make me a Yankee meal. And if I lose, which is about as likely as chicken talking French—you'll be eating grits and red-eye gravy."

"Red-eye gravy? You kidding? Isn't that coffee and bacon drippings? Forget it. You make hush puppies and it's a deal."

We shook hands and I borrowed his watch. "Go inside and call the weather number, 364-TEMP. By the time you come out, I'll tell you what it is within one degree. You'll see just what this Yankee city girl knows."

Tony walked up the steps and into his house. I pulled a pen and pad from my purse, listened for a minute, and then did my calculations.

"How about some of that shiny pink salmon on a poppy-seed

bagel with a pile of cream cheese?" Tony said as he came back down the steps.

"Ninety-two. It's ninety-two degrees out. Le cluck, le cluck, le cluck."

I watched the smile slide right off Tony's face. "I wouldn't mind some homemade biscuits, that is, if you know how to make them."

"How'd you do that? You must've heard it on the radio on the way over here."

"My radio's been broken for a year. You're not the only one with obscure interests. I took a few entomology courses in college. It's called Dolbear's formula. You can tell how hot it is by counting the number of chirps per minute from the male snowy tree cricket's mating call. Subtract forty, divide that by four and add fifty, and that's your temperature outside."

"Beat by a Yankee. This is the worst defeat since Sherman burned Atlanta. But a bet's a bet. You name when, I'll do the cooking. And of course I know how to make biscuits. Now, let's talk about Wally and who you mighta made mad enough to want to kill you."

I was more comfortable talking about bugs. "This might not be such a good idea," I said, more to myself than to Tony.

I had been scared and angry when I called Tony earlier and it clouded my judgment, although I'd choke before I ever admitted that to Henry. In fact, it wasn't until I was driving to Tony's that I even started hearing the voice of reason, that officious little man who's usually ringing a bell when I'm about to get in trouble—or having too much fun. Where was that little jerk when I was in the wash stall anyway?

He was coming through loud and clear now. A journalist working with a cop? That's like the two Jesses teaming up for the presidency. I was wading into the murky waters of journalism and I could feel the gooey bottom sucking at my feet. I knew as well as anyone that reporters shouldn't be sharing or comparing notes with the police. It raises all sorts of questions about independence, perceived and real. You want people to feel as if they can tell you things they wouldn't tell anyone, especially the police. A reporter's currency is trust and accuracy; without them she's broke.

"This is bad, Tony, any way you look at it. If I talk to you and anyone, I mean *anyone* finds out, I could lose a story I've waited years to get. If I don't talk to you, I could die. Assuming my phone caller means business."

"Talk," Tony said. "This'll be between us. One friend to another. No departmental memos, no follow-up calls. That's what's got you in a stew, idn't it?"

"You got it."

"Tonight let's forget where I work, okay?"

I took the plunge and spilled my guts, hoping I could swim to the other side and stay clean.

"The way I see it," Tony said, "half of Southern Pines and all of Camden know you're digging for dirt about Wally. That means either his killer wants you to stop, assuming it's not Stone, which I'm not ready to assume, or it's someone who doesn't want you to find something out about Wally and his little horse-killing business. That's a lot of folks who'd just as soon you stuck to writing about fanny sashes."

"This Sunday it's shoulder pads," I said. "So, what's next?"

"How about something about women dressed in men's clothes. Ooh-ooh, Lord have mercy, can't get much sexier than that. 'Cept, of course, with what she's wearing underneath."

"Very funny, I mean, what's next with my psycho caller friend? Am I going to find a dead cat boiling on my stove? Should I get bulletproof glass in my car, or what? *What* should I do?"

"Let me guess, you don't have caller ID, right?"

I nodded.

"I know someone at Southern Bell. You'll have it tomorrow. You have my number, call me if anything happens. *Anything.* I don't know what we're dealing with here. Could be nothing or it could be something. If you're worried about going home, I'll sleep on the sofa. You can have the bed. I'll padlock the door between us so no bodily urges overtake me, or you. I can make you your victory meal for breakfast. Biscuits and all."

The little man in my head was just about apoplectic. "Forget it, sister," he was screaming. *"Go home."*

"I've got to go, Tony. I'm sure everything's fine. I've got a million things to do before I take off for Camden tomorrow."

"Okay, but call me as soon as you get in. Otherwise, I'll be worrying instead of sleeping."

"I didn't know you were Jewish," I said.

"Catholic, and I'll put my mama up against any Jewish mama when it comes to worrying."

CHAPTER 13

I'd be lying if I said I wasn't scared when I walked into my apartment. But I figured the walls were thin enough for my neighbor, Mrs. Flock, to hear me being murdered. She could hear everything else that went on, and took great pleasure in letting me know it. Last month in the parking lot, she'd said to me, "That John fellow, the one who does the morning news on Channel 9, he's a handsome one. But I don't know how you can sleep through his snoring. It kept me up."

"Just bang on the wall next time, and I'll give him a shove," I'd said. That was before I'd decided there wasn't going to be a next time. I couldn't suffer through another Friday night recap of ratings and sweeps week, followed by silence and blank stares when he ran out of TV talk.

I called Tony as soon as I switched on the lights and checked the place out. Everything was fine and I was feeling pretty silly.

"I'm sure Henry was right about this, it's nothing," I said.

"Hope so. But call me if anything comes up," Tony said. "Like middle-of-the-night phone calls or strange noises. I'm right here by the phone and I can make it to Charlotte in fifteen minutes. Ten if I speed."

"I wouldn't want you to get a ticket on my account," I said.

"Po-lice don't get tickets, we give 'em."

"On that note of justice I'll say good night, and, by the way, thanks for the lemonade."

I hung up and headed straight for bed. I decided not to call Gail. I don't know what burr got under her saddle, but I wasn't about to tangle with her that night. It was hot and I was exhausted, not to mention talked out. I'd see her at the barn in the morning. I had tons of packing to do for the show, thanks to Rob. He'd given me a two-page list of essentials he insisted I bring to every horse show. I had to check off each item and then show him my checked-off list before he would let my horse get on the trailer. Rain sheet, fly sheet, boots, wraps, extra bits, bridles, saddle pads, soap, creme rinse, fly spray, etc., etc., etc. By the time I got finished, I could have opened up a small tack shop.

The night hadn't cooled off any and neither had my apartment. My windows were open wide and my bed was pushed next to them. The fan was blowing high, churning and re-churning hot air around my naked body. But it was a breeze, and mercifully I fell asleep quickly. It wouldn't take Sigmund Freud to predict what happened next. Or figure out what it meant.

Beneath my closed lids I watched a chase scene as spectacularly cinemagraphic as a Steven Spielberg movie, this one starring me and my horse:

We're galloping through the woods, cutting a cool path deep inside the heat. A sharp wind creases into my cheeks, my hands, my eyes. Tears squeeze out from the corners of my eyes and blow off before they have a chance to roll down my face. I press my legs into Brenda's flanks, urging her to move on. Faster. Faster. Suddenly a gunshot explodes behind us, the sound ricocheting against the trees. Brenda bolts, gallops faster, fleeing. Another shot, closer. Again, so close I hear the bullet whoosh past my ears. Someone's after us, faster and faster, closer

111

and closer until—Brenda stumbles, I fall, I hear a laugh, then the voice, "Back off or die . . . die . . . die." A maniacal laugh and steps racing back into the woods, away from me. I look up and see Tony Odom, standing above me, looking concerned, scared, relieved. His hands reach under my head, he pulls me up to him—thank God I don't have a broken neck—and we kiss. Hallelujah!! My blood turns to gold glitter and it swirls wildly, madly, through me. Our clothes disappear magically. We're naked together, making love so crazily, I hardly have time to notice I've dreamt myself a new pair of thighs, thin thighs.

A high-pitched ringing spirals around us, circling and circling us until we're cradled and wrapped in its translucent shimmer. I look down and see the earth slipping away, farther and farther until it's a green and blue pea in a sea of black. We come together, a blasting crescendo that's skyrocketed us into outer space, me with the added ecstasy of knowing I'd look good in a bathing suit— finally!

I wake quivering, still in the throes of an orgasm with my hips bucking to some far-off celestial beat. The female equivalent of a wet dream. Whew. If I ever considered doing it with Tony, I'd better forget it right now. Besides the fact that he's a cop, and reporters and cops don't mix, what could live up to that dream?

An industrial air conditioner couldn't have cooled me down then, let alone my measly little fan. On jelly legs I wobbled to the bathroom and turned the shower on cold, full force. Was it my imagination, or was that steam sizzling off my flesh?

I crawled back in bed, wet as a drowned rat, and fell into a deep and uneventful sleep.

The phone woke me to an even hotter apartment. Now the sun was pouring in, cranking up the heat from moist roast to searing broil. I felt like a well-done steak.

"Hello," I said. I was parched and my tongue was sticking to the roof of my mouth, making me sound like I needed speech lessons.

"Jeez, Nattie, get a drink or something." It was Gail. "Are you okay?"

"I'm fine, I'm fine. Just hot, so what else is new? This is it, I'm getting an air conditioner. Anyway, what was wrong with you last night? I thought you were gonna take an ax to me. I didn't realize Allie's show life was such a sensitive subject. I swear I'll never mention it again."

I hopped out of bed and walked to the bathroom. Bless the inventor of mobile phones. I swished some water in my mouth while Gail talked.

"It was just a bad day. Allie was a pig when I rode him. Rob was screaming at me for everything, and I'm PMSing in a big way. I'm sorry. I shouldn't have acted like that. I just, I don't know, seeing that cop here and you about to be all kissy-face with him. I don't get it, Nattie. You're going out with John, so what's this stuff with you and Odom, anyway?"

"John's over and it was nothing with Tony. I swear it."

Then I told her about the phone call and why Tony was there.

"Maybe you'd better back off, Nattie. It can't be worth your life. And even if that person's just trying to scare you, nothing good's going to come from it anyway. Whatever you write, you're going to piss off everyone on the circuit. Then try to get a ribbon. You know how political the judging is, anyway. You could put in ten perfect trips on your mare and the judge'll be looking the other way every time."

This wasn't a new thought to me. I figured whatever resentments I stirred up if I wrote a story would blow over sooner or later. At most it would cost me a few ribbons. And the trade-off would be well worth it. I didn't want to say the *P* word, but if this story turned out to be as big as I thought it was—murder, corruption, insurance fraud among the nation's wealthiest—it would certainly be a contender for the local reporting you-know-what prize.

"This could be the biggest story of my life."

"Or death," Gail said.

"Cut it out, I'll be okay. I'm just about to hop in the shower and then come out to the barn to pack up. Let's talk when I get there."

Another cold shower, my answer to no air-conditioning. I dressed and gathered my horse show clothes. Just looking at them made me hot. Heavy leather boots, stretch britches made from some kind of unbreathing man-made plastic-wrap-type fabric, longsleeve riding shirt with a matching monogrammed choker that went around my neck to seal in any escaping heat, and for the pièce de résistance—a *wool* hunt coat. All that, plus leather gloves and a black-velvet-covered hunk of Styrofoam for my head—all destined to be worn in the ninety-plus-degree heat this weekend.

As I was carrying my stuff to the parking lot, I saw Mrs. Flock coming out of her apartment to get the newspaper.

"Anything of yours in today, Nattie?" she said.

"Nope, not today. Sunday, though, a thought-provoking in-depth look at the profound effects of shoulder falsies. It's what every woman needs to know. Better not miss it, Mrs. Flock."

"Nattie, you're too much. I haven't had this much fun reading the paper since I lived in New York. It's hard to believe those editors let you write about fashion."

"Thanks, Mrs. Flock, see you Sunday. I'm off to a horse show."

"Don't break a leg," she said, and laughed.

And laughed and laughed. I laughed, too. Maybe not the best

joke, but it was a joke nevertheless. I love a good laugh and I haven't found many here in the land of small smiles. Northerners, whom southerners still refer icily to as Yankees, have a quick and caustic sense of humor, while I can't figure out what it takes to get a southerner to let loose and bust a gut.

Humor is but one small difference between the North and South. Bread and heritage are as much a dividing line as the Mason-Dixon. Go try to find a real loaf of rye bread south of Washington, D.C. It's like trying to find grits in Connecticut.

As for heritage, southerners are fixated on who your daddy's daddy's daddy was. They even give their kids last names for first names, just so everyone knows exactly by whom they've been spawned. Imagine Jews doing that. You'd have a kid named Goldberg Rothblatt Silverstein, and he'd go through life with people thinking he was a law firm.

This odd naming practice works well here. Consider Frye, Cameron, Clarke, Link, Tyler, Bailey, Jackson—first or last, either way, it sounds just fine. Every once in a while, though, you hear a name that turns your head. La Fontine—God's honest truth, some mother gave that moniker to her baby boy, and despite it, he grew up to be a Mecklenberg County Commissioner.

I waved to Mrs. Flock and asked her to take in my mail and newspaper. I wished I had a few minutes to talk to her. She always has an interesting spin on things that she picks up at Berrybrook Farms, a health food store where she works. She's the one who told me if I can't find something, just say the word "reach" to myself and it'll snap my memory synapses into action. I thought she was nuts until I lost my keys and had to be someplace pronto. After twenty minutes of hysteric searching, I mumbled "reach" and damned if at that very moment I didn't remember that I'd left my keys in my sneakers so I wouldn't forget them.

But I didn't have time to chat. I was running late and I knew Rob was probably steaming mad. By the time I got to the barn, he had the rig pulled up to the barn.

"We're leaving in twenty minutes, you'd better be ready," he said. "You're not showing if you don't school your horse in the ring this afternoon."

I've always been a sprinter. I was ready in fifteen minutes. Packed and checked. Brenda's legs were already wrapped. They were standing bandages from the night before, meant to support tired tendons. They'd do for shipping in a pinch. I slipped the wraps down over the tops of her hooves to protect the coronet band. That's what the hoof grows out of and if that gets smashed, you could wind up with a horse that grows a bad hoof, or worst of all, no hoof. In my hurry I'd forgotten to pack Vetrolin. I didn't care if Doc Loc called it fancy alcohol. If I showed up in Camden without it, Rob's shrieks would be heard halfway to Charleston. I rushed back to my tack box to grab a bottle.

"Shit," I said, and slammed down my trunk. I'd run out the other night. Then I remembered Gail always had gallons of the stuff, but she was already heading down to the show grounds to hang up the tack room drapes. I didn't want to open her locker. We borrowed horse stuff from each other all the time, but whenever she gave me anything, she made sure she was the one who got it from her locker. "It's such a mess in there," she'd say, "let me get it." I didn't want to go into her locker, but the alternative was worse—Rob's wrath. I promised myself I'd buy her an even bigger bottle of Vetrolin and I swung open her locker door. I had to rummage around because it was crammed with bottles and jars and bags of things. I thought I saw it, a dim outline of a white plastic bottle with the green stripe across, way in the back. The overhead bulb in the tack room had burned out and I couldn't see much. As I reached back, I knocked over a glass bottle. I felt something spill on my fingers.

There was no telling what equine concoction it could have been. Gail's locker was a veterinary pharmacy. I knew it wasn't DMSO, the sickening, rotten garlic–corn-syrup taste would have already hit my tongue. I pulled my hand out and looked down. My fingers were stained dark brown. I brought my hand close to my nose. It didn't smell veterinary or even vaguely medicinal. It smelled like Fridays at Mr. Robert's beauty salon. My mother dragged me there every week as a kid while she got her hair done and I sat under hair dryers pretending to be Sandra Dee.

I reached back in and found the bottle, lying flat in a pool of something. I looked at the color on the bottle and then on my hand. Unless Gail was planning a drastic new look, she wasn't going to be using this stuff on her head. Gail was a blonde and wouldn't change her hair color for anything. She said it was her only good feature. The color was so familiar. Then I realized why. Miss Clairol might have called it sable brown, but to me and any other horse person, it was blood bay.

"Nattie, this rig is pulling out in two minutes, with or without your horse," Rob shouted. "You know as well as I do it'll take me two hours to get this trailer down to Camden and I'm not driving this thing in the heat of the day with the sun beating down on these horses. Hurry up."

Quickly, I put the bottle back. I didn't have time to blot up the spill. I'd have to get it later. I grabbed a bottle of Vetrolin, which she had four of, and ran to Brenda's stall.

As I led Brenda up the ramp of the trailer, Rob said to me, "Nattie, you better have your gloves with you. You're not going in a show ring at an A show with your hands looking like that. And why the hell do you have hair dye all over them, anyway?"

That's exactly what I wanted to know.

CHAPTER 14

For the life of me, I couldn't figure why Gail stashed a bottle of Miss Clairol in her locker. I'd heard of bleaching a dirty white tail with Clorox, sometimes peroxide. I'd even used baby powder to make my horse's white stockings whiter when there wasn't time to wash them. But hair dye? Allie didn't have a scar on him, and even if he did, what would be the point in covering anything up? Gail never showed him.

I couldn't decide if I should ask her straight out, or back my way into it. If she was as hormonal as she claimed, she'd bite my head off. More emotional stress is exactly what I didn't need. I had my own horse show jitters to deal with. And I had Rob.

Rob, who was hovering by my car door before I even had a chance to get out. His arms, crossed against his chest, and his face contorted in his just-sucked-a-lemon look.

"Nattie," he said, "next time wrap your mare right, with shipping bandages. Standing bandages are meant for that—*standing* in a stall, not a horse trailer. If I'd have stopped suddenly, she could have torn her legs up."

Rob walked back to the February Farm trailer—hunter green with navy blue stripes—looking immaculate and color coordinated in a mint-green Polo shirt and pressed blue jeans. I stepped out of my car, and in my haste landed a foot smack in the middle of a pile of horse shit.

Rob rolled his eyes and I think I even saw a bit of a smile.

"Come on, get her off and into the schooling ring. Let's see if you can't repeat last night's performance. She was fabulous, it gave me goose bumps to watch her jump around that course. You rode her as well as any amateur rider here could ride a horse."

"Thanks," I said. Rob could be gruff, nasty, petulant—any of those and more. But he could also be kind, on occasion. He knew I felt outclassed by the big name, big money ammy-owners (that's what riders in my division—amateur-owner hunter—are called), and this was his way of making me feel better.

"Have you seen Gail?" I said as I lowered the ramp of the trailer.

"She's on her way back to Charlotte. I got a call from the barn about a half-hour ago. Allie started colicking. I called down to the show grounds and had her paged."

"If anything happens to that horse, you'll have to dig a double grave. Is Maryanne there yet?" Maryanne is the vet who took over Doc Loc's practice.

"Nattie, just get your mare off the trailer and saddled up," Rob said. As he turned to walk toward our stalls, I heard him say, "Maryanne isn't coming. Gail won't let anyone but Doc Loc work on Allie. Now, hurry up."

I had lots more questions, but I knew Rob wasn't about to answer any of them. If Doc Loc got caught treating horses, he could lose his license for life. So why risk it? And why was Gail so insistent on Doc Loc? Maryanne knows what she's doing. Three weeks ago she saved another horse in the barn that colicked.

I took a reporter's pad from my purse and wrote down all my questions, along with the Miss Clairol stuff. I'd had a feeling something about this story would pop this weekend, and I'd come fully armed: notepads, tape recorder, Rollermatic, even a camera if I needed to take a quick mug shot of someone. Henry could dig through all the arcane records he wanted, I had a gold mine here, and I planned to excavate.

Every big-name pro from Atlanta to Richmond would be at this show. It was rated A-3 by the ASHA (the American Horse Show Association), which meant lots of money and lots of points up for grabs. To get an A-3 rating, a show has to offer more than $18,000 in prize money, along with those pretty little ribbons that wind up in the trash if they're not blue or red. But prize money isn't the biggest draw. A3 shows are Mecca to point chasers looking to win end-of-the-year championships that will then allow them to add a few more zeros to the end of their horse's price tags. Every time you win ribbons at an A3 show, it's extra points, and lots of them. At best, you can rack up an extra 140 points, which could easily mean the difference between Horse of the Year and almost Horse of the Year.

Points were beyond my realm of concern. I couldn't afford to show enough for them to matter either way. The bucks, however, I could use. Between entry fees, stall fees, training fees, trailering, half of Rob's hotel and meals, my hotel and meals, and braiding, I was looking at blowing close to five hundred dollars. Usually I made at least some of it back. Given the state of my checkbook, if I didn't win anything, I'd be stewing in my apartment for the rest of the summer. This was my air-conditioner money I was using.

"Nattie, quit daydreaming and come on," Rob shouted to me. "They're closing the rings in twenty minutes. You've got to show that mare these fences today, before you take her around with a judge watching you tomorrow."

"Be right there," I said, which wasn't really the truth. I couldn't put a saddle on Brenda the way she looked, not in front of Rob, anyway. She was soaked in sweat. Even with the doors open, a trailer can be like a big oven. I washed her quickly and rubbed her back with a towel, watching patches of shiny copper pop up on her as the sun dried her coat. For the first time this summer, I was happy to be this close to the equator. She was dry in about two minutes.

I put my clean saddle, clean saddle pad, and clean bridle on her. I was wearing a clean pair of britches, clean white Polo shirt, and freshly polished black boots. None of this is my normal state of being. Around Rob at a horse show, it's the only way of being. Still, I had to admit, when I hopped on Brenda, we were both so squeaky clean, I felt like I'd just come out of a warm bath into a fluffy turkish towel.

I walked her on a long rein down the sandy hill into the ring. There must have been twenty horses in there, each one fancier than the next. *Fancy* is horse lingo for very beautiful, very able, and very valuable.

A course of eight jumps had been set at about three and a half feet, the height my division jumps. There was an assortment of fences—brush boxes, three ugly oxers, a chicken coop, which is a long triangle that's supposed to look like its namesake, and a roll top, a giant half–Tootsie Roll covered in green miniature-golf-course carpet. I've yet to figure out what that one's supposed to simulate in the hunt field.

I walked past Rob, who was standing next to Jack Thompson, Keith Rollings's trainer. One thing I have to say about horse pros, scandal doesn't bother them in the least. Here you had a guy who was just arrested for murder, and everyone was talking to him as if it were just another horse show. It was "Hi, Rob" this, "Hi, Rob" that. I'd been watching since we pulled into the Tri-Color show grounds. Not one person snubbed him. But then again, no one came rushing up, asking to help. It was as if nothing had happened. And maybe to them, nothing much had. Wally was generally regarded as a blight on the profession. So I'd bet most everyone here was just as happy to see him wiped away.

"She looks great, and you look normal," Rob said. This time he did smile. Normal to him was clean and pressed. "Trot and canter around the ring for a few minutes, get her warmed up."

I slid the reins up my hands and pressed her forward with my legs into a trot. She arched her neck and came right down on the bit. This was where my two and a half years of training/abuse from Rob paid off. Brenda was perfect. Soft and round, Rob calls it when she's going this way. Meaning she was so soft in my hands, the slightest flex of my fingers could make her slow down and shorten her stride; or just a faint touch of my leg could make her go forward, extending and stretching her stride out. You've got to be able to adjust your horse's stride when you're jumping around a course, otherwise you'll crash through or into fences if you get there wrong, no matter how athletic your horse is.

"She looks fabulous," Rob called to me as I cantered around the ring, avoiding the multitude of other fabulous horses. *Fabulous* is the word on the circuit when fancy horses are going well.

Brenda hadn't been a fancy horse when I got her, she'd been a problem horse who kept ditching one famous pro after the next. That's why she was so cheap, by horse show standards. To me she cost a fortune, my entire fortune, as a matter of fact. I blew my life savings on her—$4,500. But I had a feeling she could be something special. And I had been right. Last month I turned down $35,000.

"Start over the cross rails," Rob said.

I trotted her over the X fence. She barely lifted her legs.

"That's enough of that," Rob said. "Let's not bore her. Do the outside line, the brush box to the oxer. It's a long five. Then canter down the diagonal line, the chicken coop, to the other oxer. It's a short six."

Horse talk for five long strides between fence one and two. So I had to extend her stride between the first and second fences and then pull her together to fit in the short six strides between the third and fourth fences.

I put my left leg against her side, the signal for her to take the right lead, which she did. We cantered to the first fence and she jumped it as well as any quarter-of-a-million-dollar horse. I

123

pressed her forward to make the five long strides to the second fence, the ugly oxer. She couldn't have gotten there any better or any prettier. Around the corner to the chicken coop. I didn't see anything, more horse lingo for the rider doesn't know where the hell she is so she can't adjust her horse to a good takeoff point. I got her to the coop so wrong, she practically had to climb it. Normally, I can fix the second fence in a line because Brenda is so adjustable. But as I was thinking about adjusting her, a tall blonde walked past the in gate. She caught my eye because she looked so annoyingly familiar.

I was thinking about who she was when I should have been thinking about where I was. Instead of fitting in six short strides, Brenda left out the last stride and started flying. About halfway there I knew we wouldn't make it. Not unless she sprouted wings. And Pegasus she's not.

I hate this moment more than any other part of falling. It takes about an hour for your body to find its way to the ground while you're watching each movement in super slo-mo, freeze-frame by freeze-frame, wondering what's going to break, rip, or tear.

Crash.

She landed smack in the middle of the oxer, scrambling through a network of poles, thrashing her legs wildly. She made it through on four feet. I wasn't so lucky. I somersaulted over the fence and Brenda practically twisted herself into a pretzel to avoid stepping on me.

I looked up to see Rob standing over me, wearing an expression I'd never seen before: panic mixed with concern. I stood up, nothing felt broken. And Rob's face turned to anger.

"Nattie, what were you doing down that line, planning your grocery list? I told you it was a holding six. What in God's name made you leave out the last stride? There's not a Grand Prix jumper on these show grounds that could do that line in five.

You're lucky you're not both dead. I ought to take you off that horse for good. Are you okay?"

"I'm fine," I said. Then I remembered who the blonde was. La Donna Mobilay, Lucy's Aryan circus queen friend. No sense in telling Rob who she was and how she'd discombobulated me. A good rider should be able to filter out everything when she's on course, even if Jesus Christ himself floats by. It was my fault and I felt horrible making such a stupid mistake. Rob was right, Brenda deserved better.

"Now get back on her and do it again," Rob said.

I would rather have gone to the gynecologist. Rob brushed the sand off my hat, I brushed it off my britches and shirt. He gave me a leg back up into the saddle, and I took a deep breath, chanting silently my scared-shitless mantra: Throw your heart over the fence and go catch it. Which I did. And this is why I turned down the big bucks for Brenda: Any other horse would have been skittery the next time around after a scary fall like that. Brenda cantered around all four fences as sweetly and calmly as if nothing had happened.

"Ride her that way tomorrow, and you'll win every class," Rob said. "Now put her up and wrap her legs."

As I led her back up the hill, I scanned the show grounds for La Donna. Good luck, it was like looking for Waldo, except I didn't have the advantage of a red and white striped shirt separating her from the crowd. She was a tall, leggy blonde in a sea of tall, leggy blondes.

What was she doing in South Carolina, anyway? Lucy said she comes east only for the indoor shows, and they don't start until the fall.

I could find La Donna later, first I had to tend to Brenda. I gave her a good washdown with Gail's Vetrolin. Then I rubbed her legs with liniment and wrapped them with a clean set of

standing bandages. The bandages still smelled of Clorox and
Downy.

I took my time, and not just because I didn't want to listen to
Rob complain. Wrapping a horse's legs is an art. There's a hand-
ful of grooms in Camden who are legendary wrappers; some
trainers won't let anyone else but these guys touch their horses'
legs because you can cripple a horse if you pull the wrap too tight
or bunch it up on top of a tendon. I'm no artist, but I can put on a
decent set of wraps. The quilts go on first, three-foot-long rectan-
gles of white quilted cotton wrapped counterclockwise on the left
side and clockwise on the right side. Tight enough to support the
tired tendons of the horse's lower leg, but not too tight to bind or
bunch. Then the flannels, rolls of six-inch-wide strips of white or
light blue flannel that wrap on top of the quilts, always going in
the same direction as the quilts. The trick is to keep consistent
tension as you unroll the flannel around the horse's legs. You
don't want any parts tighter or looser than the next, and you want
to start at the top and finish at the top. Fold the end corners into
themselves like hotel toilet paper and wrap a strip of masking tape
two or three times around the top. Do that four times and you've
got a wrapped horse ready for rest, or whatever it is they do in
their stalls all day.

I got a bag of carrots from my bulging tack trunk and let
Brenda have half of them. She rubbed her head against me for
more, and I gave her the rest along with a kiss on her nose. It's true
what they say about horses' noses, softer than velvet. I led her into
her stall, made sure her water buckets were full. One last thing before my search for La Donna—hay. Inside the trailer were bales of
alfalfa-timothy mix, smelling sweeter than a thirteen-year-old on
her first date. I jammed my knee against the center of the bale and
grabbed one of the two strings of bailing twine bound lengthwise
around the hay. With a good jerk, the taut loop of twine I was
holding sprung off to the side and the flakes of hay fanned out into

neatly divided sections. I piled four flakes into my arms and dumped them at Brenda's feet.

"Here, your highness," I said to her. "Is there anything else you desire?"

She dove her head into the hay and didn't come up as I left.

I walked up and down the aisles, looking for La Donna. I didn't know what I was going to say to her, but I wanted to make sure I'd really seen her. Maybe it had been just another statuesque blonde with chiseled features and Heidi-blue eyes. But if it had been her, she must be with Lucy. Why now? Lucy made a big deal about how she never sees La Donna because she has to baby-sit her eighty-something tissue-paper-heir husband and run her barn because her husband is too cheap to hire someone. I was willing to bet La Donna knew Wally, or at least knew of him. The A-circuit horse world is small and tightly woven, everyone knows everyone else's business, and even if they don't they'll gossip about it anyway.

Searching for La Donna was really just an excuse to roam the show grounds. I love walking the aisles at A shows. It's like window-shopping. I stop in front of the stalls and check out the horses. They're so groomed and polished, the hair on their coats runs together in one shiny mass, making them look like life-sized versions of the plastic horses on my mantel—the same ones my mother gave me twenty years ago.

Grooms are pressed by the horses' sides with rub rags and soft boar-bristle brushes, circling and circling to raise even more of a shine. The grooms that aren't caring for the horses are running around setting things up: hauling tack boxes from the van, stacking bales of hay, arranging saddlery, polishing boots and hanging tack room drapes. The drapes are elaborate custom-made affairs, the colors of that particular barn. February Farm's are hunter green with deep scalloped edges piped in navy blue. The fanciest barns go all out; the entrances to their stabling area look like something out of *House Beautiful* with Louis the whatever tables and chairs, big vases of fresh flowers or bowls of fruit, and a wall full of framed photographs of their winningest horses and riders.

Even though it was the day before the show, the grounds were already packed. There were rows of big semi-tractor rigs, all painted in the appropriate barn colors. Nearby were matching RVs for owners and trainers to cool off in between classes. And, of course, the requisite Mercedes, millions of dollars worth of them. In mechanical horsepower alone there was probably enough power packed onto the sandy fields of the Tri-Color horse show grounds to run a small country for a year.

I didn't see La Donna or Lucy in the stabling area. But I did see Lucy's jumbo-jet Mercedes sitting in the fleet. They were probably in someone's icy-cool RV, sipping spiked tea. Well, I wasn't heading off the show grounds anytime soon, so I figured I'd run into them sooner or later. In the meantime, I headed over to the entry booth to get my number and also to call Gail. I was more worried about her than Allie.

"Hey, Nattie. Don' just love these shows at Tri-Color?"

I turned to see who was talking to me. The face registered, but the name wasn't coming up. Dark brown hair, shoulder-length, pushed back by a yellow and white polka-dot grosgrain headband. A long face—handsome maybe, but ultimately horsey—and a big set of white choppers that looked like even an expensive set of braces hadn't been able to tame. Baggy but pressed khaki shorts, Gucci belt, white Polo shirt, white Polo socks, and yellow and white polka-dot sneakers.

"Hi," I said, frantically searching my mind for a clue.

"Did you see the coolers they're giving out to the division winners? Blue with red and yellow piping. They are just darling!"

Bingo!!!

"Bryce Whit," I said. "How are you? Is Keith showing this weekend?"

"Not hardly. He's just been beside himself since that horse of his died. And none of his other horses are ready yet. He's here this weekend, though, hoping to find himself a new ammy horse. How about you? Are you showing your mare, Lois Lane?"

"Brenda Starr and, yep, we're both here." Yippee, I thought, no Keith Rollings and his quarter-million-dollar machines to compete against. I reined in my smile—it would have been poor sportsmanship on my part to let my glee show. Plus, Keith's horse did die, and I felt badly about that.

"I'm not here completely for fun, if that's what I have at these shows," I said. "I'm working on a story about Wally Hempstead's murder."

"You, working on a story about a murder?" Bryce Whit was holding her manicured hand over her mouth as she laughed. Either that was southern politeness, or her mother must have told her early on to cover those choppers. "Oh, that's just too funny. You must be teasing me. Why would the fashion editor be writing about a murder?"

Maybe it hadn't been such a good career move to take this job after all. "First off," I said, "I'm not the fashion editor. I write about fashion sometimes, and other things other times. This time it's about Wally and Ruskie and who wanted them dead."

"Well, I'm sure I wouldn't know anything about that," Bryce Whit said. "I hardly knew the man. He was always polite to me when he came to see Keith. Isn't it just awful what happened to him?"

"Not from what I hear. Everyone I talk to is pleased as punch that he's dead. What did you think of him? Did you know him pretty well?"

Bryce Whit's hand dropped from her mouth to her narrow hips. "He came by right much," she said. "He used to come to the house, even though Keith told him once if he didn't tell him a thousand times that he liked to keep his horse business confined to the barns. I guess Wally was a bit stubborn, because no matter how many times Keith asked, Wally kept coming to the front door. But he was always nice to me and couldn't have been nicer to our daughter, Hastings. I remember the last time he came, about a week ago. He was just talking up a storm about how lovely our daughter was and what a wonderful family Keith had. Keith seemed a little irritated and directed him out to the barn. Other than that, I didn't see him much. Like I said, I didn't really know him.

"You know, I never did get a chance to thank you for that darling article you wrote about the Women's Auxiliary Symphony Society. And by the way, we all found the most darling hot-pink dresses for our daughters to wear in the school play—as a matter of fact, thanks to you. After you wrote about it, the owner of a little shop in Columbia called and said she had five hot-pink dresses that would be perfect. And are they ever! Why don't you stop by for tea this afternoon? You could see the dress yourself. We're just down the road not three miles away. You've never seen our farm, and I'd love to show you around."

"Maybe," I said. "I'll have to see what Rob has planned for me. Knowing him, I'll have to polish every hair on Brenda's coat. But thanks. And thanks for talking to me about Wally."

"It was my pleasure. Though I can't imagine I helped you any."

More than she could ever know. I waited for her to walk away, and before I forgot a word of it, I took my reporter's pad from my purse and let my Rolling Ball rip, writing down exactly what she'd said. Then my observations, questions, and speculations.

Wally was blackmailing Keith. I knew it as sure as I knew my name. That's why he kept popping up at the front door, talking about Keith's "lovely family." Rubbing in what he had to lose if he didn't pay up. That's why Keith was "a little irritated"—southern speak for rip-roaring red-faced rabid-dog mad. And that's why

Keith didn't tell his wife that a reporter had been by their farm, asking questions. He must've wanted this whole Wally mess buried with the bodies. But what did Wally have on Keith? A dead horse? Keith didn't need to have his horse killed for money. Or did he? I'd have to ask Henry to do a records check on Mr. Rollings and his financial security. I had a feeling that wasn't it, but what could it be?

CHAPTER 15

I never did have tea with the lovely Mrs. Rollings. By the time I got through all the things Rob wanted me to do, I could barely make it to the hotel.

And I never did find La Donna. After running into Bryce Whit, I called the barn to check on Gail and Allie. Gail wasn't taking phone calls. In fact she wasn't moving an inch from her horse's stall. One of the boarders, a teenage girl named Rankin, answered the phone and told me the vet pumped Allie's stomach with a gallon of mineral oil—the standard course of treatment for colic. If the impaction wasn't too bad, the oil would loosen things up enough for him to pass the balled-up manure and be out of distress. If that didn't work, he'd have to be shipped off to Raleigh for the expensive and oftentimes unsuccessful surgery.

"They think they caught it in time and Allie's going to be okay," Rankin said. "I don't know about Gail, though. She hasn't stopped crying since she got here. Oh, by the way, someone by the name of Henry Goode's left a message on the answering machine here, says to call him as soon as you can. You want his number?"

"Thanks, I've got it already. Listen, tell Gail I called and tell her I said to call me on Rob's car phone if she needs anything. Okay?"

I toyed with the idea of going back to Charlotte to be with Gail. I knew she'd be spending the night at the barn and I was sure she wouldn't have minded some company. Friendship aside, I owed her a night at the barn, not to mention the week's vacation she used up on me and my family. When I first moved south, Brenda ate a bag of carrots. Literally. Plastic bag and all. I had to stay with her all night to make sure she passed the plastic—which she eventually did. Gail brought her sleeping bag to the barn and pulled it up next to mine. She'd also brought a milk carton full of Whoppers for herself and a couple of bags of strawberry Twizzlers for me. We ate ourselves sick and talked through the night. About horses and men and mothers.

I was torn between friendship and selfishness. The selfishness won out, with a lot of justifying on my part. I figured I'd call the barn every couple of hours to check on Allie and Gail. If things got dire, I'd head back, regardless of what Rob had to say.

In the meantime I went over to the horse show office and got my number. Lucky me, my favorite number twice, 44. As for Henry, I was having too good a time to be upset by him. I'd call him when I got home on Sunday night.

Lucy's big Mercedes was gone by the time I got back to the parking area. I cursed myself for not hanging around. Henry probably would have stayed put. Henry probably would have found La Donna and asked her just the right questions, in just the right tone. Shit. Maybe I deserved to be fashion writer. And just maybe I was making myself feel bad because I felt guilty about Gail being alone with a sick horse.

This is why I like jumping horses. The unwavering simplicity of it. You jump in big to the first fence, you know you've got to hold for the second fence. You jump in tight, you know you've got to push ahead. No hidden agendas, no super-ego back talk. Just straightforward math.

"Nattie, what are you doing standing there in the middle of the sand with the sun beating down on your head? You've got to ride tomorrow in two classes and you can't ride in them if you've got sunstroke."

It was Rob. Last show, he'd yelled at me for running down the hill, thinking I'd be too tired to ride. Now he was getting on me about the sun. Next, was he going to start regulating my period so it wouldn't coincide with horse shows? (Which is done with mares.)

"Gail's a basket case," I said. "Maybe I should go back to Charlotte to be with her."

"That's the stupidest thing I've ever heard, even from you. Gail's a grown woman. Now, come on and help me hang the drapes and set things up. It's a mess."

It sure wasn't when we left, five hours later. I was beat. I passed up dinner with Rob, stopped by McDonald's, and went to the hotel, where I planned to spend a quiet night. Just me and my McSalad. And John Hawkes's book, *Sweet William, a Memoir of an Old Horse.* Cross Dostoevsky with Anna Sewell and that's *Sweet William*—a dark and highly literary tale told first person by the horse, making it a twisted and bitter Black Beauty tells all.

I called Gail as soon as I got into my room. I'd called her three or four times when Rob and I were setting up the show barn. Gail was plastered to Allie's stall like a fly around fresh manure. She wasn't taking calls, I'd been told by various boarders, workers, and, one time, even old man Clarke, the owner. The old man said Allie was no worse, but in his words, "the horse still hadn't had a gratifying bowel movement." Maybe Clarke's daughter, Lally, had been on the money when she claimed her father was perverted.

It was well past nine and I knew no one would be at February Farm except Gail. The phone rang twenty-three times before she picked it up. Someone must have forgotten to put on the answering machine.

"Hello," Gail said. She was panting. She'd probably dashed to the phone from Allie's stall, cursing the caller.

"Gail, it's me, Nattie. I'll make it quick because I know you're watching Allie. Anything new with him? Want me to come back to Charlotte? I can sleep on one of Brenda's blankets."

"Holy Mother of Mary, what a day," Gail said. She had that same small, beaten-down voice my grandmother used to have after spending the day in the hospital with my grandfather, who died a slow, horrible death of colon cancer. "But I think it's over. I think he's going to be all right. About fifteen minutes ago he started pooping. A little bit at first, then more and more. It wasn't the right texture to start with. You know how Doc Loc says a colicked horse's manure can be dry? Well, that's how his was, even with all that mineral oil tubed down his nose and into his stomach. And the color was off. Doc Loc says . . ."

Allie was clearly out of the woods, because for the next fifteen minutes Gail described every aspect of her horse's manure. She devoted as much attention to Allie's excrement as she did to his lead changes.

". . . Finally, a few minutes ago, a pile of the perfect poop came out. Green, plump, each one about the size of a small peach and nice and moist. That was a close one, but it's over now. I'm gonna stay here tonight, just to make sure. I'm fine, though. Really. Don't even think about coming back. That would make two murders Rob would have to stand trial for. How's he doing, anyway?"

I took a bite of my salad and tried not to crunch in Gail's ear. I hadn't eaten since breakfast, and even Gail's poop talk hadn't deadened my appetite any. "Well," I said with a quick swallow, "you know when you're riding and something bad happens? Allie or Brenda bucks or goes too fast? Your riding faults become exaggerated, you start grabbing or leaning forward and become a caricature of yourself. Well, I don't think it's any different off a horse. Something bad happens, and you become a caricature of the worst aspects of your personality.

"That's how Rob was today. He makes the pre-murder Rob look laid back, sloppy even. He was so damn exacting, it took us five hours to set up the barn. Every nail had to be hammered in exactly right. If it stuck out more than a half inch, he made me nail it in again. We had to clean all the tack, and if there was one small spot of dirt, clean it again."

"Sounds like your afternoon wasn't much better than mine," Gail said.

I laughed. "You've got that right. Before that I had a major fall when I was schooling Brenda. I splattered all over the sand like road kill, except there wasn't any blood, thank God. I couldn't have gotten Brenda any more wrong to a monster oxer if I'd tried to. I lost my attention halfway down the line because I saw La Donna, remember that friend of Lucy's I told you about? Then I spent an hour looking for her so I could ask her some questions about Wally and Lucy. I never did find her."

"Just as well," said Gail. "You better stop being so nosy down there. Just do what you went there to do, show your horse. Forget the story, you're gonna get yourself killed. Do I have to remind you about that phone call?"

"No, you don't, thank you very much. But you should have seen Brenda go. Afterward she clocked around the course as good as a horse could go. She could've beat anyone, even Ruskie. Ruskie, *alevasholom*."

"I can tell you're feeling pretty good about things with Brenda. That's when you slip into your Jewish talk. What do you mean, you'll show him? You'll show him what?"

"Shiksas," I said. "No wonder you goys are born with straight noses and thin thighs. God had to give you something to make up for your hearing problems. It's *alevasholom*, and you're supposed to say it after the name of someone who's dead."

"Like Nattie Gold, *alevasholom* if you keep asking all those questions about Wally. I'm not kidding, Nattie, I'm worried about you. Henry called here. He must have said fourteen times how 'concerned' he was about you. He didn't know where you were, thought you might be lying dead someplace. I told him you were at the show and would be back Sunday night."

"That's interesting," I said, forming each syllable like Henry does. "So the man has something other than ink running through his veins. Look, stop worrying, I'm fine. Rob's in the next room and he can rescue me if a psycho comes calling."

Gail and I burst out laughing. I was probably stronger than Rob, and the idea of him going fist to fist with anyone was hilarious. He'd get his hands dirty.

"All I've got to worry about is getting Brenda around the course."

"Then you've got nothing to worry about. Brenda is a machine. She takes care of your ass, and you better do the same for her. There's nothing stopping you from being ammy-owner champion this weekend. Not Keith or Lucy. It's there for you. Now, get some sleep so you're not tired tomorrow. And thanks for calling. I needed to unload and I couldn't have talked to anyone else but you about all this."

Guilty no more. Allie was fine and so was Gail. I hung up feeling better than I had all day. Who cared what La Donna had to say? It probably wasn't much, anyway.

Even Sweet William's scurrilous adventures couldn't keep me awake. I fell asleep just as the big, surly horse attacked a man for peeing in his stall and stinking it up.

CHAPTER 16

What's wrong with this picture? Woman sleeping deeply. No light outside or inside. Answer: It's four-thirty in the morning, and the alarm clock starts blasting.

Four-thirty in the damn morning. The chickens aren't even out of REM sleep and my alarm is squealing like an angry jackass. Which is what I feel like.

Then the telephone starts ringing. In my fog I pick up the buzzing alarm clock and shout hello into it, like I'm in a bad sit-com. Finally I sort things out and grab the phone.

"Are you up?" It's Rob.

"Of course I'm up, would I be answering the phone if I weren't?"

"I'll be in the lobby in ten minutes. We don't have that much time to get Brenda and the other horses ready. And you've got to eat. I'm not letting you ride on an empty stomach. So hurry up."

"Rob, it's four-thirty. The show doesn't start till eight. We've got plenty of time." The second the last sentence left my mouth, I knew it was the wrong thing to say to Rob. Especially this weekend.

"Nattie, find yourself another trainer. Find yourself someone who can get you and your horse ready in ten minutes. Because that's how you always do things. If it weren't for me, you'd go in that ring with your tack unbuckled and your hair hanging out of your hunt cap. Find yourself someone else. I've had it."

"Whoa, Rob. Take it easy. I don't want another trainer. I'll be in the lobby in five minutes."

Rob was right about me going into the ring half done if not for him. I'm not a detail person. There've been many times when Rob has had to slide a loose strap into its keeper or tell me to redo my hunt cap because my hair's sticking out.

I got dressed fast and was in the lobby before the clock got to four-forty. It was still dark, but what did I expect, sunrise for my benefit?

The air was thin and cool inside the hotel. I don't know why I thought it'd be the same when I walked outside. I was in South Carolina, not Maine. It was as dark and steamy as a bowl of the miso soup my father eats all the time. I'd been hoping it would have been hot enough for the judges to excuse braiding. They didn't. That's why we were heading out to the show grounds before the sun even thought about rising. Rob was going to braid the horses and I was going to bathe them. That way, I worked off his braiding fee.

Show grounds always look eerie this time of the morning. Everything's dark as dirt, except for a few round splashes of white here and there. They're the spotlights and under them are the sleepy horses with their heads hanging as low as they can make them. Which isn't too low, because right next to the horses are people standing on stools, flicking their fingers back and forth, working the horses' manes into tightly woven braids. Maybe I'd been reading too much *Sweet William*, but I couldn't help thinking how much these horses must hate being woken up in the middle of the night to have someone twist and tie their hair into fussy little knots.

"Go give Brenda a bath, I'll start on the other horses," Rob said.

I took Brenda to the wash stall the long way, weaving in and out of the rows of stalls, hoping to find Sully, Lucy's braider. She

139

was the most popular braider on the circuit, so I figured she'd be at one of the big show barns. Sully loved to gossip, and I wanted to hear what she'd heard about Wally and Rob.

I walked past the fanciest barns, where there were plenty of horses being braided. None of them by Sully. I couldn't dally for long because Rob would be apoplectic if I came back late.

I gave Brenda a quick bath, with a drop of olive oil in the soapy water to make her coat shinier. Once I'd sprayed her whole body with Show Sheen, an equine hair polisher, and the saddle kept slipping off. Now the Show Sheen just goes on her tail, as instructed by Rob, who has an unnatural passion for tails. He can talk as long about a good tail as Gail can talk about her horse's poop. He showed me "the only way" to groom a horse's tail—separating it strand by strand with your fingers. Never a brush. God forbid, that tears the hair out.

I scraped the excess water off Brenda and toweled her legs dry. If you leave a horse's legs wet, they become petri dishes for fungi.

I walked Brenda back the other way, still hoping to find Sully. She wasn't at the smaller barns either. She must be at another A-3 show. I'd get her number from Rob and call her on Monday.

Rob was still working on the first horse when I got back. He hadn't gotten much further than when I left and I could see why. He was tearing out each braid that he finished and redoing it.

"I can't get these things tight," he said. "Did you put Show Sheen on this horse's mane?"

"No, I didn't even wash that horse yet and I never wash a horse's mane you're going to braid. I know you can't braid a clean mane tight. Rob, the braids look great. Stop worrying about them."

He didn't answer me, but he did stop ripping out his work. I couldn't tell if it was the weird light or what, but Rob's eyes looked awfully shiny to me. I would have liked to say something like I didn't believe he killed Wally and I was working my butt off to prove it. But I shut up, finally listening to the little man in my head.

I got all the horses bathed and Rob got them braided with time to spare. Brenda looked like a star standing in her stall with her glistening coat and braided mane and tail.

"She looks fabulous," Rob said.

I was standing next to him, close enough to reach my arm around his shoulder. I did. It was the first time I'd ever touched him.

"Thank you," I said. "I don't want to get mushy or anything, but you know I couldn't have gotten to the A shows without you. I know I can be a pain in the ass to teach and I'm sloppy as hell. So thanks. And listen, I know I shouldn't say this, but I know you didn't kill Wally, and you're not going to jail, not if I have anything to do with it."

Rob looked at me and I couldn't read what was on his face. He could have slapped me or hugged me—either way I wouldn't have known what was coming.

Instead, he stood there for a second with my arm wrapped around his shoulders.

"Go get the hoof polish," he said to me finally.

I did. By the time I got back, Rob had vanished.

He never said a word about what I'd said to him. Then again, he didn't yell at me for the rest of the show. Probably because all his horses gave the performances of their lives. Including Brenda.

My first trip around the course was the best I'd ever ridden. Everyone clapped after the final jump and I was smiling so big, the white dust from the sand crusted over my teeth and gums, cementing my face into a grin. Rob met me at the in gate with a paper cup full of diet Coke and a hug. This sudden intimacy made me giddy enough to want to kiss him. It was a good thing I couldn't lower my lips over my teeth to pucker up. That would have pushed Rob over the edge.

"Nattie," he said, "that was fabulous. I'm almost afraid to send you back in the ring, to give you a chance to screw up. You can't do any better than that."

I grabbed the paper cup and gulped, freeing my frozen mouth.

"Thanks, Rob," I said. "That felt great. God, I can't believe we nailed every fence. You know that second fence, the roll top, I thought I was getting there too soon and then—"

Rob cut me off in mid-sentence. "Stop, stop it. I've told you a million times you think too much. You're your own worst enemy. Stop analyzing. Just go do the same thing again. Now walk your horse around before she falls over dead."

I walked her around for a few minutes and then went back into the ring.

As I started to canter I heard the announcer. "Number Forty-four, Brenda Starr ridden by Nattie Gold of Charlotte, North Carolina."

I cantered past Rob. His voice trailing me as I left him behind: "Remember, don't suck back in the corners."

There's not much difference between jumping a horse around a course and writing a good feature for the paper—when they both go right. You click into a lead, and if it's good, you sail right through the story with your fingers clacking across the keyboard like you're possessed. Which in a way may be true. One of my father's gurus told me I may not know it, but I go into a trance when I write and then my spirit guides take over. I figure the same is true for riding.

All I can say is whoever was riding my horse that day—either me, my spirit guides, or both of us—did a hell of a job. The second trip was more brilliant than the first. Rob was whooping and jumping up and down when I finished. People I hardly knew were coming up to congratulate me. I slid off the saddle and loosened my horse's girth. Sweat was dripping down Brenda's face, and she rubbed her head hard against the front of my shoulder, pushing me backward. I would have fallen flat on my butt had it not been for the firm piece of flesh I landed into. I braced my fall by shooting my hands in back of me, directly into someone's thighs. They felt like marble columns.

"I'm so sorry," I said as I turned around. I looked up and into the arctic-blue eyes of the Aryan poster girl herself, La Donna Mobilay.

"Honey, don't you worry yourself one bit," she said in a southern accent thicker than cafeteria gravy. "That's the sweetest horse I've seen in all my days. I was just telling Lucy here she should offer you half of L.M.'s stock in his granddaddy's tomato soup company just to get that animal on her farm. Isn't that right, Lucy?"

Lucy smiled, sort of.

"Well, you're certainly riding much better," Lucy managed to say to me. "La Donna, I've got to go. Joey's showing me a horse at his barn, says she's a ringer for Lady. Then I've got to pack, so let's go."

"Oh, Lucy, Lord have mercy. Be a little nicer to this girl. It's not her fault your horse is dead." La Donna smiled at me and then swung her arm around Lucy, who was still scowling. "I love this woman better than my own sister, but she sure doesn't like to lose, even when she's not competing. Lucy, go easy, sugar. This ain't the Olympics. I'm sure what you meant to say is 'That's a lovely horse you've got there and you ride her beautifully.' Isn't that right, Lucy?"

I expected Lucy to hurl around and land a punch into La Donna's face. I've seen her rip into judges for less. To my surprise, she burst out laughing. "La Donna," she said, "you're a friggin' pain in the ass. Yeah, I like to win. Is that such a bloody crime?" Then, in the ooziest sugar-blossom-sweet south-ernese she said to me: "And, Nattie, you darlin' thang, that was truly the most spec-*tac*-ulah trip ah've ever seen in all mah born days. Give that little horse a few kisses from me, whah-dontcha."

She swung La Donna around the other way, and the two started walking off.

"Wait, wait," I said. Brenda was parked in the sun, her eyes closed. It took me a few pulls of the reins to wake her up and get her going. Reluctantly, she followed me as I chased after La Donna and Lucy.

"Lucy, one second," I said, catching stride with them. "I wanted to ask La Donna a few questions."

"Christ," Lucy said. "Is this about that little story you're writing?"

"Yes, and I'm hoping it won't be such a little story." I stuck my hand out to La Donna and introduced myself so thoroughly even Fred, the shoe salesman/editor of our paper wouldn't be able to find fault. I explained who I was, where I worked, and that I was trying to gather as much information as possible about Wally for a story about his murder and how it fit into the horse world.

"Lucy honey, why don't you go on," La Donna said. "I'll meet you in just a few minutes at Joey's. This girl's got a job to do, so why shouldn't I help her? Not that I knew Wally that well."

"Oh, all right," Lucy said. "Just don't be too long."

Lucy walked away and La Donna turned to me, a beatific smile across her unlined face. Either she'd stayed out of the sun better than Lucy had, or she had one hell of a plastic surgeon.

"Now, what can I help you with? Nattie Gold, right? Are you kin to any of the Golds in Neenah, Wisconsin? They run the little clothing store on Wisconsin Avenue. They're a lovely family. They're Jewish."

After two years of southern living, I still hadn't decided if this was anti-Semitism or just plain ignorance. I run into this kind of thing all the time. People who haven't been around Jews much find the most creative ways to slip my religion into a conversation. Like when I interviewed the Gaston County Fair pecan pie champion, she segued from lard pie crusts to what she called "those flat crackers y'all eat around Easter" as if matzoh held the key to her flaky-crust successes. Then there was the time I covered a party at the opera. I was talking to a violinist by the name of Morris Steinberg, the only Jew in the orchestra. The head of the Women's Opera Auxiliary, an alcoholic old-line Charlottean named Fuzzy Crenshaw, asked me if Steinberg and I were "kin."

"Gold's a really common last name," I said to La Donna. "I have no relatives in Wisconsin. My people never made it farther west than Sixty-ninth Street in Philadelphia. So, tell me what you know about Wally."

"That ain't more than a mouthful," La Donna said. "Hardly knew him at all. I can tell you this much, he had the best behind I've ever seen on a white man. I used to tell Lucy all the time that it was just a crying shame he liked boys instead of girls. But that's the way it is in this business. Anyhow, I can't imagine why someone would have killed him. He seemed perfectly lovely to me, found me my best horse. You probably can't tell, but Lucy's broke up about this pretty bad. Wally did wonders for Lady. And the way Lucy talked about Wally to me, she loved him like he was her kid brother."

"Kid brother?" I said.

"Oh, don't tell me you believe all those ridiculous rumors about Lucy and Wally? If Wally was interested in anyone in that family, it would have been L.M. Now, look, I'm going to write

145

down my phone number in Neenah. If you have more questions, you just call me, now. I'll be back home tomorrow night doing battle with the lake flies. Okay? I've got to run. Lucy may seem strong as nails, but between Wally and Lady, she's about to fall apart. That's why I'm here and that's why she's coming back to Wisconsin with me. Who knows, maybe she'll find herself another Lady there. It was lovely talking to you. And good luck on your story."

Before I had a chance to figure out what that was all about, Rob was by my side, red-faced and screaming.

"Nattie, they're about to pin the class and what are you doing? Hurry up, get back down to the ring. Take her saddle off and wipe down her back. You'll have to jog in, and you're not doing it with a sweat-stained horse."

I raced down to the ring and was rubbing the marks off Brenda's back when the PA system started crackling with the announcer's deep voice. "For class number thirty-two, Amateur Owner over Fences, will the following numbers jog back in this order. Number forty-four, number thirty-seven—"

"Yes!!!" I heard Rob shout. I grabbed Brenda's reins and Rob gave her a slap on the rump to get her into a trot. I led her into the ring and trotted her past the judge, so she could check Brenda's soundness. If your horse is lame, you're out of the ribbons. I stood there while the rest of the horses trotted past the judge. Then the voice of the announcer: "The blue ribbon in class number thirty-two, Amateur Owner over Fences, goes to Nattie Gold of Charlotte, North Carolina, on Brenda Starr."

I threw my arms around Brenda's neck, and the ringmaster, a bowlegged man in tan jodhpurs, handed me the blue ribbon and a pewter cup.

"I wouldn't go too far away if I were you," the ringmaster whispered to me. "My guess is you'll be jogging past the judge again in just a few seconds."

He was right. The announcer called the jog order for the second class and it led with lucky number forty-four. Two blues in one day. Hot damn, there was nothing that could go wrong now!

Or so I thought.

CHAPTER 17

Sunday was better than Saturday. If that was possible. I walked away with the division championship and that "darling" cooler Bryce Whit had been cooing over. I'd won a first and a second in the remaining jumping classes, giving me enough points to win the whole shebang without having to take Brenda in the flat class. That's where the judge watches all the horses walk, trot, and canter and then pins the best moving animals. Brenda isn't much of a mover, too much knee action. But she's a hell of a jumper. Ammy owner champion at an A-3 show—Holy Manoli!!

Even Lucy Bladstone congratulated me, along with an offer to buy Brenda for fifty grand. I turned her down.

Lucy and her checkbook were long gone by the time we got all the horses wrapped and everything packed to go. Truth be told, I was in a slo-mo mode. I wanted to savor every last minute of this and make it last as long as possible.

Rob came up to my car just as we were about to pull out. It was twilight, everything was warm and fuzzy—including, apparently, Rob. I was sitting in the driver's seat, too happy to care about the sweat rolling down my face, between my breasts, in back of my ears. He handed me a clean navy blue towel. I pressed the embroidered FF part into my face.

"Nattie," he said, "I don't want you going home overanalyzing this weekend. You would have won the division if George Morris

148

had been riding in it. No one could have beaten the trips you put in on Brenda. You earned the championship."

Well, mercy, mercy, mercy. Rob must be a red-haired Jew in disguise. Either that, or God gave blond Baptists something extra, too. Rob knew exactly what was harboring in the back of my mind, one small step behind my glee. Despite est, Outward Bound, Freudian therapy, and three sessions with a Reiki master, my demons had only been muffled, not exorcised. If I listened carefully, I could still hear them sneering, "Sure you've won Ammy Owner Champion, but go do it against Keith and Lucy."

"Funny you should mention that," I said. "I was going to ask you about that on Monday. I've been thinking about that, you know how Keith can—"

Rob grabbed the towel and held it over my mouth. "Stop it, stop talking. That's your problem, you think too much. Let's go, it's 145 degrees out, we can't keep these horses on the trailer all night."

Rob walked to his truck and I noticed his jeans still had knife-blade creases, front and back. I don't know how he did it. I looked like a discarded rag doll that had gone ten rounds with a hyperactive toddler.

I put on a James Taylor tape and drove down the dark roads with just the red taillights of Rob's trailer in front of me. When we got back to the barn, I looked for Gail, hoping she might be there. She wasn't. I'd been calling her since the previous night. I wanted to tell her my good news and ask her about the hair dye in her locker. I'd been calling the barn and her home, with no luck on either front.

It was pushing nine when I finally pulled into my parking lot. I rolled onto the blacktop, my headlights on high beam. Two sweeping triangles of white washed over a familiar silver Accord. A car door slammed and out unfolded Henry with two little Goodes in tow, screaming at their father.

"Can we go now, we've been waiting a century," the littler one said.

"Yeah, let's go," said the bigger one. "I don't see why we had to wait so long, anyway. She doesn't look that great to me. She's got red hair, I hate red hair. She probably has freckles, too. Yuck central."

Henry took the boy by his arm and said, "Chet, that's enough out of you. Another word and no new computer game next month."

I guess it was time to buy Henry that book on parenting. I got out of my car and walked over to the bickering trio.

"If it isn't Clark Kent himself," I said to Henry. Then I reached my hand out to Chet and said, "Hey, I'm Nattie. You bet your butt I've got freckles. Plenty of them, and I wish I had more. They may look like regular old freckles to you, but they're magic freckles bequeathed to me by my great-grandmother, the first freckle-faced, red-haired Natalie Gold, otherwise known as the Gypsy Queen of Odessa. I can cash in every freckle on my body for someone's secret. So far, I've used up 237 of them. Now I'm going to make it 238. Your favorite computer game is Gabriel Knight—even though your father shouldn't let you play it since it uses bad words like shit and bastard—aaaannd, you hated your father's girlfriend Wendy. Am I right, or what?"

Chet's eyes got big enough to make him look like he was re-lated to those alien invaders who abduct midwestern farm wives and drunken loggers. "Dad, how'd she do that? Is she some kind of witch?"

"Some days," Henry said, and actually winked at me. So he did have a sense of humor. "Nattie, how did you do that?"

"Like I said, I'm Gypsy royalty. Isn't it kind of late for you to be here?"

"I've been trying to get in touch with you all weekend. About Friday, in the newsroom. I was an ass."

His boys laughed and singsonged, "Ooohhh, ooohhh asssss, assssss . . ."

"Chet, Hank, that's enough. Anyway, we baked some chocolate chip cookies, and we thought you might like some. Can we come in?"

I didn't have the heart to tell him I hated chocolate. "Sure, of course. Here's my key, it's the first door on the right. I'll meet you there, I just have to grab a few things."

I heard Henry and his boys arguing the whole way up. "Just a few minutes and then we'll go. . . . Will you stop that, no more fart talk, please. . . . Don't ever call me an ass again, young man. . . ."

I gathered my cooler and ribbons and followed in their footsteps. I was halfway to them when Henry called out, "Nattie, are you sure you locked up?" I heard a door swing open and saw the lights flick on. Then Henry in a controlled, but alarmed voice, "Chet, Hank, get out of here fast. Run down to the car. Get out of here. *Now*!!!"

I bolted up the steps and felt the wind woosh by my face as the boys scrambled past.

I ran to my door. Henry was standing in my living room, blanched whiter than the Lone Ranger's horse. I looked around and saw why. I felt like I was going to vomit—if I could. I threw up once in my life and was so repulsed by it, I've never been able to again.

If ever there was a time to throw up, now was it. Scrawled in big red lipstick letters across the fireplace mirror was QUESTIONS = DEATH. STOP NOW, WHILE YOU CAN. Beneath that lay a pile of plastic horses—the ones my mother had given me twenty-five years ago, the ones I still kept on my mantel—battered and broken. Across the flanks of each one, this sicko had written BRENDA USED-TO-BE-A-STARR.

151

"Don't come in until I look around and make sure no one's waiting for you in a closet," Henry said.

I puddled to the floor in a heap, the wind knocked out of me more than any fall from a horse. I heard Henry opening and closing doors. A few minutes later he came back into the room and sat down next to me.

"No one's here," he said. "And it looks as if your bedroom is undisturbed, except for one peculiar thing. Your bed is pushed against the window with the pillows hanging into the open ledge. Maybe the person got in that way."

"No, no, no, that's the way I sleep." Henry gave me a funny look. I didn't have the air inside my lungs to explain it now. I waved my hand, meaning "let it pass."

Henry crinkled his forehead into deep furrows. If he'd have been a woman and my place hadn't been just broken into, I'd have told him to quit that or else he'd etch himself a set of crevices he could shoot pennies across. Instead, I took a deep breath.

"An anonymous telephone call is one thing, but this is entirely a different matter," Henry said. "This person means business. I'm calling the police."

I nodded and continued re-airing my lungs. I was able to speak again. "I wasn't happy being fashion writer. Oh, no, I had to be Nellie Bly. Well, I'll tell you what. If this asshole gets within one mile of my horse, I'll kill him. I'll kill the son of a bitch. I'll rip this bloodsucker to shreds, so help me God. I'll track him down across every state in the country if I have to."

I heard Henry pick up the phone and realized what he was doing. I grabbed the cord.

"What the hell . . ."

"Wait," I said. "Don't call the Charlotte police. Let me call Tony."

"What's with you, Nattie? Just two days ago you couldn't criticize me enough for not wanting to call the police. Now you're telling me to stop so you can call your Union County white knight. Come on, Nattie, can we have some consistency here?"

I took the telephone from his hand and pressed memory 4. It was busy.

"You've stored his number in your telephone's memory?" Henry said, sounding strikingly similar to his eight-year-old son's earlier whine about being here.

"Well," I said, "you were right about one thing. You sure as hell can be an ass sometimes. Yes, his number is in my phone's memory. He wanted me to be able to reach him quickly in just this kind of circumstance. I'd like to remind you, Tony was the only one that took this lunatic seriously to start with. And he's not my white knight. He knows what's been happening with this whole thing and I just don't feel like going over it again and again. Do you have a problem with that? I mean, it is my apartment that got broken into, not yours."

"Call whomever you want," Henry said. An iceberg the size of the one that sank the *Titanic* had replaced the whine in his voice. "Would you like me to stay until someone with a gun arrives?"

"Suit yourself."

Henry got up and started to leave.

"No, wait," I said. "Look, I'm sorry. I'm upset. I'm scared. Please stay."

"All right, let me go down and get the boys."

While Henry fetched his kids, I called Tony again. I told him what happened. He barely said good-bye. All I heard was "I'll be right there."

And he was. Fifteen minutes later he walked through my front door. I'd have offered him a chocolate chip cookie, but Henry's kids had already scarfed them down.

Henry and Tony exchanged pleasantries. The usual hello-how-are-you's. Then Henry turned toward his kids and said, "Boys, say hello to Detective Odom." It was as if a word never passed through Henry's lips. Chet and Hank didn't even look up from what they were doing, which was working a bottle of Elmer's, trying to piece back my horses. I'd told them I'd give them a buck for every one they made sound.

Just as Henry started marching over to the pile of plastic equine parts, Mrs. Flock, my next-door neighbor, knocked on the open door.

"Nattie, is that you again?" She craned her neck toward the living room. "Oh, my God! What happened here?"

"Some high-heel freak got mad when I called for a ban on spikes," I said.

"Nattie, stop the jokes. Tell me what happened."

I made her swear to secrecy before I told her the truth. "So now I come home to this mess. Say, what did you mean, 'is that me again?' Again when?"

Mrs. Flock looked a bit confused. "Last night I heard you banging around in your living room. At least I thought it was you. That's what you said when I called through the wall."

"Exactly what did you say and then what did I say?"

"Well, I was surprised to hear any noise from your apartment because you told me you were going to a horse show. So when I heard a few knocks and bangs, I called out, 'Nattie, is that you? Back already?' Then I heard someone, I just assumed it was you, say, 'I left my nightingale here.' I had no idea what you were talking about. I assumed it was some kind of joke. I went to sleep and didn't hear anything else."

"I never left Camden," I said.

Mrs. Flock's faced whitened. Then she clamped her left thumb and left index finger over the soft mound of flesh between her thumb and index finger of the other hand and started rubbing vigorously. The headache point. My father taught her that—how to use acupressure instead of Excedrin.

154

"Looks like our perp's a woman who can sound like a Yankee—or is one," Tony said. .

"Maybe yes and maybe no," I said.

"What do you mean, maybe no?" Tony said. "Just the other night you were telling me your walls are so thin you can hear your neighbors snore." Tony looked Mrs. Flock's way and added quickly, "Not that you snore, ma'am."

"Hold your horses, Tony," I said. "Mrs. Flock, mind if I go into your apartment for a minute?"

"Of course, anything I can help you with?"

"Yeah, just stay here with Tony and listen. Henry, you come with me."

Henry and I walked next door and stood in Mrs. Flock's living room. I'd never been in her apartment and was a bit surprised by the decor. She always talked about her glory days as a former Rockette, so I expected a lot glitz and pizzazz. A monk could have lived there. It was sparsely furnished, a couple of wood chairs suitable for sending a kid to the corner in, and an uncomfortable-looking sofa. It was remarkable its utter lack of ornamentation anywhere. No paintings, no pictures, no tchotchkes. No old issues of *The New Yorker*. Nothing, except the most sumptuous Oriental rug I'd ever seen. She had it hanging on her living room wall, edge to edge, floor to ceiling. It was huge, banquet-size, straight out of *The Arabian Nights*.

Henry walked up to it and ran his fingers across the blues and reds. "This is spectacular. Look at the colors and the detail in those panels. It's a Persian Bakhtiari from the Chahar Mahal region."

"Whatever," I said, "It's a wonder she can hear anything through it. Here's the test. First I say it, then you say the exact same thing just as loud. Say it in a high, muffled voice. Put your hand over your mouth or something."

Henry nodded.

"I left my martingale," I called out. Then I whispered to Henry. "Your turn."

"I left my martingale," Henry called out in a most convincing Henrietta voice.

"Now let's go back to my apartment."

"Wait a second," Henry said. "Your neighbor said the person said 'nightingale.' Why did you say martingale? What is a martingale?"

"I'll explain everything in a minute. Come on, let's go. Don't you have to get your kids to bed sometime before midnight?"

Chet and Hank were still working. Judging by the stable full of pieced-together horses standing proudly on my mantel, it looked as if they'd be walking out of there with a good share of my prize money.

"Okay," I said to Tony and Mrs. Flock. "Which voice was me? First or second."

Tony guessed the first, Mrs. Flock the second. The point being, the rug on the walls muffled words beyond recognition. James Earl Jones could have been in my apartment and Mrs. Flock would have thought it was me.

"See, just as I thought," I said. "Neither of you could tell which one was me. Henry, here's where the martingale comes in. I knew something was different about Mrs. Flock's living room wall the minute she told me what she heard."

I turned toward Mrs. Flock and said, "You've recited back conversations I've had in my bedroom word for word. Your accuracy rate is better than *The Appeal*'s. So when you told us the person said 'I left my nightingale,' I knew something was wrong. Whoever said it didn't say *nightingale*. They said *martingale*—it's a piece of tack used to keep a horse from throwing his head around. So that means the only thing we know about this creep is that he or she is a horse person. Which is what we knew to start with. It could have been anyone. Man, woman, even Yankee."

"My bet's on the last—given the nasty nature of his or her visit," Tony said. He was smiling.

"Oh, really?" I said. "You think we Yankees have a monopoly on evil? Where'd the last serial killer come from? Charlotte. And your brother officers didn't even know he was a serial killer until the sicko's tenth victim turned up dead—same type as the others, same M.O. used to kill her and found within a block of the other nine. This person could be anyone from anywhere. Let's just find the bastard before my horse gets hurt."

Hank cocked his head and looked up. Kiddie radar. "Ooooooo-ewwww," Hank singsonged. "She said the B word. So that means I can. Bastard. Bastard. Bastard."

Henry was in Hank's face before the kid could get another syllable out. "That's it, son, another word out of you and you start losing privileges. Now, let's go. It's time for bed."

He wrapped his hands around each boy's arm and led them to the door.

"Wait," I said. "A job's a job. I owe these guys some money. Let me count up how many horses they fixed so I can figure out what I owe them."

"Not now," Henry said. "You can give it to me tomorrow and I'll give it to them. Nattie, call me in an hour and let me know what you and the detective are doing about this. I'd like to stay, but . . ."

Chet and Hank were like a pair of fractious colts trying to break free. Henry led them out and down the steps. They weren't happy about the delayed payment plan their father had arranged.

Meanwhile Mrs. Flock excused herself. Tony gave her his card and said to call him if she remembered anything else—if she noticed a strange car, other noises, unusual smells. Anything out of the ordinary.

It was just me and Tony in my ransacked apartment.

"We've got to call the Charlotte fellas in on this, Nattie. I know you don't want a big to-do about this, but I'm out of my jurisdiction here. I can't do anything official. And this is getting more serious by the incident. Someone's gotta come in here and dust for prints. I've got a friend in your ward. I'll call her. First, show me all the damage, other than the writing on the mirror."

Oh, no. The plastic horses. I hadn't told Tony about them being smashed. I hadn't figured on fingerprinting. I wasn't keen on calling in the Charlotte cops and having them swarm around my apartment poufing baby powder all over, or whatever it is they use to get prints. Now the only swirls anyone could lift off my horses would be the pint-size prints of Chet and Hank.

I pointed to the mantel where my stable of pieced-together horses stood. "Those, whoever broke in thought it would be funny to break my toys. They were in a pile when I got here."

"Oh, Lord," Tony said. "We can kiss those prints good-bye."

"Well, the person was probably wearing gloves, anyway," I said.

"Look, just don't touch anything else until I get someone here, okay? Just sit down and meditate or something."

Tony called his Charlotte kin and mumbled a bunch of police mumbo-jumbo into the phone. God forbid cops use plain English and say something simple like "Someone broke into Nattie Gold's apartment." Instead, it was a lot of perp and number talk. Though, every group has its secret code and decoder rings. Someone who didn't know horses wouldn't be able to decipher a conversation between me and Gail. And the same goes for my newspaper cronies. When we get together, it's sidebar this, news hole that.

"They'll be here in fifteen minutes," Tony said. "I'm going to look around. You stay put, hear?"

I heard Tony clumping around in my bedroom. Cowboy boots on hardwood floors. I was splitting split ends, pulling each side of a forked piece of hair as far as it would go. That was about all my mind could handle. I was physically exhausted from the horse show and mentally spent from the break-in.

Tony clunked back in. "Nattie, by the way, I found out something real interesting about that rich fella in Camden you told me about. The paper guy. It seems like he had a little problem in Georgia. Young girls. And I do mean young."

That cut through my fog. "You mean Keith Rollings?"

"That's the one. His daddy makes the paper that you print stories on. And that makes him rich enough to buy just about anything, including a good future for his pedophile son."

"Slow down, Tony, tell me exactly what you're talking about."

"You're telling me to slow down? Wasn't it just two nights ago you were complaining I talked so slow you could plan your grocery list between my sentences?"

"Okay, okay, okay, I wasn't complaining, I was observing. Anyhow, what do you mean Keith's a pedophile, and how do you know?"

I should have known better than to ask a southerner who once aspired to be the next Faulkner the how-do-you-know question. That was like dumping a flatbed full of cow manure on an already fertile field. When Tony told a story, there were no straight lines from point A—Keith Rollings—to point B—pedophilia. Tony utilized the whole alphabet of points, talking in long, circuitous sentences that ambled along the countryside of his life and everyone's life around him.

It turns out Tony's father had been a cop, too. Worked in the same office as Tony. About twenty years ago Tony's father was investigating a case about a four-year-old girl who had been snatched from her front yard. That was way before picking up a milk carton could scare the crap out of a parent, so a missing kid was an oddity.

Months went by and no clues, no body, no nothing. Just a

mother whose hair turned white overnight and a cop who got obsessed with the little girl. That's all Tony's father could think about. Weekends, nights, any time he could steal away from work—his bosses had already given up—Tony's father tracked down known pedophiles. He started in North Carolina, working the courts and police stations. When those leads turned up cold, he moved on to South Carolina. When nothing turned up in South Carolina, he made his way through Georgia.

"He came home spitting mad one night," Tony said. "Complaining and cussing about rich people and how money can buy anything. I was only a kid at the time, but I still remember how mad he was, telling my mother about a nineteen-year-old in Georgia whose daddy owned paper mills and forests and practically the whole damn state. That boy got caught doing the wrong kinds of things to a three-year-old girl. But the little girl was the maid's daughter and you can bet that maid wasn't about to press charges, not after that boy's daddy bought her off or near scared her to death. Either way, the end was the same. The kid walked away like nothing happened, and his family got the records sealed so no one knew about it."

"How come you didn't tell me this when I told you Henry and I had been to Keith Rollings's farm?"

"I didn't know the fella's name," Tony said. "My father never did say what it was. Even if he had, I wouldn't have paid much mind to him. I wanted nothing to do with his police work. But I never did forget how mad he was that night. Those kinds of things stick with you. After I took down that list of names of all the people you talked to, I got to thinking. I remembered reading something you'd written a couple weeks ago. Something about a party in South Carolina. You had a bunch of women talking about how important it was for their children to all be in the same shade of pink for their school play when they dressed up as talking azaleas. You were making fun of those Junior League types something awful, but I'm sure they thought it was a real fine article. Anyway, one of those ladies was Rollings's wife, or, as you put it, 'Bryce Whit Rollings, who prefers to be known as Mrs. Keith Rollings. That's Rollings as in Rollings Paper of Georgia as in the paper you've got between your fingers.' "

"So did you ask your father if it was in fact Keith?"

"Can't hardly do that. He passed three years back. But I called the fellas in Brunswick and got someone on the phone who remembered my father. Asked after him and that little girl he'd been investigating. I was sorry to tell him they never did find her. The day my father died—pancreatic cancer, got him fast—he told me he was heading out to find that little girl, ask her what happened and who did it. He said if he couldn't solve the case when he was alive, then he'd just have to do it when he was dead."

I looked at the clock. Fifteen minutes had passed. The Charlotte cops would be here any minute. "I'm sorry about your father. I didn't mean to stir up sad memories," I said. I didn't want to be a jerk, but I had to knock the detours out of Tony's story before we were interrupted. "So what'd the guys in Brunswick say about Keith?"

"I don't know what Jewish folks believe, but for me, I think my father solved the crime. He just can't make an arrest."

"Tony," I said, trying to be as gentle as possible without shrieking, which is what I felt like doing. We could talk metaphysics later. "What about Keith?"

"Oh, yeah, those boys down in Brunswick didn't want to talk much about the Rollingses and their pedophile son, Keith. Rollings is a big name down there. But that one man who knew my father did allow as how the police were only too happy to see Keith's daddy pack his sick kid up and send him off to school in South Carolina."

That explained it. That's what Wally had on Keith. Not a dead horse, but a perverted past. Wally's father was a cop in Georgia, that's how he knew about Keith's little problem.

Just then I heard an officious pounding on the door.

"Odom, you in there?"

"Sure am, come on in," Tony said to the pair of starched blues standing by my threshold. Introductions were made, they asked me the standard cop questions, and then Tony showed them around.

It was pushing midnight. I'd been up long enough to see two black skies in one day. I sat back down on the sofa and the next thing I knew the sun was shining on my face.

CHAPTER 18

"Nattie, telephone." It was Tony. He was standing by my bedroom door, holding the phone in his hand.

I was in my bed. "Huh?" I said, propping myself up on my elbow.

"Telephone, for you. He's been calling all morning."

I looked down to see what I was wearing. Same clothes as last night.

Tony handed me the phone. "Hello," I said.

It was Henry. "What you do is your own business, and I certainly don't want to interrupt anything, but I hope you're planning to come into work soon. Fred wants us to download and then sit in on the weekly story meeting to tell all the editors what we've discovered so far. They're interested in promo-ing this story to the hilt; extra editions in Columbia and Camden, rack cards on all the paper boxes. Et cetera, et cetera, et cetera. Also, I never did get a chance to tell you what I found when I did a records check on your friend Melissa Mayfield's father. Some very intriguing and implicating facts. So, if it isn't too much of an interruption, could you make it your business to get here as soon as possible?"

Henry was a master of modulation. His voice was level and cool as the penguin slide at the zoo. The words racing down were anything but. What a Puritan. No doubt the *Mayflower* was carrying his seed when it landed, but that was three hundred years ago. I wanted to tell him times have changed, that women actually have

163

sex without their clothes on now—and sometimes even with men whom God has not joined them to. Not that that was the case with me and Tony. Besides, why start a fight? We had a story to finish.

"You're not interrupting anything," I said. Not now, at least. I could have danced down Queens Road naked last night for all I remembered. "I'll be there as soon as I take a shower and get dressed. And wait'll you hear what I found out. Tighten your seat belt, 'cause, baby, this'll take you for a ride. See ya soon."

I handed the phone back to Tony. "Okay, Tony, talk. How'd I wind up here? The last thing I remember was sitting on my sofa with those two Columbos sprinkling fairy dust all over my apartment."

"I carried you in. You were deader than Bambi's mother last night. Funny thing, though, you never do stop talking, even in your sleep. Something about being chased—you mentioned my name."

That dream again. My face must have turned redder than my hair. No dream talk now. "So what did your Charlotte brethren find, anyway?"

"Then you got real loud about an oxer. You kept saying, 'No, not an oxer.' What's an oxer?"

"It's a kind of jump that scares me but doesn't bother Brenda. Now, can we get back to what happened last night?"

"You were right about the gloves. There were no prints to be found anywhere. But that's one strong, or very angry, perp who broke into your apartment. The lock, the door, the jamb—smashed badder than that big horse. That's why I stayed here last night. I wanted to make sure you didn't have any return visitors."

"I thank you and my mother thanks you," I said. "I'll get the locksmith, the doorsmith—whatever it takes—to get it fixed today. I don't mean to be ungrateful, but I've got to run if I want to make it down to *The Appeal* for the ten A.M. budget meeting."

"You still don't have a lock. I'll leave when you do. So go take a shower or whatever it is you want to do."

"No, that's ridiculous, you go on."

Tony sat himself back down on my sofa and picked up a back issue of *The Chronicle of the Horse*. I wasn't going to argue with him. I'd never had a bodyguard before, and after last night it didn't feel too bad having one now.

Ten minutes later Tony and I were standing by my battered door. I was pushing the clock and getting nervous. Tony wanted to explain in minute detail about the kind of lock I needed.

"I got it," I said. "A double dead bolt. I gotta run, Tony. Thank you for everything. You're a good friend."

I reached my hand around his neck and kissed him on the cheek. After a night out, his five o'clock shadow had grown into a three A.M. thunderstorm and it felt like I was sliding my lips across the sidewalk.

I ran to my car and headed to work.

CHAPTER 19

"Nat-ola, Nat-ola. I wish I had the kind of night you had last night. You don't look like your head hit the pillow once. Anyone I know?"

It was Jeff, his ear already attached to his phone, with his hand over the mouthpiece so he could talk, or, in Jeff's case, scream to me.

"Lower the volume about thirty decibels, would you please?" I said with more bite in my bark than I intended. "I don't want the entire building knowing about my sex life, or what you perceive my sex life to be."

"A might bit touchy are we?" Jeff said. He looked hurt. "What's wrong with you today, anyway? It's Monday morning. Why should this Monday morning be different from any other Monday morning? *Mah-nish-tah-nah ha-lilal ha-zei?*"

"*Mikall ha-lay losh,*" I said. It was the next line of the four questions, the famous four all Jewish boys and girls ask at Passover. Jeff was the only other Jew in the newsroom. We had our own little ghetto back in Features.

I leaned over and hugged him. "I'm sorry, sweetie, I had a rough night, and not the good kind of rough night, if you get my drift. I've got to rush to the ten A.M. budget meeting. But I promise I'll give every last gory detail later. It is, after all, Monday morning."

That washed the little-boy-with-a-boo-boo look off his face.

166

He started to say something else to me, but the person he'd been on hold with must've come back on the line.

"Look, it's pretty simple," I heard him saying into the phone. "Just get me the exact number of *Mr. Ed* shows that ran. Also, see if you can find out how they made that walking bottle of glue talk. This request is coming directly from my publisher. He's got a nut case of a nephew, a wacked-out little bureaucrat in Washington who has nothing better to do than fixate on old *Mr. Ed* shows. No one in the capital of our great nation can access this classified information, so he called up our publisher, his uncle Rutger, who was only too happy to help. And lucky me, I got the assignment. See what you can do, okay?"

He blew me a kiss as I walked away. Despite Jeff's computer hogging, we hit it off the minute we sat down next to each other two and a half years ago. If I could have chosen my brother, he would have been it. He had a tongue sharper than mine and didn't mind using it. Jeff was witty and wry, a regular Oscar Wilde, except he was Jewish and heterosexual. Wildly heterosexual. Jeff might have been Trojan's leading individual purchaser of ribbed condoms in the Southeast.

Jeff's relationships never went past the tingly stage. Once the newness was gone, so was the woman. And I heard about them all—as he did mine. At the start of every week, we'd Monday-morning-quarterback over cups of bad coffee from the back shop. Detail for lurid detail, we'd match each other's story with the tales of our weekend revelry.

Jeff hung up the phone. "Gold, I want to know *everything*!!!" he called out after me.

Inside the glass office, the whole gang was gathered, every editor and mid-level editor this side of South Tryon Street. And Henry. Reporters aren't usually privy to the machinations of the newsroom except when he or she has got the goods, as we clearly did now. I sat down next to Henry; he handed me a printout of today's agenda. We were item 6. They were on item 2, news-hole size. The big guys and gal were talking about the latest directive from Miami, chain headquarters, to reduce our costs. Though we've run countless page-one stories about other companies' shameful track records concerning minority hiring, there is still only one woman in our newsroom with power, my boss Candace. And being head of Features, her stick isn't too big, not yet at least. As for other minorities, the hierarchy at *The Appeal* is a sorry sea of paleskins, with the whitest of white boys, Fred Richards, at our helm.

News hole, budget, contingency. Yackety-yackety-yak. More stuff about how badly we were doing. The truth is, we are the chain's cash cow, with a thirty-cent return on every dollar of our investors' money. The Miami muckety-muks have yanked our belts so many times, we reporters already felt like Scarlett's waist. Cinched any tighter and we'd pop. I tuned them out, it just made me mad to listen to it.

I was trying to fit all the pieces together: Wally, Melissa, Keith, Lucy, La Donna, Gail. . . . I must have been pretty deep in thought, because we were already on item 5 the next thing I knew. Ken Grant, the city editor with the soft spot for short young women, was giving a weekend wrap-up and what follow-ups he planned to assign to reporters. I was barely listening, I had too many things on my mind. Although I did tune in enough to hear him zing Fred about his circulation/profitability fixation.

". . . and I'm going to have Cynthia, the new intern from Duke, chase down whatever she can find out about a body that turned up in a ditch in Southern Pines. I realize it's out of our penetration area, so don't start in on me on that. How many attractive young women, fully dressed and completely devoid of ID, turn up with their heads battered? I don't care if it's one hundred miles outside our 'penetration zone,' we're tracking it. The police don't know who she is, how she got there. . . ."

I had to find Gail today, ask her about that hair dye, and where she's been for the past two days. Also, I had to find out more about Keith. Then there was that stuff Henry uncovered about Melissa's father . . .

Ken was droning on. ". . . a couple of things odd about this one. The police said her fingernails were caked with a tarry black substance—definitely nothing resembling Carolina clay. And this is even odder, she had small bruises, abrasions, and scars on the insides of her knees. Go figure that? What would give a person those kinds of marks?"

"Riding," I said before I realized I'd said it.

Everyone looked at me. Candace was smiling. I was one of hers. Her stick was growing bigger by the second.

"Riding bruises, those are riding bruises," I said. I was fully aware of what I was saying now. A dead rider. The hair stood up on my arms—this was another piece to my puzzle. "Here, look at my legs."

I was wearing a mini, so it was easy to see the faint purple scars and bruises of healed-over rubs on the insides of my legs. On my left leg I had a newly worn patch of red, right where my calf and thigh connect, right where my jeans rub me raw every time I ride. On my right leg I had a matching set.

"You can get them when you ride without britches or chaps," I said. "And in this heat, those are about the last thing you want to ride in."

I looked at Ken. "Do you know what she looked like? Hair color, height, weight? Anything?"

"Let me get Cynthia."

Ken picked up the phone and punched in some numbers. Through the glass walls I saw a short young woman with curly brown hair and extremely large breasts pick up the phone on the copy desk. Cynthia, no doubt. She was the right hiring height— shorter than Ken. He mumbled into the receiver, "Dead body . . .

notes . . . more details . . ." I watched Cynthia's lips move, "Be right there, boss." No one except Lois Lane called her editor "boss."

Cynthia put down the phone. Her face was flushed—with excitement over the job or Ken, who knew? I watched as she fished a mirror from her purse, checked her hair, her lipstick, and whatever else she could check in a two-by-two-inch reflection. Poor girl, she was new enough to the newsroom not to realize the implications of these glass walls. New enough not to know that we all were watching her primp like she was getting ready for the senior prom.

"Ahhh, she'll just be a minute," Ken said. "She said she had to get her notes together."

I nudged Henry's leg under the table and he winked at me.

Cynthia finally made it into the glass office. She walked up to Ken with a reporter's pad in her hand and a look of absolute adulation on her face. I had to turn away. It was embarrassing. The only time I've been looked at that way was by my dog, Mutchka. And he was retarded. His genes were more strained than English royalty. The poor dog's father was his grandfather and he thought I was his soul mate.

"Cynthia, Nattie thinks she might know something about the dead woman. Give us whatever you've got on her," Ken said.

Cynthia faced me and turned into Robo-reporter, reciting detail after detail. This was no bimbo.

". . . five-foot-six, slender build, 110–115 pounds, blue eyes, blondish hair, late twenties, wearing Levi 505 jeans, white Polo, no insignia, new Nike 780s. The Southern Pines police will fax me a picture as soon as they get one; however, I asked them to describe her face to me until then. They said, 'She looked rich.' I asked what rich looks like, and they said, 'Straight teeth with a lot of expensive dental work, hair that was probably light brown but dyed to look like it'd been bleached by the sun, and solid gold horse-head earrings."

She just described half of the horse show world. I'd have to work the phones, see if anyone was missing, which would be problematic because the thing with the idle rich is just that. They're idle and rich. They don't have to be anyplace they don't want to be and they can go anyplace they want to go.

"She was a rider," I said, "and I'm betting she has something to do with the story. Cynthia, keep me posted on anything else you find out."

"Sure thing," she said to me. She turned to Ken. "Anything else I can do for you, boss?"

It was a challenge, not a question. This kid could take care of herself. Ken's cheeks pinked up and he cleared his throat. "No, no, not right now. Keep on the coroner and the cops. Let's get that photo asap."

Next it was our turn. For the next thirty minutes Henry and I held court. We started with the facts: the bloody corpses in the stall, the other dead horses, Rob's arrest, the telephone threat to me, and the break-in at my apartment. Then we mapped out the direction we thought the story would move. We wanted to give the readers more than a *National Enquirer* look at a grisly murder. If Wally's death had to do with insurance fraud—and not a jealous boyfriend as the police believed—we wanted to paint a vivid and accurate picture of the horse show world and explain how killing horses, and possibly people, fit in.

"It's a fascinating subculture we've got here in our own back-yard, so to speak," Henry said. "Before I started working on this story, I had no idea any of this existed. And from what Nattie tells me, the Carolinas are the hub of the horse show industry. An in-depth look at these people and their world would not only be

171

very interesting, but timely as well, thanks in large part to Wally's murder."

The head of the copy desk, a professional nitpicker, had that faux-pained look of concern on his face, the one editors wear when they're about to mutilate your copy.

"What if the police are right?" he said. "What if it's merely a crazed-gay-lover story. Then why would your story be any different from something that would run in the tabloids?"

I was waiting for someone to say that. "Because we're taking a look at a part of Carolina culture that we haven't explored before. Millions of dollars a year are spent in North and South Carolina on show horses, and have you ever read anything about it in the pages of *The Commercial Appeal*? Not likely. Not at all, in fact. I ran a library check and couldn't find a word other than the standard tailgate party coverage of the Carolina Cup. So that's why. As far as I'm concerned, we don't have to worry about justifying running a smutty gay-lover story. Because I'm sure that's not what it's going to turn out to be. Rob didn't do it. I know he had motive, opportunity, and not much of an alibi, but he didn't do it."

"Then who did it?" The $64,000 question from our leader, Fred Richards.

"Well," I said, "that *is* what we're trying to find out. Any number of people could have done it. Wally made a regular cottage industry of blackmail and horse murder. Knowing what I know now, I'd have liked to kill him myself."

"Have you got any leads?" Candace asked.

"As a matter of fact, we do," I said.

I told them about Keith's nasty little secret and what Keith's wife, Bryce Whit, told me at the horse show, how angry her husband used to get by Wally's unannounced visits. "Blackmail," I said. "I'm sure Wally was using Keith as his personal bank machine. Maybe Keith got fed up or ran out of withdrawal slips.

Who knows. One thing's for sure. Keith had a life to lose if Wally starting yakking. His fancy, well-bred wife, his fancy, well-bred daughter, his fancy, well-bred horses—gone, forgotten, history— if all those South Carolina high-noses found out about his preference for toddlers. Now, what remains to be seen is if he had the opportunity."

As I unraveled the Keith connection, I'd kept an eye on Candace. It was like watching Bill Bixby turn into the Incredible Hulk.

"Great stuff, Natalie," she said. "Forget Sunday's column. We'll plug it with wire copy. Just focus on this story. Hell of a story, hell of a story."

Yes! I was on my way to becoming a full-time feature writer.

"Then there's the stuff about the Mayfields," I said.

"Mayfield as in Edward Mayfield as in SouthPark Mall, Eastland Mall, and the Arboretum?" Another entry from our astute editor.

"The one and only," I said. I filled them in on my Melissa connection. Candace practically burst when I got to the part about Melissa telling me *on the record* about Daddy commissioning Wally to kill her horse for insurance money.

"Here's the kicker," I said, "the kid lied to me about shopping with Mommy on the night of the murder. She said they'd gone to Montaldo's. Trouble is, Monty's was closed that night for inventory."

"How'd you know that?" Fred again.

"I called and asked," I said.

"Oh, yes, well, good digging, Nattie," Fred said. "Anything else?"

"Henry's been doing his own brand of excavating," I said. "Henry?"

Henry, lover of history, took the editors through a brief tour of Charlotte development as it pertained to Edward Mayfield. It was pretty interesting stuff—how Mayfield had transformed a small southern city with a few dry goods stores downtown into the land of the suburban shopping mall.

"Mayfield had the foresight to buy up thousands of acres south of Charlotte," Henry said. "Cornfields and cotton fields, that's all it was then. Mayfield couldn't find any investors to go in with him, so he got the capital from his first wife's family."

That explained how the marriage stayed together as long as it did—and also that Melissa wasn't going to be forced to go to any state school. Another lie from the kid. Henry's information wasn't coming from court records. I couldn't wait to get him alone to find out how he knew all this and pieced everything together.

"What luck," Richards said. "The man buys cornfields and they turn out to be in the middle of the city's major development."

"Not luck," Henry said. "Mayfield is very smart; however, it goes beyond that. People who know Mayfield say he can recall any conversation he's ever had, a sort of idiot savant, except this man is no idiot. It seems in 1959 Mayfield, then a senior at Chapel Hill, was at a cocktail party given by his future in-laws. There he met a man, a geography professor who was discussing Charlotte's rock patterns and air flow. The man told Mayfield that the city's development would have to be in a southeasterly direction, given the geography of the region and its air currents."

Henry went on to explain how Mayfield must have mentally filed the conversation under future investments. A few years later he married his college sweetheart, Shay Stanier, of Stanier Mills. Her father offered him a big job at one of his mills, but Edward Mayfield had other ideas. He got in his new blue Cadillac, a wedding present from the Staniers, and drove seven miles southeast of Trade and Tryon streets—the heart of Charlotte. He waved his checkbook in front of every farmer's nose there and bought everything he could. Which was just about everything.

Even I, a newcomer to these parts, realized the foresight that took. Back then, Dilworth was considered a suburb of Charlotte and that's only a mile or so from downtown.

"At one time he owned most of southeast Charlotte, the most expensive zip code in the Carolinas," Henry said.

"I guess that's how he could afford to support his daughter's riding habit," I said. "I heard he paid almost $200,000 for the horse Melissa rode in the large junior hunter division. And then he had to lease another horse so Melissa could compete in the equitation divisions. That was at another sixty grand a year."

I stared into a collection of lost faces. They had no idea what I was talking about.

I explained: "All the really rich kids have at least two horses, a junior horse and an equitation horse. The junior horse jumps big and arches its back over the fence—very spectacular to watch. Problem is, it's hard for a rider to look pretty on a horse that jumps so big because it throws you out of the saddle so much. That's where the other mount—the equitation horse—comes in. Equitation classes are judged on the rider, and more or less how pretty she looks atop her horse. An equitation horse doesn't jump as brilliantly as a junior horse. The arc to its jump is much flatter, so the rider looks better over the top of the fence."

Ken looked especially annoyed. "You know," he said, "some people just have too much money."

I had to agree with him.

"He certainly *had* an enormous amount," Henry said. "Put that in the past tense, however. His current holdings are minuscule compared to his previous holdings. He did manage to avoid bankruptcy, however, and that's the interesting part."

Interesting with four syllables, all capital letters. Henry had already uncovered a gold mine of information and I was sure the best was yet to come. I couldn't bear to dig through court records. The sheer tediousness of it would drive me crazy. Henry seemed to thrive on it, boring deeper and deeper until he found blood. He reminded me of a picture I saw in *Smithsonian* magazine. It was a story about moles, illustrated with an X ray of a pelican that had swallowed a mole whole. The mole, still alive in the pelican's stomach, bored out through the bird's intestine and almost through its skin before they both croaked. I hoped this wasn't a metaphor for our story.

"From what I gather," Henry said, "Mayfield believed that Fort Mill, South Carolina, was about to become the next southeast Charlotte. Fort Mill is not even fifteen interstate highway miles from downtown, and Mayfield must have figured the development would go that way. He bought everything that Jim Bakker didn't. The trouble was that the development corridor headed north instead, circling the university. Mayfield, like Bakker, was left with acres and acres of extraordinarily expensive cotton fields—and numerous creditors and lawsuits.

"I know several of the attorneys who represented his creditors and they showed me their depositions, everything. He was precariously close to losing everything if he didn't come up with enough money to meet his monthly mortgage payments.

"Why didn't he go to his father-in-law for a bailout?" I asked.

"According to court documents, Shay Stainer Mayfield had filed divorce papers at about the same time, but later withdrew them." Henry said.

"What grounds?" I bet I knew, given his track record.

"Adultery," Henry said.

Mayfield's loose zipper went way back.

"Then at the proverbial last minute he came up with enough money to begin satisfying his creditors and start building again. Somewhere he found a half million dollars."

Poor Waysie. "Somewhere in the form of Equitable Equine Life," I said. "That's how much Waysie had been insured for. I've got a friend whose husband runs a pretty big insurance adjusting company. And he happens to know the agents at Equitable Equine Life and they happened to remember the Mayfield claim, because it was such a whopper."

Candace was beaming. Ken was smiling. Fred still looked a bit confused. But all in all, the energy in the room was high. Everyone knew we had a big story on our hands. Ken started in on extra-edition talk, which replaced the look on Fred's face from one of confusion to utter discomfort.

"I don't know if we can sell anything extra to Miami," Fred said. "Especially with this last directive to cut the news hole by seven percent. I just don't know if it's a can-do kind of thing."

Ken's face reddened, not pinked, as it had around Cynthia. Ken may not have a deep reservoir of integrity when it comes to glandular decisions. However, when it comes to newspapering, he's one of the best. It was a major coup for *The Appeal* to land him, and they've always treated him with kid gloves, which is why they ignore his intern problem and his Big Daddy attitude toward women. I may hate his sexual politics, but he's a hell of a newsman and refuses to compromise his standards. I've always respected him for that. And today was no exception.

"When Henry and Nattie crack this thing, we're going to run every inch of copy they've got," Ken said, slipping into his television voice of authority. I used to listen to it as a kid when he reported on the Vietnam War. It gave me a shiver then, and it did now. "We're also going to rack-card the shit out of this story and run extra papers to Camden, Southern Pines, and anywhere else we think it'll sell. And if we don't, if Miami starts pulling the plug on this thing, they'll have to find themselves a new city editor."

"Well, there's no reason to get in a huff," Fred said. "Let's all just stay calm. I'm sure everything will work out. I'd like to compliment the person who thought of teaming Henry and Nattie up. Excellent idea. I see this as the start of many more interdepartmental collaborations."

I didn't know if Candace would be able to fit through the door. Her personal space had expanded to the size of the Bullwinkle float in the Macy's Thanksgiving Day parade.

"I gave Nattie the go-ahead on this," Candace said. "I've always said if a reporter is gung-ho on a story, the best thing I can do is open the gate and let her fly."

I had to rein in my eyeballs to keep them from rolling. When Candace cornered me the other day, it wasn't the sound of opening gates I'd heard.

CHAPTER 20

Miracle of miracles, Jeff was off the phone *and* the computer. He had his head buried in his file cabinet, so I swung the computer terminal around before he had a chance to grab it.

"I hear you, Gold," he said. "Don't think you're sneaking anything past me. I don't need the computer right now. The column's done, finito, pain in the ass-o. So clack away all you want, my little short one. Hey, I don't know what you and Goode were unloading in there, but I haven't seen all those editors so excited since Jessica Hahn's nudie photos came out in *Playboy*—you know, the first set before she got her tit job, the ones that proved Galileo's hypothesis of gravity. So tell me, what's up besides Jessica's new and enhanced chest?"

"Jeff, you're such an oinker sometimes," I said. Truth is, everyone in the newsroom talked about Jessica's plastic surgery—even our token radical feminist copy editor.

I gave Jeff an abbreviated version of the events, which satisfied him since he has the attention span of a hyperactive first-grader, pre-Ritalin. Just as I was wrapping up my two-minute history of the past few days, his phone rang. He swiveled his chair, back to me and whispered, as best as he could, into the phone. Because it was Jeff, I could hear every word. Not that I needed to. It's the same spiel every week, "Yeah, I had a great

179

time, babe, et cetera, et cetera, et cetera. I'll be talking to you. . . ."
I could set my clock by it, three or four minutes of lies and then
bam, the phone's back in the cradle.

Normally, I'd have been interested in the who, what, where,
and when of Jeff's latest. But I had too much to do. That dead
girl in Southern Pines gave me the heebie-jeebies. I had to find
out who she was. I made a list of twelve people to call, many of
the same I'd called the other day asking about Wally. After four
calls I was no closer to an answer. No one knew of anyone
not accounted for, and I had a feeling this was how it was going
to be.

I stood up and stretched. Jeff was still on the phone, back to
me, and trying to whisper. Ten minutes had passed and he was
still cajoling. He looked like a fly trying to get his little feet unstuck
from flypaper.

". . . It's okay, I said it's okay," he said, "just hang there if you
want. I can't make any promises about tonight, it's sweeps week
supreme. I'll be here till they find me slumped over my computer. . . . I'll call as soon as I know, yeah, yeah, I promise . . . give
me a couple hours and . . ."

Serves him right. Whoever this one is, was pinning him to
the mat. I went back to working the phones. By call number
nine, the only thing I'd gotten was a stiff neck. This approach
wasn't working. I was spinning my wheels for nothing. I'd have
to wait on the photo, and hope whatever creatures had been
sharing the ditch with the stiff had dined on parts other than
her face.

Gail, I had to find Gail and get this hair-dye business settled.
It was driving me crazy. Besides, I hadn't heard from her since
her overnight at the barn. I called her apartment again. No
answer. I called the barn and old man Clarke picked up the
phone.

"Oh, hey, Mr. Clarke, this is Nattie Gold," I said in my most obsequious voice. Rob may have convinced him to take me as a boarder, but it was clear he didn't like me any better than the paper I worked for. "Would you please put Gail on."

"She's not here," he said. Click.

I slammed the phone down and said, "Thanks for all your help, jerkface. I'll find her myself."

That was unlikely. Given the way my morning was going, I couldn't find my way to the bathroom.

"Try my house."

It was Jeff.

"What?" I said.

"I said, 'Try my house.' She's still there, probably has a moving van on the way over."

"Gail? Your house?"

"Nattie, you're operating on two cylinders this morning. Don't you remember the Great Fix-up? 'Call my friend Gail, she's great, you'll love her, be nice, et cetera, et cetera, et cetera'?"

"That was *Gail* you were talking to a few minutes ago?"

"Yes, any other questions? Like when she's planning to leave my house or stop calling me? That was the fourth call this morning. Nats, I know she's your best friend, but why didn't you tell me she's unbalanced?"

I can't say I wasn't warned. Before I left home, my mother told me two things. "Never play matchmaker—that's how I met the gonif you call a father," she'd said between drags of her Chesterfield Light. "And always wear A-line skirts. It'll help your figure type." I was seventeen, so whatever she said, I reversed and did the opposite. I must still be rebelling.

"Define unbalanced," I said.

"Okay, how's about sticking to me like a Post-it after one unremarkable date," Jeff said.

"Unremarkable to you maybe, but apparently not to her. She's not crazy, she's just lonely. Give her a break, the last guy she was with dumped on her pretty good. I told you to be nice, didn't I?"

"I couldn't have been any nicer. Dinner, made by *moi*, movie, walk in the park, tumble in bed. That's nice, isn't it? You didn't ask me to marry her, you just asked me to take her out. Which I did."

"I'll call her, I've got to talk to her, anyway. What's your number?"

I dialed. I wasn't sure what I was going to say. How do you tell a friend the man she's obsessing over isn't interested? As I listened to it ring three, four, five times, and tried to figure out a gentle way to get her out, I slipped into my usual telephone habit and started playing with my hair. I didn't have the patience to split ends; instead, I flipped around three thin strands into a braid. Eight rings, no answer. As I started to put the phone back on the cradle, the braid fell across the handset. I looked at it. Same color as my horse's mane. It looked just like one of her braids. A horse's braid.

I dropped the phone.

"Hello, hello." Gail's voice coming from the other end. "Jeff, Jeff, is that you, I was in the shower and—"

I ran across the newsroom. Ken was standing by the copy desk.

"Where's Cynthia?" I said.

"She's at the cop shop to get last night's report," Ken said. "She left about twenty-five minutes ago, she won't be much longer."

"Who's her contact with the Southern Pines police?"

"I don't know, let's look on her desk, see if her notes are out."

Just as I was about to rifle through her piles of papers and notebooks, I heard, "Can I help you?"

Cynthia didn't look too happy to see me messing with her stuff.

"Did the police say anything about her eyes?" I said.

"The dead woman's?"

"Yeah," I said.

"Just that they were blue."

"Do you have someone there who doesn't hate reporters? Someone who'll give you more than the standard press release?"

I didn't call the police myself for that reason. *The Commercial Appeal* has an uneasy relationship with most of the police agencies in the state. It's virtually impossible to get anything more than the official write-up—unless you've worked up a source.

"There's an Officer Shelby Hines who was quite helpful," Cynthia said.

"Well, do me a favor, would you? Call him and ask him about her eyes. Ask him if there was anything unusual about the color."

She looked at Ken. He nodded. She dialed.

"Officer Hines, please. Yes, this is Cynthia Morrel from *The Commercial Appeal*. . . . I'm fine and you? How's that little girl of yours? Swimming yet? Great. Maybe you could help me with something, if you have a minute. A colleague of mine wants to know about the dead woman's eyes. Was there anything unusual about the color? Anything at all?"

After a few "oh, reallys" and "that's so interesting," Cynthia said her thank-yous and good-byes and hung up.

"It looks like you're on to something," Cynthia said. "Her eyes were blue, but not your everyday blue. Officer Hines said they were a weird shade, with very little color to them. He said they were so pale, he felt like he was looking inside her. The only time he'd seen eyes like that were on his brother-in-law's dog. A Siberian husky."

I slipped into Ken's chair. I felt like I'd had the wind knocked out of me.

I mumbled, "That's why her fingernails were so dirty."

CHAPTER 21

"That connection would have never come to me," Henry said. We were sitting by a window at the Pewter Rose, the best lunch place in town. I'd worked the frost off the iced tea glass, wrapping and rewrapping my fingers around it and then running my chilled hand across my forehead. It was plenty cool inside, between the air conditioner and the paddle fans. But I felt like I'd gone three hours on the Stairmaster and couldn't cool down. If I'd been a horse, I'd have tied up by now and the vet would be pumping me with tranquilizers, which might not have been too bad.

"Yeah, well knock me over with a feather," I said. "Sully wasn't even twenty-five years old and she's dead. I can't convince my brain that the half-eaten corpse in Southern Pines was the same person I shot the bull with at every horse show."

My hands started shaking again. I started to reach for the glass, and knocked it over.

"God, look at me," I said. "My first run out the gate and I'm a basket case. So much for how dirty I can get my trench coat."

Henry blotted up the tea with his napkin and signaled to the waiter for another one.

"Go easy on yourself, Nattie," he said. "Death is hard to deal with under the best circumstances. The only thing worse than murder, I suppose, is suicide. I'm sure you know this, but my partner in Investigative killed herself. About four years ago and it's still painful to think about it."

I'd heard about it. She was a hotshot, a real golden girl. Everyone thought she'd be at *The Post* or *The Times* before she hit twenty-five. Instead, she wound up in a coffin at twenty-four.

"She was gifted, she was funny, she was smart. But she had no private life, nothing outside *The Appeal*. That's one of the sad things, at her funeral it was just her mother and a room full of reporters, the same people who can joke about plane crashes and run office pools on the number of victims, all of us, crying. The minister, clearly disturbed by such a young suicide, could offer no solace. In his eulogy he said, 'She was just too broke to fix.' Too broke to fix, how does a person get that way?"

Henry's voice trailed off and so did his eyes. He was staring into his glass of iced tea like it was a crystal ball. Meanwhile, my hand was still shaking—what a duo we were, a dysfunctional Woodward and Bernstein. I didn't know what to say next, and Henry seemed stuck in bad-memory land. The restaurant gods must have been smiling on us, because before that awkward moment had time to grab hold, the waiter showed up with two large platters of green and red baby lettuce.

"Balsamic or lemon poppy-seed dressing?" he said.

"What, what did you say?" I grabbed his wrist. I was shaking and holding the poor guy's cuff like it was going to keep me from drowning.

This waiter was truly a food industry professional. He replied as coolly as the plate of chilled greens. "I said balsamic or lemon poppy-seed dressing."

"Lemon poppy-seed! Lemon poppy-seed! That's it! That's it! You must be Nellie Bly reincarnated, here to help a sister journalist. Talk about synchronicity, three times in one day!! My father's right with all his mumbo-jumbo talk about the universe taking care of you. Yes!!!! Thank you! Thank you!"

That yanked Henry right back into reality. There wasn't much room for maudlin thoughts of dead reporters, not with me hooting and hollering about lemon poppy-seed dressing and synchronicity.

"I'll leave them both here for you to decide," the waiter said. He unlatched my fingers from his wrist and walked away.

Henry had that concerned-school-nurse look in his eyes. He looked fatherly, which made him look vulnerable, which, I have to admit, made him look even more handsome. "Are you okay?" he said.

"Yeah, yeah, of course I'm okay. Don't you remember? Lemon poppy-seed? Lucy's maid, Dorothy? Sully's bread?"

I spilled a little of the lemon poppy-seed dressing on my salad plate, dipped my finger, and licked it. Tart and sweet, with tiny balls of crunch. Nothing can bring back a memory like taste or smell. I assumed it was the same for everyone. I dipped my finger again.

"Here, taste this," I said. I was so excited about what I'd re-membered that sticking my finger in Henry's mouth seemed like the natural thing to do for two reporters working on a story. Once inside, I realized I was in much more familiar terrain than I wanted to be.

"Oh," I said, and pulled my finger from his lips.

Another awkward moment. This was turning out to be the lunch of revelations and regrets.

"Anyway," I said, hoping my face wasn't as red as the radic-chio, "remember that taste? Don't you remember what happened when Lucy's maid brought the bread in?"

Henry shook his head. "Sorry, I don't."

I guess taste doesn't catapult everyone back in time. So I walked Henry through Dorothy's weird reaction, how just touch-ing the bread hurt her.

"Remember how she didn't even want to bring it into the room at all? She said it felt like someone hit her 'upside the head and down the back' when she pulled the bread out of the freezer. She kept rubbing the left side of her head while she was talking. The same spot where Sully's head was bashed in."

Henry was shaking his head. "Coincidence. Maybe the woman suffers from migraines. Maybe the flu was coming on. There could be any number of plausible explanations."

"Henry, here we go again. It's not coincidence. The only plausible explanation is that she knew Sully was dead before any of us did. I know this woo-woo psychic stuff doesn't compute in your logical brain, but even you must admit there are some things that happen on this earth that can't be scientifically quantified."

Then I told him what my friend's grandmother told me umpteen years ago about redhaired Jews and green-eyed blacks.

"I'm not saying every redheaded Jew or every green-eyed black person can tell your future, but this woman's got a gift, Henry. She knows things. I knew it the minute I saw her. We've got to go to Camden to find out what else she knows. Let's go. Hurry up and finish your salad."

We'd just begun eating and I could tell that Henry had no intention of leaving a plateful of fancy lettuce behind. He speared a fork into a curlicue of frizzee.

"And here you go again, Nattie, rushing off half cocked. I'm not discounting any possibility, even the one that Dorothy—for whatever reason—knew Sully was dead. We can't barge into a place with no plan. Let's finish our lunch and map things out. I find it helps if we have a framework to work from."

He pulled out a reporter's pad and pen and started scribbling. I looked over. An outline, a goddamned outline he was drawing while the clue to our murder was an hour away. "Look, I'll tell you what," I said, my voice remarkably calm given the fact I wanted to dump his plate of salad over his ash-blond hair. "You get started on the framework. I've got a phone call to make. Then when I come back, we'll go, okay?"

I got up from the table and started heading for the phone.

"I'd thought we'd draw up a plan together, that's what I used to do with—"

I cut him off. "I'm not her. When I get back, you can tell me what you've written. Then I'll give you my thoughts—in the car, on the way to Camden. Deal?"

I don't know what he said, because I was halfway to the phone booth when he said it.

I dialed Gail's number. No answer. I'd hoped she'd left Jeff's house by then and gone home. She was really making a mess of things. I dialed Jeff's. She picked up before the first ring finished.

"Jeff?" she said.

"Sorry. It's me, Nattie."

"Oh, Nattie, the most incredible thing happened. I think I'm in love. Last night was the . . ."

She started going into more detail than I had time for. I looked for a gentle way to enter her monologue, but she wasn't leaving many spaces between sentences. I broke in.

"Gail, I can't talk now. I think something big broke in my story that I've got to chase down. I just wanted to check in with you, 'cause we haven't talked since I got back from Tri-Color. I want to hear all about your date with Jeff—tonight, when I get back. In the meantime, take it one step at a time with him. I don't want you to get hurt."

"Why? Did he say something to you. Is there something you're not telling me?"

I lied. Now wasn't the time and the phone wasn't the way.

"No, no, no. Just don't get so involved that if things don't turn out how you want them, you'll be okay. Okay? Oh, yeah, there was one other thing. Right before the show I took some of your Vetrolin. I ran out and you know how Rob gets. Anyway, I went into your locker to get it and by mistake knocked over a bottle. It was hair dye of all things. I'm going to stop by Eckerd's and get

189

you some more. But what's with the Miss Clairol, anyway? It's the same color as Allie. Does he have a bad scar you're covering? I can't imagine why, it's not like you're showing him conformation hunter or showing him at all."

Maybe she was dreaming about Jeff, because I didn't hear anything on her end for the longest time.

"Hey, Gail, you still there?" I said into the dead phone.

"Who've you been talking to?" she finally said. Her voice was tight. I could almost see the fury splotches erupting across her face.

"What do you mean, who've I been talking to? I'm talking to you."

"You know that's not what I mean. I mean who have you been talking to about Allie? That time Sully told you she thought Doc Loc and I were an item, was that little bitch spilling her mouth about anything else? Did she—"

There was a break on the line.

"Hold on, Nattie, that's Jeff's call-waiting. It's probably him."

It must have been, because she never came back on the line. I hate call-waiting. I hung up, not liking what I'd just heard. Gail sounded mad enough to kill, and she was talking about Sully, who'd just been murdered. This was a street I didn't want to walk down.

CHAPTER 22

Another blistering-hot Carolina day. Henry's car is air conditioned, but that doesn't help much when you step out of it. And when you step out of it in Camden, South Carolina, you step out into a double broiler oven, between the sun above and the sand below.

"Lord, Lord, Lord, y'all come in here now. That white skin of yours ain't meant for a sun like this. Ain't nothing meant for a sun like this, 'cepting my daddy, bless his soul. He done passed thirty years ago, but he could've stood this sun. He was blacker than Muddy Fork Creek at midnight, he was. Nothing got through that skin of his. Come in and hurry on up about it, before you start frying right here on this front step."

It was Dorothy, opening the Bladstone door to me and Henry. She was downright garrulous away from her employer, going on and on about skin color: her father's, her mother's, hers. I had to agree with her about white skin; under this kind of sun, it's like wearing a nylon jacket in the Antarctic.

She led us into the living room, talking all the while. "I wish I had my daddy's skin, I do. You won't find many black folk be wanting darker skin, 'cepting me. The Lord come and told me hisself that we was to inherit the earth. The blackest-skinned people, he said. He done told me in a dream. He said, 'Dorothy, peoples been tearing at my earth, ripping the sky out from under me; soon

191

there won't be nothing left to protect your brothers and sisters
'cept the color I gives to them when they was babies.' "

At this point, I'm sure Henry had filed Dorothy away in the
wacko category and was wondering why the hell I'd dragged him
down here. But her vision made sense to me and I loved the irony
of it. "Well," I said, "that would certainly shut the Ku Klux Klan
up for good."

Dorothy laughed. "Lord have mercy, it sure would."

I looked around the living room. It was immaculate. Not a dog
anywhere. "This place looks different."

She smiled, happily and territorially. "When she's away, those
nasty, filthy, stinking dogs don't come inside here tearing Mr.
Bladstone's things all apart. That woman don't have the sense she
was born with when it comes to dogs."

Then she launched into an impassioned diatribe about dogs
and worms and Lucy Bladstone's poor personal hygiene, proving
that Henry had worried himself needlessly on the way down. He
assumed we wouldn't be able to pry anything out of Dorothy,
given that she was a poor black maid in a rich white southern town.
He thought this was going to be a repeat of our talk with Keith
Rollings's tight-lipped farm manager, Lawrence. He all but said this
was a wasted trip and he was going to humor me—"in the spirit of
interdepartmental cooperation," he called it. Ha-ha, the joke was
on him. This woman was a veritable faucet.

And it's not as if we took her by surprise and caught her with
her guard down. Henry insisted we call first to make sure Dorothy
was there and Lucy wasn't. He said it wasn't that he doubted my
information—Lucy's being in Wisconsin with La Donna until Saturday—but suppose there'd been a change of plans? Rather than
argue, which is pointless once Henry gets his mind made up, I
called. Lucy was in Wisconsin and Dorothy was home and said
she'd be glad to have the company.

She told us to sit down, and she'd be right back with something to drink. Last time we were there, it took her fifteen minutes. This time she returned pronto, carrying the same silver tray and talking about Wally—not that we asked her.

"Alls I got to say about Mr. Hempstead is bad and I don't even like thinking bad things. It dirties the soul, it does. But since you're here, I'll tell you. He was the Lord's bad brother in the flesh. Yes sir. An evil man. Can't say I ever met anyone else I'd say that about. No, I can't. I told Mrs. Bladstone the day he come into the kitchen that we was looking at trouble when we looked at him. I prayed and prayed when he died, that he'd stay dead and stay away from me."

I wondered what went wrong in Wally's life to make him so mean. I'd never met anyone so universally despised. Sap that I am, I was starting to feel sorry for him.

Dorothy looked at me in a funny way.

"Don't you be thinking this man deserved a kitten's tooth of pity. He was nasty to every creature that crossed his path. I seen him kick these dogs, for no good reason other than his own nastiness. He never did it in front of Mrs. Bladstone, knowing how crazy she is about them. But me, it didn't matter none what I seen."

Dorothy stopped what she was doing, which was pouring us some tea. "I know the Lord says to forgive, but I'll bet even the good Lord hisself had a hard time with that when Mr. Hempstead came calling."

The tea was sweet. Again my teeth ached. Dorothy didn't pour herself a glass, even though we asked her to join us at least three times. She wouldn't sit either. But she sure did talk. About Wally, and Wally and Lucy—"never saw nothing funny between them"— and L. M. Bladstone—"a sweet-souled man that don't know half the things go on around here."

I love a good story, and even more, a good storyteller. Dorothy had a mellifluous voice, deep and rich with a rolling cadence to it. I felt like I was riding the surf on a wave of words; I could have listened to her talk all day and she would have gladly obliged. Henry, on the other hand, was a hard-facts kind of guy. Between that and the hard fact that he had to pick his kids up by six, he was getting antsy.

"Dorothy," he said, "do you remember the lemon poppy-seed bread you served us?"

"Do I remember that bread? Do I remember my mama's first name?" She laughed, loud and hard, and then went on about her mother, a Mrs. Maybelle P. Dobbins of Cheraw, South Carolina. Reining Dorothy in was going to be no easy task.

I tried. "Sully baked that bread and you didn't want to handle it. . . ."

" 'Course I know who baked the bread, like I know my own mama's name. Something bad happened to that girl, and I told Mrs. Bladstone, told her something real bad happened upside the head. There was nothing but pain in that bread, no life, not anyhow. Mrs. Bladstone hates when I tells her things. She says she don't believe. But I thinks she does and that's why she can't stand me talking that way. It scares her. Scares her bad that someone's watching and someday she'll be up there explaining to that someone why she done been so nasty to everyone but those filthy dogs of hers. That girl's dead, ain't she?"

That perked Henry up. No one outside the Southern Pines police and a few reporters knew about the corpse in the ditch. And no one outside of us—and the killer—knew for sure who it was. The Southern Pines police were still working on an ID, chasing the lead I'd given them. But Dorothy knew, and she surely wasn't the killer. She could barely lift the tea pitcher, let alone whack someone upside the head.

"Most likely," I said. "The police found a young woman in a ditch. I think it was Sully."

"You do more than thinks. Otherwise you wouldn't be here

wasting your time talking to a crazy old black woman. I knows it's her. I been knowing things my whole life. Somes say it's a gift from the good Lord. But I just as soon he gave it to someone else. I'd like to go 'bout my business without feeling everyone else's hurting."

She looked old and pained standing there with her bony fingers pressed into the sofa for support. "I gots enough hurt in my life to last me more than forever."

That's when I saw the look. It's in the eyes where that kind of grief settles. I'd seen a roomful of those eyes a few months back. I was covering a meeting of the Compassionate Friends, a support group for parents who've buried children. It's a look I'll never forget; the eyes, desperately searching for a way back, to just before, when life seemed all right. Good even. To the moment that plays back and forth, sideways, up and down. Examining, dissecting, looking for a chink, looking for a way to change things. For a way to stop death.

"I'm sorry about your child," I said.

"Children," Dorothy said, and for the first time since we'd arrived, stopped talking.

Finally, Henry broke the silence. Dorothy's eyes were glassy and so were mine.

"When you told Lucy about Sully, what did she say?"

Dorothy pulled back her shoulders, shook her head slightly, and wiped her eyes clear of any memories. "In front of y'all, she told me to stop my 'voodoo talk.' That's what she says all the time when I tells her things. 'Course, as soon as you walks out the door, she be hurrying her skinny self into the kitchen, asking wheres I thinks Sully is. She done look plenty worried, too. Mrs. Bladstone don't care a stick about many folks, but she sure did about that child. Maybe on account she can't have none of her own. She was always fussing over that girl, give her clothes, money, even had me to fix her breakfast, 'cause she be coming here so early to put plaits on those horses. Hair plaits on a horse? Ain't that the stupidest thing you ever done heard of?"

Before I had a chance to agree, Dorothy went on with her story. After Lucy rushed into the kitchen, Dorothy said she made a flurry of phone calls trying to track down Sully.

"Even called the girl's mama and daddy in Georgia. Made it seem like nothing important, just a calling call—seeing's how she didn't want to worry them none."

"Georgia?" I said. "Do you know where in Georgia?"

"I don't want you to be thinking I know all Mrs. Bladstone's business and I ain't got nothing better to do. I was cleaning up after those dogs and that's when I hear her tells the operator she's looking for a telephone number of Mr. Trowbridge Cameron of Brunswick, Georgia."

Brunswick, Georgia. Home of Sully Cameron, Keith Rollings and Wally Hempstead. Henry and I were going to have one hell of a post mortem on this interview and I swore to myself not one I-told-you-so.

That was assuming he could talk, drive, and worry about making it back by six—all at the same time. I could tell he was getting nervous. Every thirty seconds for the past fifteen minutes, he'd been flipping his wrist over, watching his watch. We were pushing the clock if he wanted to make it back by six. And I knew he did. That wasn't negotiable. When it came to his kids, they came first. I think if the president himself called Henry and it was close to six, Henry would ask him to call back another day.

"One last question," I said. "You knew Sully was dead before anyone else knew. So who killed her?"

Dorothy smiled and nodded her head. "I knew you'd be asking that. Mrs. Bladstone kept after me on it, too. But I can't figure who killed that poor girl. The Lord works in a funny way. He gives you what you need to know, sometimes a little more, but never enough to hurt you. That's his way. He done gave it to you, too. You just do too much worrying, so things inside you get all mixed up. I never did me much worrying because I didn't see no sense to it. All the worrying in Jesus' kingdom couldn't stop the bad things from happening. Just hush up all that worrying, it makes too much noise inside your head, makes it so you can't hear what you're supposed to be hearing, the voices of God's children talking to you. Just never forget we all be God's children, except that Mr. Hempstead. He be Satan's boy, like I said. . . ."

I stood up to start the good-byes. As it was, we were going to have to court speeding tickets to get back in time. Henry shot me an appreciative look. A good father is hard to come by, and when you find one, even if he's not yours, why not help him out? I eased myself into Dorothy's stream of words and told her she'd been more help than she could have imagined. Then I wrote my home and office telephone numbers down on a piece of paper—I'd lost all my business cards.

"If there's anything else, call me," I said. "Even if there's not, you can call me, too. I'm always up for a good story."

Dorothy piled our glasses on the tray. "Child," she said, "you take care of yourself." She looked Henry's way and said, "Your husband don't smile much, but he's a good, honest man. A fine man and he cares about you."

I looked at Henry. She was right about one thing. I hadn't seen him do much smiling up till now. We both started laughing.

"He may be a good man," I said. "But he's not my man."

"Uh-huh," Dorothy said.

She laughed along with us. "You remember what I said about taking care, now. Two people dead's enough, even if one of them wasn't fit to live. You hear what I'm saying?"

"Loud and clear," I said. "You and my mother could have worry sessions."

"Thank the Lord for that. There ain't no one who loves you like your mama."

I reached to shake Dorothy's hand good-bye, and when I did, her right leg buckled under her. She stopped herself from falling by grabbing Henry's arm and stood that way for a few seconds. I noticed little beads of sweat raised on her forehead.

"These old bones can't hardly hold me up," Dorothy said. "I never had a pain like that in all my days. Felt like my leg was being branded outside from in."

She took a few deep breaths and was about to let go of Henry's arm, when he reached around and lifted her up.

"Hang on," he said. "You should be sitting down."

He carried her to the sofa and she started to protest.

"I think it's important that you sit down," he said. "At least until you've got your breath back."

"My breathing's fine, now leave me be," Dorothy said. "I ain't the one you should be worrying about."

Henry wanted to call a doctor or a relative. Dorothy seemed embarrassed by the whole thing and insisted she was fine. She pushed herself up from the sofa and walked us to the front door without even a limp.

"Whatever it was done passed," she said. "Now I got work to get done. Don't you?"

CHAPTER 23

Nothing good happened the rest of the week. No synchronistic revelations, no big leads, no psychic arrows pointing us anywhere. Of course, nothing bad happened either. The nut case who liked to crack plastic horses and leave messages in lipstick was laying low.

So was everyone else, apparently. We struck out on every interview we tried to arrange. Keith Rollings was back in Ocala until Saturday, we'd left messages with his wife saying we wanted to talk to him about Wally. Melissa and Mumsy were at the family beach house in Duck—no answer, probably the maid's day off. And Daddy Mayfield refused to return our calls. Lucy was with La Donna somewhere other than home in Wisconsin according to La Donna's near-deaf and, as far as I could tell, near-dead tissue-heir husband.

"You're calling from Hershels' Pier, is that a fish store?" he said in a shaky voice.

"No," I yelled into the phone. "It's *The COMMERCIAL APPEAL*, a newspaper in North Carolina. Please tell Lucy we'd like to talk to her about Wally and Sully."

It took the man seven tries to get my name and number right. You think with all that toilet-paper money he could have bought himself a hearing aid.

In the meantime, Henry continued his excavations at the courthouse. I continued phoning every horse person I knew, looking for leads about Wally and now Sully.

The Southern Pines police officially confirmed she was the corpse and the cause of death was a blow to the left side of her head—exactly where Dorothy had felt the pain. As to motive, rape wasn't one of them. Sully hadn't been sexually assaulted, though she'd been stripped of any identification. The crime lab in Raleigh was running all sorts of tests, looking for clues. Hair, fingerprints, fiber fragments.

I wasn't the least bit surprised when Cynthia told me what the stuff was under Sully's fingernails. In fact, I'd predicted it at the previous day's story meeting. I know the cops were hoping for traces of someone else's skin or blood. That someone else being the murderer Sully might have been fighting off. No such luck. All the white-coats found in the black, tarry goo under her nails was a combination of horse hair, dander, and dirt. Braiding a mane is a dirty business, by demand. Braiders, a surly bunch to start with because their fingers hurt all the time and they start work in the middle of the night, have a hissy fit if you wash your horse's mane before a show. A clean mane is a slippery mane, and a slippery mane makes for loose, sloppy braids.

Candace, my boss, was impressed that I knew what the lab report said before it said it. But that was three days ago. Daily journalism is a real what-can-you-do-for-me-today job. And what I was doing for Candace today wasn't much, according to her. She didn't like running wire copy in my fashion column slot and she especially didn't like her department not being the center of attention. Three daily budget meetings had gone by without me or Henry wowing the big boys and without the spotlight casting any beams on Features. The best she had to offer up was an it's-not-happening-here-yet trend story on canine Prozac abuse and a disease-of-the-week tearjerker about aplastic anemia, complete with a Where-to-Go support-group-information box at the end. She'd been marching up to my desk repeatedly, assigning me to cover one dumb party after another. I had an excuse for all of them.

"Gee, I'd love to do the Designer House," I said to her on her last go-around, "but I've got four different phoners lined up with people who can't wait to tell me who they think killed Wally, and why."

"All right," she said, not happily, "just make sure you turn in your list of whom you've interviewed. And don't forget the phone numbers."

I smiled, at least my lips turned up. I don't know what my eyes were doing. "Sure thing, Candace."

That would add another hour to my day. I hadn't been logging my interviews, so now I had to mentally backtrack to everyone I'd spoken to that week. Then I had to go find their phone numbers and then I had to call each number to make sure it was the right number. Any source that was off the record—and God help us if there were any—had to be labeled as DT (for Deep Throat) and thoroughly discussed with Fred. This was all part of his new reader satisfaction policy. At the end of the week, he'd select twenty or thirty names from the list and then call them all. He'd introduce himself as the editor of *The Appeal*, tell the lucky interviewee he was calling to make sure we at *The Appeal* were doing our job right, and with that in mind, he wanted to know if the reporter that called had been polite, thorough, and professional.

I can just imagine Ben Bradlee calling Woodward and Bernstein's sources to check if they'd been polite. Somewhere along the line, *The Appeal* had turned from a newspaper into a public relations firm. And as long as the gray suits at corporate headquarters controlled the shekels, we'd always be that way. No sense in brooding about it. I could still be collating grocery inserts on Wednesday like I had been at the first newspaper where I worked.

I wanted to get out before the sun set, but that wasn't looking likely. Not that it really mattered. Saturday was coming up fast, I had no plans for the weekend other than long trail rides through the cool woods. I'd broken it off for good with John, the pretty-boy news anchor who didn't mind as much as I'd thought he would. My father had talked about coming to visit. Instead, he decided to go to an ashram in the Poconos. He wanted me to join him.

"It'll be my treat, airfare and all," he said. "You can choose any workshop you want."

He said that because the last time he roped me into going with him, he signed me up for Explorations in Colon Integrity without telling me. Colon Integrity turned out to be new age mumbo-jumbo for water-trough-size enemas.

"Is it air conditioned?" I said.

"Air-conditioning? Are you kidding? This is an ashram. These people are ascetics."

"Forget it," I said. "I'll stay here and roast. But I promise I'll meditate."

I didn't say where. Atop a horse was as godly a place as any. Since I hadn't been able to get ahold of Gail, it looked as if any trail riding I did would be contemplative—and solo.

I didn't know what was up with Gail, and I was worried. About her connection with Sully and her encampment at Jeff's. He said he had to get a forklift to pry her out of his apartment. "Don't do me any more favors with fixups," he said afterward.

When I'd gotten back from Dorothy's, I'd kept calling Gail until well past midnight. No answer at her place, Jeff's, or the barn. On Tuesday I went to her house. I saw no signs of life. Mail was falling out of her box, newspapers were piled up on her step. No lights on inside. I knocked. No answer.

From a pay phone I called the barn. The last thing I needed was for old man Clarke to pick up, which he did. I hung up. He wasn't going to tell me doodly-squat, and I wasn't going to put up with his foul humor. Later that day I got Rob on the phone. He told me Gail called in sick and said she was going to her mother's for a few days. Peculiar. She hated her mother, never talked about her other than to say she was a pathetic drunk who ate only the green olives at the bottom of her martinis. No one at the barn knew where Gail's mother lived, including me.

I made my phone calls, which led me nowhere, finished my list, and checked in with Henry before I left. Though Keith Rollings was due back the next day and Henry and I could have taken ourselves a trip to Camden and shown up at his front door, working this weekend was out. Henry was taking his kids to see their grandmother, who was in Hilton Head, golfing. We planned to meet first thing Monday morning to map out our week and figure out a strategy for interviewing Keith. You just can't say to a guy, "So I hear you're a pedophile and Wally was blackmailing you and by the way, you and Sully grew up in the same town and she's dead, did she also know about your preference for three-year-olds?" Nope, can't say that if you don't want the door slammed in your face. This was one we were going to have to finesse. For once, I was glad Henry was my partner. Finesse and subtlety don't come natural to me.

On the way out, I made a quick call to Tony. He'd been calling every night and morning, just to make sure I was still alive. I told him I was going to the barn to ride, and not to panic when my telephone didn't answer after the sun set.

"I'll be right down the road if you need me," Tony said. Then he oozed into his deepest southern accent, "Me 'n' Rin Tin Tin'll jes' be sittin' there countin' cricket calls to see how hot it is. Have yourself a fine ride on that pretty mare."

I intended to.

And I did. Back in glory land with my horse. Two and a half hours deep through the woods, a kaleidoscope of colors and smells and sounds. I could have died happy that night.

CHAPTER 24

B etween Tony and Mrs. Flock, I had my own protection service. She made it her business to come out of her apartment and watch me walk up from my car to my front door. She didn't shut her door until I was safely past mine.

The same was true when I went out. She'd hear my door close and hers would open.

I didn't mind it one bit. If some wacko was gunning for me, the more eyes that watched my comings and goings, the better.

"Nattie," Mrs. Flock was calling from her front door as I parked my car. "I've got something for you."

I was hot and sweaty, not from the ride on my horse, but from the ride home. "I hope it's a bucket of ice water to dump on my head. But if I had to guess, I'd say it was a tracking device for my car."

Mrs. Flock was the kind of woman old men look at and say, "She must have been a beauty." I thought she still was, especially with that easy smile of hers. But she wasn't smiling now.

"You know I like to laugh as much as anyone," she said. "Not about this. There's nothing funny about your apartment getting broken into and there's certainly nothing funny about those death threats. This is a serious matter that should be taken seriously."

I walked up to her door. "I couldn't agree with you more. I always laugh when I get nervous. It's an annoying habit, I got it from my father."

She handed me a bundle of weeds tied tightly with purple twine.

"I brought this for you from Berrybrook." Mrs. Flock runs the juice bar there. How a former Rockette wound up grinding carrots and beets at a health food store is anybody's guess.

"It's sage, and I understand you're supposed to burn it to clear away the negative energy in a room. That's what our herb expert told me. I know it sounds preposterous. Give it a try. I'm not a Sensitive, but even I could feel the bad energy in your apartment that night."

She wants me to take my situation more seriously and then hands me a pile of herbs to burn. I know she meant well, but so did my father when he signed me up for Enemas 101.

I thanked her and promised I'd do the bad-energy rites as soon as I got in. Which I did. After a few minutes, my place smelled like I was cooking a turkey and went crazy with the seasonings.

I called Tony. "I'm home safe and sound. Thanks for worrying. But stop now, okay?"

"I'm not worried, I'm just being cautious. By the way, according to your professor, it's eighty-nine degrees outside. Call me before you leave tomorrow and let me know what you're fixing to do this weekend. I won't be around Saturday night, but I'll give you the number of a fella who works with me."

"Oh, ahh, well, okay," I said, and took down his buddy's number. Then we said good-bye. I hoped the chill I felt hadn't crept into my voice. I had no reason to feel jealous. That didn't mean I didn't.

The next morning I checked in with Tony and hightailed it to the barn for a nine-thirty lesson with Rob. I was running late as usual, and rushed to my stall.

"Don't bother." It was Rob. He was raking the front in that crazy zigzag. "She threw a shoe. The blacksmith's on his way out."

"You know, I thought it was loose last night, I could put that easy boot on her and we could still jump . . ." I started to blather.

Rob waved his hand. "Stop, stop. It's just as well. You're not going to a show next week and I don't feel like schooling anyway."

Something was wrong. Rob never misses a school. He's like the mailman; neither rain, nor sleet, nor nuclear attack stops him. I've schooled in every weather condition imaginable.

"Bad news from the lawyers?" I knew I was crossing his boundaries.

He didn't say anything and kept raking. I went to Brenda's stall and patted her neck, gave her a kiss, told her how beautiful she was in a high-pitched voice: just the kind of behavior girls are supposed to grow out of by the time they get interested in boys.

I was walking to the tack room, figuring I might as well clean my saddle and bridle while I was there.

"No news," Rob said. "I've gotten no news from the lawyer. The way this is going, I'll be lucky if I end up in jail for life. Otherwise, I'll be working forever to pay his bill."

Three complete sentences and one half sentence. This sudden loquaciousness took me by surprise. I was about to give him some platitude about his lawyer being the best in town, when he really shocked me.

"Your saddle's clean enough," he said.

First shock: that anything can be clean enough to Rob.

Then the second shock: "So put the saddle soap down and come upstairs. I've got some tea ready."

I followed behind, forcing myself to shut up. Inside, it was white. White sofas, white carpet. White at a barn where the soil is red clay. Now, that's chutzpah—anal-compulsive style. Complementing the study in white were the prerequisite tasteful antiques, a sideboard here, an old trunk there, and the essential hunt prints everywhere.

Rob's eating-disordered Jack Russell lay on a hunter-green doggie bed with his name stitched in navy blue: Moon Pie.

I sat on a burgundy tufted leather stool next to the coffee table, which was an old barn door, bleached and pickled near white. My jeans were clean, sort of. Not clean enough to sit on a white sofa.

He went into his kitchen and I heard him banging around.

Admittedly I am a snoop and I have looked through more than a few medicine chests not my own. However, I feel anything on a coffee table is fair game. And on Rob's coffee table was a hunter-green-leather photo album, navy-blue monogram FF—for February Farm. The first pages were filled with photos of faces I didn't recognize. Then there were a bunch of Melissa Mayfield and her horse, Waysie, everywhere. The Garden, Washington International, Harrisburg. She was wearing a shadbelly and top hat, the most formal and expensive show attire possible, and carrying an assortment of victory mementos: championship coolers, trophies, tricolor ribbons, silver bowls.

A few pages later, a younger-looking Gail appeared. A few were of her holding a small chestnut mare, a few more were of her and that mare atop some old-fashioned fences. Meaning outside course jumps; big logs and real hedges, obstacles one might actually come across while fox hunting. Although hunter classes are supposed to test a horse's mettle in the hunt field, virtually all of them take place in a ring. Go figure it.

On the next page, there she was, leading Allie in an expensive-looking leather halter covered in sheepskin. It was a very fat and shiny and well-cared-for Allie. I saw Doc Loc's silver hair and pink skin in the background. He always looked like he'd been in the sun too much.

"Want sugar in your tea?" Rob was standing by the table, holding what looked like a crystal glass.

"No thanks. Boy, Gail looks like a kid in that picture. How long ago after she got Allie was this picture taken?"

"Five minutes. That was right off the van."

This wasn't adding up right. "Are you sure?"

"I took the picture, mainly because I'd never seen Gail so happy. Look at the smile on her face. You never see that around the barn."

Certainly not around Rob. "So what's Doc Loc doing there? Hadn't Allie been vetted before she bought him?"

Rob gave me a funny look.

"She got that horse *from* Doc Loc. Didn't you know that?"

I didn't. Gail told me she found an ad for Allie in the Henderson paper. A backwoods mountain guy had the horse in his yard, half starved to death and looking like a bag of bones. That's why, she'd said, she got him so cheap, for seven hundred dollars.

"I thought all Doc Loc's horses came from his million-dollar stud and his brood of extra-fancy mares."

"They do. Waysie, Melissa Mayfield's horse, was one of Doc Loc's. A fabulous horse, the best horse I ever trained. Allie's not as good as that, but he's not bad. Not bad at all. He's a half brother to Waysie."

No wonder Melissa cried when she saw Allie come into the barn. This was all new—and disturbing—to me.

"How could Gail afford Allie? Gail told me Waysie cost at least two hundred thousand dollars, and that was years ago. Even if Allie was worth a quarter of that, Gail could never have gotten that kind of money together."

"You know Gail worked for Doc Loc, don't you. You do know *that*, right?"

I nodded.

"She said he ran into money problems. I heard it was gambling. Anyway, he couldn't pay her and gave her a horse instead."

I said, "A fifty-thousand-dollar horse for a few months of vet-tech work? That doesn't make sense."

"Supposedly the horse had soundness problems in its hocks, but I've never seen him take a lame step. And she works that horse to death trying to get lead changes," Rob said.

He took a few delicate sips of his tea and continued. I couldn't believe how much he was talking.

"I never thought about it much. You know, how Gail got Allie. But Wally thought about it a lot. He kept saying that horse was too damn fancy to waste on her and Doc Loc must be out of his mind. He wanted the horse, but Gail wouldn't speak to him, much less sell him her horse. They hated each other. Wally wanted me to fire her. I told him that was ridiculous. She's a fabulous worker. Then a few months before he left, he stopped bothering himself about Gail or Allie. Wally was moody and I thought that was just one mood he'd gotten over."

I put down the glass, which was crystal—I tested it—on a hunt scene coaster and picked up the photo album to take a closer look at the pictures. There were three pages of Allie and a happy-looking Gail over what seemed to be an assortment of seasons.

"Can I borrow this book, just for the afternoon?"

Rob didn't look happy and probably was about to say no.

"I'll be very careful with it. It's important and may have something to do with your case."

He thought for a few seconds, then said, "Don't crinkle the pages or get the pictures out of order."

I looked at him sitting on his sofa. He seemed smaller, deflated, though still immaculate and crisply pressed.

"I know you don't like me to talk about it, but hear me out."

For the next ten minutes I told him what had happened with our investigation so far, though I didn't go into details about Keith, just that we suspected he, along with the Mayfields, were being blackmailed by Wally. When I told him about Sully, it jolted him. Either he was a great actor or truly surprised. I used to pride myself on knowing the difference, until I interviewed Jessica Hahn, a true talent of the untruth. She swore up one side and down the other she had never had an affair with her old minister—and I believed her. Then, not a month after, I read another interview where she blabbed about sleeping with the same man of the cloth I'd asked her about.

For what it was worth, my gut told me Rob was telling the truth, but I didn't know how much of that was just plain old hope.

"It would be nice if my lawyer were working as hard as you," Rob said. That was his way of saying thank-you.

A vehicle pulled up by the barn, I could hear the gravel crunching.

"It's Eddie," Rob said. "Go down and cross-tie your mare for him. If he doesn't get those shoes on today, you won't see him for another month."

I took the photo album and thanked him for the tea. Downstairs, Eddie was waiting by my stall.

"Where's Rob?" he said.

"Hey, Eddie." I could smell the beer from across the aisle. "He's upstairs. I don't think he's coming down. He's not feeling great."

"What'sa matter, that time of the month? Has he got his period?" He laughed and shot a wad of brown spit into a Hardee's coffee cup.

Eddie thought homosexuality was hilarious. He was always making jokes about the gay guys on the circuit. Maybe if I were a shrink I'd see it differently, like maybe Eddie had latent tendencies.

Though that would be a hefty psychoanalytic leap. Eddie was as good a good old boy as they came. When he wasn't shoeing horses, he was hunting coons, when he wasn't hunting coons, he was fixing his truck, and when he wasn't doing that, he was passed out from all the beer he drank doing all of the above.

Latent or not, it's giving Eddie's sense of humor more thought than it deserves. No matter how he finds his yuks, he's the best blacksmith between Washington and Florida. The reason he's so hard to get is that he's constantly being flown up to one fancy show barn after another to shoe a string of half-million-dollar horses.

"What's that you're working at, Nattie, the third grade?"

"Do what?" I said in my deepest country drawl. Eddie also thought it was funny to hear a northerner talk southern.

"Listen, girl, you gotta make that 'what' a lot dumber and longer before you start soundin' like mah kin." Eddie pulled at the center of his plaid shirt, trying to free up some room. His gut was so big, nothing short of liposuction or temperance could dent the mass. "The third grade. That must be where you're working, because that's the last time anyone checked up on me like they did you."

"Oh, yeah," I said. "I was going to warn you. I guess that means you got a phone call from my editor, Fred. Did you tell him how *po*-lite and *re*-spectful I was on the phone when I interviewed you about Wally?"

"Hell, no," Eddie said. "I said that little Yankee Jew ain't been polite since the day she moved her carpetbag down here and I don't expect she ever will."

"I hope to hell you did, you nasty redneck," I said. "Now, stop flapping that ugly mouth of yours and let's get some Nikes on this girl."

I led Brenda into the aisle and cross-tied her by the halter.

"Ooohhh, mama, how you talk. Two years of living here ain't

done nothing for your temperament. You could use a fixin' of my southern gentility."

"Yeah, right," I said.

CHAPTER 25

"**I**'m back. And in for the night," I called to Mrs. Flock, who was standing like a sentry by her front door.

I was looking forward to spending a Saturday night home and alone. I had a box of Lorna Doones and a new man to keep me company. His words, at least. Sometimes a good book is better than a man, certainly less complicated. The lady at the bookstore had directed me Michael Malone's way, said I'd be twitching to skip pages to find out what happens but I wouldn't let myself because the writing so's rich. Sounds good to me, I said. I could use a literary diversion.

Before Michael and I got to know each other, I picked up the phone and dialed Tony's cop friend. "Nattie Gold reporting in," I said. We chatted for a few minutes. I made myself not ask where Tony was.

I took a shower, slipped on a clean T-shirt, and headed for bed with cookies and book in hand, hoping for a long, satisfying night. That lasted three sentences. They were:

Two things don't happen very often in Hillston, North Carolina. We don't get much snow, and we hardly ever murder one another. Suicide is more our style.

Suicide. I hadn't even considered the possibility. Where the hell was Gail? She was acting loopy, but loopy enough to do herself in? I didn't know.

I did the telephone rounds. Her place, the barn, Jeff's just in case they reconciled. Then I tried Jeff's desk at *The Appeal.*

The phone rang ten times, and just as I was about to hang up, someone answered. I say someone, because no one said anything.

"Jeff," I screamed into the phone.

"Oh, Nats, it's just you. Thank God."

"What are you doing there?" I said. "It's Saturday night, don't you have another conquest to make? Don't want those condoms to get stiff and crack, now, do we?"

"Very funny. It's your fault I'm here. I'm hiding from *your* friend. She's been calling and hanging up and calling and crying and calling and calling and calling. *Ahhhhh.* She's driving me fucking crazy, Gold. I'm spending the night on the friggin' floor here just to get away from her."

"I thought she went to her mother's."

"No, she didn't. She's here, in Charlotte, in the lovely Queen City, torturing *me.* Get her off my back, Nattie. Please."

I didn't know what to say. My best friend was having a psychic break before my very eyes, but I couldn't get close enough to keep her from shattering.

"I'll go to her house right now and talk to her," I said.

"Don't bother, she's not home. She's at a bar somewhere and she sounded like she was tanking up."

It was getting worse by the second. Gail was a 12-stepper, AA meetings twice a week. She'd been on track ever since I knew her; now it sounded as if her current track didn't have a staircase anywhere near it.

"Shit," I said.

"Shit is right," Jeff said.

I couldn't go back to reading now, no matter how "vivid, compelling, and beautifully rendered" *The New York Times* said Malone's book was.

215

I picked up Rob's photo album to look at the pictures of Gail and Allie. What was missing? I remembered Mrs. Flock telling me to say "reach" when I lost something. She said it stimulates the synapses to tap deep into the collective unconscious, where all answers lay.

"Reach," I said. If I could burn sage, I could say reach.

It did about as much as the sage. Nothing. My eyes were getting droopy and I fell asleep. I was in the middle of a dream when I woke up. I didn't mind leaving it, because it was a stupid one about Allie being a waiter at the Pewter Rose. He was HIV positive, but otherwise a picture-of-health muscle-man kind of guy who washes his hair with Grecian Formula 16 to hide his gray. He was having a fight with a customer who demanded his plate be served on his right side, but Allie served plates only on the left.

"Shit," I said, again. It was four-thirty, the lights in my apartment were on because I'd fallen asleep without turning them off. That's not what woke me up. My notes, I'd left all my notes on top of my desk for anyone to look through. I wasn't used to locking anything up. Who'd want to rifle through pages and pages of speculation as to which way the hemlines were going—up or down. But these notes were different.

Then I remembered Jeff was at the office. A small stroke of luck. I'd call him and ask him to stash the notes in a locked drawer of his desk. The phone rang and rang. This time, no answer. Either he was still hiding from Gail or asleep on the floor.

I looked out the window, knowing what I'd see. Nothing. It was dark as dirt and I felt like I was at a horse show. That's the only reason to get up this early.

"Shit," I said again, and really meant it. The notes were nagging at me like a whiny six-year-old. I couldn't leave them there. I slipped on a pair of shorts and my Birkenstocks (a gift from my father after graduating from est, also a gift from my father) and headed out the front door.

I couldn't believe it. Mrs. Flock's porch light snapped on. Then she opened her door.

"For heaven's sake, Nattie, is everything all right?"

"Everything's fine, Mrs. Flock. You must be part bird-dog to hear that. I didn't mean to wake you."

"Well, where *are* you going at this hour?"

"To the office. I left my notes out and have to put them away."

Mrs. Flock didn't want me to go in the worst way. She just about convinced me it could wait until at least the sun edged into our hemisphere. Then I remembered my friend who carried his notes everywhere with him because he'd once had a set stolen.

"I gotta go, Mrs. Flock. I have people's names and quotes written down who don't want it known they were talking to me. I owe it at least to them. Go back to sleep, I'll be back before you wake up."

I'm used to traveling the roads this time of morning and it always makes me feel the same way. Peaceful, but a bit lonely. I pulled under *The Appeal* building and parked in Fred's reserved-for-the-editor-only space. I would have parked in Rutger's reserved-for-the-publisher-only space, but Jeff's 1967 red Mustang was there.

There wasn't a soul in the lobby. I rode the escalators to the fifth floor, wondering how much it cost to run them twenty-four hours a day. If we were in such a fiscal pickle, why not turn the damn things off and cut our Duke Power bill by half?

There wasn't a soul in the newsroom, either. Not that I could see right off. Every light in the place was on, though, rows and rows of fluorescents. I could have performed microscopic brain surgery on the copy desk.

Features is tucked around the corner and to the back. Candace, who believes proximity is power, has been lobbying to get our department moved, anywhere, because you can't get any farther from the glass offices than Features. Even the janitor's closet is closer.

I like the isolation. We don't have to deal with the nutsos who come in off the street. Especially with Fred's be-polite-to-every-one-including-Charles-Manson edict. My friends over in city side say the constant stream of wackos is swelling because word's out that *The Appeal* listens to anyone and then gives them a cup of coffee and a doughnut for their trouble. That's also part of Fred's community relations campaign.

I turned the corner and saw Jeff. Poor guy, his head was cradled in his arms on his desk like a ninth-grader catching a snooze during algebra.

I come by guilt genetically and I was feeling plenty of it just then. Jeff was hiding out on account of me—strike me dead or doom me to a life of straight skirts if I ever attempt another fix up.

I called to him: "Jeff, wake up. I'm taking you back to my place. You can have my bed. I'll take the sofa. I'll even make you breakfast. Lox and bagels."

I thought that would perk him up. To a Diasporaed Jew of the North, an offer of lox and bagels is like the ram's horn call home. But Jeff's head didn't move. He must have been exhausted. A person, this person, can bear only so much guilt. I was about to start reaching for the Maalox.

I felt worse when, from across the newsroom, I could make out what was on his desk: a half-eaten Big Mac and fries, plenty of ketchup. Jeff, my friend who'd rather be celibate than eat fast food, had been forced to do both this weekend because of me.

"Come on, Jeff, let's go. This is all my fault, I'm really sorry. I'll throw in some whitefish and sable *and* I'll tell you how I lost my virginity."

I walked up to the back of his chair and put my hand on his

shoulder to shake him. He felt heavier or thicker. Something. Whatever it was, it wasn't right.

I shook him harder and he didn't move. His arms had a funny bluish tint. I looked on his desk. It wasn't ketchup.

I screamed. No one was there to hear.

I screamed again and again.

I kept screaming. Then words came to me, like a mantra, I kept repeating them to calm myself down. "Call the police, call the police. I've got to call the police."

My hand was shaking, my body was shaking. I didn't know what the hell I was doing.

"Call the police, call the police," I said, trying to force myself out of hysteria and into reason. I couldn't make my hand get to the telephone.

I screamed louder and louder. Then I shook Jeff's chair.

"Wake up, wake up, goddammit, wake up," I yelled as I yanked his chair back and forth.

Back and forth until Jeff tumbled to the floor and I saw a bullet hole in his head.

Then I crumpled to the floor.

"Nattie, Nattie." From down deep I heard someone calling my name. Then shaking my shoulders. Then calling my name again, louder and louder. I followed the voice through the darkness, back to the surface.

It was Tony, leaning over me, his face white, sheet white.

"Thank God, I thought you were dead when I saw you lying there."

He was talking. But I was having a difficult time figuring out what his words meant. I was dreaming. I was dreaming. Please let me be dreaming.

He lifted me up and carried me away. Away from Jeff's body.

I wasn't dreaming.

"Oh my God, oh my God. Oh my God. He's dead. Jeff's dead. He's dead." Tears were streaming down my face, I couldn't catch my breath.

"Easy, easy," Tony said. "Take in a deep breath, start with your stomach and work up. Easy. That's it."

I looked at him. I wanted to ask him how he knew I was there. I couldn't get my mouth to string all the words together.

"How . . . how . . . I must've call—"

"Shhh," he said, "don't talk until you can breathe. Your neighbor's one hell of a detective. She tracked me down and called me right after you left your apartment. Jesus, Nattie, what were you thinking coming here by yourself at four-thirty in the morning?"

"I—I . . . my notes. My notes were . . ."

"Yeah, she told me all about your God-blessed notes. They weren't worth dying for, were they?"

I looked on my desk. It didn't matter whether they were or not, now. They were gone.

After a few minutes I could breathe normally. I was still wobbly on my feet. Tony put me down in my chair while he called the police. I heard him murmur law-enforcement-club talk into the phone.

"Jeff's dead because of me," I said.

"Now, hush, Nattie, you don't know anything yet. Maybe someone was looking for Jeff, you don't know."

"I know this," I said, and swung the computer so Tony could see it. "Read it."

I looked at the lime-green letters across the black screen. I knew what they said, but to me they looked like little gargoyles laughing and sneering at me.

NATALIE GOLD,

   I WAS HERE, BUT WHERE WERE YOU? PLAYING BRENDA STARR? HA! HA! GET IT?

SPEAKING OF GETTING IT, DON'T YOU LISTEN? I TOLD YOU TO BACK OFF. BACK OFF, DO YOU KNOW WHAT BACK OFF MEANS? DO I HAVE TO MAKE MYSELF CLEARER? MAYBE A VISIT TO YOUR BARN WOULD CLEAR THINGS UP ONCE AND FOR ALL. OR A TRIP TO THAT NICE LITTLE SCHOOL IN THE WOODS WHERE YOUR PARTNER SENDS HIS KIDS. IT'S AWFULLY SECLUDED THERE—ANYTHING COULD HAPPEN. JUST LIKE IT DID HERE. YOUR DESK MATE WASN'T TOO HAPPY ABOUT FINDING ME AT YOUR DESK WHEN HE GOT BACK FROM MCDONALD'S. AND I WASN'T TOO HAPPY THAT HE FORGOT THE KETCHUP.

I DON'T LIKE TO BE UNHAPPY. YOU'VE BEEN WARNED.

CHAPTER 26

I'm sitting on Tony's front porch, with Rin Tin Tin's head in my lap. He's drooling again. I see it running down my leg, but I don't really feel it.

I'm not feeling much of anything.

"Tea?"

It's Tony.

"Sure, why not."

He hands me the glass and sits between me and Rin Tin Tin. Neither of us says a word.

The tea is cold and sweet. I think. It's difficult to tell what anything is. I feel like I'm underwater and I don't know how to swim.

"If you want to talk, I'm all ears," Tony says.

I didn't have the energy to tell him I was talked out. I'd spent half the day in the newsroom, being interviewed by one cop after another. They didn't want me to leave in case anyone else had any more questions. Tony must have used a little insider pull, because when it looked as if I'd pass out for good, Tony stood me up, put his arm around my shoulder, and led me down to his car.

I cried when I saw Jeff's Mustang.

Tony drove me right to his house. He said it was unsafe at mine. Who could argue?

I couldn't, even if I wanted to. I felt like my soul had gone ten rounds with Mike Tyson, pummeled, bruised, shell-shocked. I'd felt this way one other time in my life—when my stepfather died six months ago. He raised me after my father left; he was the one who brought normalcy into my chaotic childhood. But most important, I've never felt as loved by anyone as I did by him. When Gail told me he'd had a heart attack in a shopping mall, the first thing that came out of my mouth was "But I loved him." I did, and his death dug a hole deep in my heart that time can't seem to fill.

Then, like now, I was a zombie. And Tony couldn't have been more wonderful. Whatever I needed, he got for me. Tissues, a different shirt—the one I'd been wearing had blood on it—a blanket to cut the chill even though it was eighty-nine degrees out, anything. Mostly, he sat by my side the rest of the day and into the night.

We watched the sun set over the pines. It was a beautiful sunset full of orange and pink and gold. I told Tony I didn't deserve to be seeing it, that I should be the one dead, not Jeff.

He leaned across Rin Tin Tin and put his arm around me. "Shh, now" was all he said.

Then we watched the sky turn from blue to black. Rin Tin Tin didn't move a muscle, and neither did I.

"Come on, Nattie, you've got to get some sleep," Tony said. He stood up and reached his hands under my arms to lift me up.

"Okay." I followed him inside to his bedroom.

"I'll be on the sofa if you need me."

He turned to go out his door and I grabbed his shirt. "I can't be alone. Stay with me. Please."

I wanted his arms around me. I wanted his body next to mine. I felt so empty, I wanted his aliveness in me.

"Please," I said again, and wrapped my arms around him. "Please don't go."

I moved my face to his and kissed him.

His lips were soft. I thought of baby blankets. Soft and sweet and innocent. I didn't want to leave. I leaned into him and kissed him more. I wanted to lose myself in his lips.

Tony put his hands on my cheeks and edged my face from his. "Nattie, Nattie, we've got to stop. I promised this wouldn't happen."

"It's okay, I know what I'm doing. Tonight. Just for tonight. One night."

I moved closer and kissed him again. He started to say something, and I pressed into him harder. I slid my tongue in his mouth, ran it against his tongue, along his teeth, on his lips.

He kissed my neck, my ears, my nose, my eyes, my tears.

We fell onto his bed.

Our clothes came off.

"Easy, easy, Nattie. Let's take things real slow." Tony's voice was as soft as his touch.

I lay my head on his pillow and closed my eyes. I was lost in the darkness. This time it was a soft, velvet darkness and I could feel it swirling around me. His hands, his lips, his skin against mine. All over.

I'd never been able to take anything slow in my life. ". . . A condom," I said breathlessly. "Do you have a condom?"

I reached my hands down.

"Oh," I said.

I didn't know what else to say.

I opened my eyes. Tony had a sort of resigned smile on his face.

"Sorry, Nattie, I had an inkling something like this might happen. This dawg just ain't going to hunt tonight."

I burst out laughing. "What do you mean your dog won't hunt, Rin Tin Tin's too damn old to hu—Oh, oh, I got it now. Sorry, I'm a little slow on the uptake tonight. Let's see if we can't just get him a-barking again."

I kissed his stomach and started to follow the line of curly brown hair below his belly button.

He leaned over and pulled me back up.

"I appreciate the offer, but it won't help. I got torn up pretty badly when Sharon left. I hadn't even looked at another woman since, until I saw you at that barn. Things are real complicated right now between me and Sharon. She can't decide if she wants back or . . ."

Sharon, his wife. He'd told me a little about her, but never wanted to talk too much about it. All I knew is that she left him last winter. He said she wanted to think things out. Last I heard, she was still thinking.

"That's all right," I said. "Just stay here with me. Put your arm around me and let me fall asleep feeling safe."

"You are safe," Tony said. "I'm not going anywhere."

CHAPTER 27

I woke up—hoping, making pacts with God. Just let this all be a dream. I'll never say goddammit again, I'll work for the homeless, I'll be nice to the fashion nitwits, I'll be satisfied with my life. . . .

Sometimes it works. I wake up and all the horrible stuff really was a dream and I stop saying goddammit for a few weeks. Not this time. I woke up in Tony's bed and I remembered why.

I sat up. He lifted one eyelid. "Nattie, what in the good Lord's name are you doing up this early?"

"Well, I was hoping none of this was real. You know, like Bobby's bad dream on Dallas."

"Do what?"

"Never mind. It doesn't matter. It's not a dream. Jeff's still dead."

I slammed my head back on the pillow, thinking I might force myself back to sleep where I didn't feel so bad. I bounced back up.

"Dammit, dammit, dammit," I said. "I didn't call Henry yesterday. I wasn't thinking straight and he's back in town with his kids and that lunatic knows where they go to school. . . ."

I jumped out of bed, forgetting that I wasn't wearing anything. I was too worried about Henry to worry about my thighs.

Tony leaned up on his elbows. "Nattie, stop worrying. I called

Henry yesterday. His kids are going home to Connecticut with his mother. He's plenty worried about you, though, and would probably appreciate a phone call."

I saw my shirt, or, rather, the shirt Tony had given me to wear instead of my bloody one, on the floor. I picked it up and put it over my head. It was anybody's guess where the rest of my clothes were.

Tony handed me the phone and I called Henry. I woke him up, but he did seem very happy to hear from me—and very worried.

"Do you want off the story?" he said.

"Goddammit, no," I said. "This psychotic asshole's already killed three people, and it's going to be me next if we don't find out who it is first."

"Okay, it's your call," Henry said. "If it's a go, we need a plan."

"I'll meet you at the office in an hour."

Tony rolled out of bed.

"I knew this wouldn't stop you," he said.

"Would it you?"

"No. I'll take the first shower—women are slower than a slug in a desert at high noon."

"Not this woman," I said, and sprinted to his bathroom. I was clean and dressed in less than five minutes, while he took a good fifteen to do all his ablutions.

Tony swung me by my apartment so I could change into work clothes. The police had already been there to make sure no one else had.

I pulled together some kind of outfit and grabbed a pair of riding jeans and boots, for after work. If ever I needed to be atop a horse, this was it.

"Take a toothbrush and whatever it is you usually sleep in," Tony said.

I looked at him. Neither of us had mentioned what happened the night before.

"Tony, I can't stay at your place forever, look what happened. . . ."

"I'm not asking you to stay forever. And I'm not asking you to sleep with me. Just in my house. Where I know you're safe. Another night, until we work something out. Maybe someone can come stay with you—your momma or daddy?"

"I can't tell my mother. She still worries when I go out past sundown. I'll call Lou."

"Lou?"

"My father, the flake. He'll be back from the ashram tomorrow, cleansed, purged, and vibrating with energy. I'm sure he'll come down. Maybe he'll even astral-project himself here. Tonight I'll stay at your place—after I tell Mrs. Flock, but that's it."

"Fine," he said. "I'll be looking forward to meeting Lou."

Tony pulled up by *The Appeal*'s curb. There was a new set of police officers swarming around. We got out and I told him I'd be at his place no later than nine, since I was going riding after work.

"Spare me a twisted gut and make it before it gets dark, okay, darlin'?"

"Okey-dokey," I said. One colloquialism deserves another.

I headed to the front door and Tony walked over to a female officer examining the bushes. "I was hoping to see you here, Tony." She stood up and I saw her name tag: Sharon Odom.

I tried not to stare while I took a mental picture. Light brown hair, wavy, tied back in a ponytail; sensible glasses; milky white skin, thin lips, five six, 110 pounds. In my mother's words, plain as pudding. I heard her say something about Saturday night being a start. I walked faster.

In the lobby, two officious-looking guards stopped me.

"Identification, please."

All I had was a Harris Teeter check-cashing card, which convinced the guard of nothing. A few months ago I left my purse at a store and never got around to replacing my driver's license or *Appeal* ID.

"Wait," he said, and picked up the phone. "Got a woman here, says her name is Natalie Gold. . . . Yeah, short, red-haired, late twenties . . . okay."

He looked at me and said, "You can go up."

"I'm thirty-six," I said to him. "But thanks for the compliment."

He didn't smile.

There were still plenty of cops in the newsroom. Henry saw me walk in and was by my side in seconds. His face was ashen, like every other reporter's and editor's in the place. He put his arm around my shoulder.

"Are you all right?"

"No, but let's get to work."

We headed toward his desk.

"You know there's something I haven't told you," I said.

That wiped the concerned look off his face.

"No, no. I mean it's not that I didn't tell you because I was hiding something. I just didn't think it had anything to do with anything except my personal business. Now I don't know."

"Is this about your police friend?"

"Oh, Henry, give me a break. It's not about me, it's about Gail, my best friend."

I filled him in on her connection, rather obsession with Jeff, the lies about Allie, and what she'd said about Sully.

"That's three pieces of the puzzle staring me in the face," I said. "Why can't I put the damn things together? There's something I'm not getting."

Henry had taken notes on the computer as I spoke.

"Give me a few minutes," he said. "Let me read back over this. Maybe a new set of eyes can come up with something."

I picked up the phone and dialed Gail's house. No answer again. "Dammit," I said, and slammed the receiver into the cradle.

"The vet," Henry said. "The vet that was in the picture of Allie. Last week, didn't you tell me something about the vet losing his license for falsifying vaccine records?"

"Not exactly, but close," I said. "It was a Coggins test for swamp fever, technically known as equine infectious anemia. You can't take a horse anywhere without a Coggins and the owner wanted to go to a show to chase points. As a favor, Doc Loc wrote out the form before he got the results. But he got caught."

"What about the horse?" Henry said.

"Oh, he was fine. He tested negative and got a clean Coggins."

"What if he hadn't?"

"Then he would have—oh, my God! Henry you're a genius, a goddammed genius. That's it. The piece that fits everything together. Allie, Doc Loc, the hair dye, Wally, Sully, even the stupid dream I had the other night, everything."

I grabbed the phone and dialed 411. "A number for Charles Lockton, he's a veterinarian. . . . Great, thanks."

I started to dial, Henry took the phone.

"Before you go off half-cocked, just calm down. Tell me why I'm such a 'goddammed genius,' and what the picture looks like now that you've put the pieces together. Then, let's work out a plan. Okay, partner?"

Henry was right, I was going off half-cocked.

"Sorry," I said. "Sometimes I get swept away in my excitement, in case you haven't noticed."

"It would be hard to miss," Henry said. "However, I have to admit, that's one of the things that makes working with you so interesting."

"In-ter-est-ting?" I said, pounding out the four syllables just like Henry does. "Is that like, 'she makes her own clothes'?"

Henry laughed. "No, not at all. Interesting, unpredictable—and, all right, even enjoyable."

"Okay, okay, okay, enough," I said. "Here's what the big picture looks like. I can't believe it took me this long to figure it out. Part of me must have known it. That explains the dream. Or Mrs. Flock was right about saying 'reach' and tapping into the motherboard."

"Nattie, what motherboard are you talking about? No, never mind. You're as bad as Dorothy with these tangents. Let's just stay on the main track, at least for the next five minutes."

Just as I was about to tell Henry everything, Fred came up. He didn't look any better than the rest of us.

"Nattie, are you all right?" he said, and I could tell he meant it. I nodded. "Remember the last time something like this happened? Daniel Bolles, working on a mob story in Arizona. I knew him. He was a hell of a reporter. They never really got the sons of bitches that blew him up in his car. We can't let that happen with Jeff. He was a hell of a reporter, too, one hell of a reporter. . . ."

I started crying again. "Be right back," I said, and headed toward the women's room for a tissue.

"Nattie, one more thing." It was Fred.

"Yes?" I said, trying to choke down the tears.

"The other day I called Eddie Heffner, your blacksmith."

"Yeah, he told me."

Fred leaned toward me and in a quiet voice said, "Well, ah, I was just wondering. A woman who said she was his wife answered the phone. She sounded white. Ahhh—is she? I mean, this is the South, you don't find that kind of thing too often."

I wanted there to be an afterlife more than anything at this moment, just so Jeff could've heard what just passed through Fred's lips.

"Fred," I said. "Eddie's wife *is* white. And so is Eddie. He's a black*smith*, that's his job, not his color."

"Oh, of course, of course it is. Right. Well, nevertheless, he's quite a character. Keep me posted, all right?" And with that, Fred turned the other way and made a beeline for his office.

And I made a beeline for the bathroom. I don't know if I was crying or laughing—probably both. I splashed cold water on my face and walked back to Henry's desk with my face as splotched as an Appaloosa's.

"In a million years, you'd never guess what Fred just said to me," I said to Henry.

"Maybe you can tell me, then," he said. "First—the puzzle, remember?"

"Right." I sat down, because suddenly I felt sick to my stomach. My going off on tangents had been a way to stall—not only to Henry, but to myself. I didn't want to voice what I suspected, that my best friend could be capable of murder.

Then, in almost a whisper I spilled it out, for both of us: Doc Loc must have had one of his horses turn up with a positive Coggins. State law says you either have to destroy the animal or freeze-brand a coded number down its neck and then isolate the animal forever. Knowing Doc Loc's contempt for the accuracy of the Coggins test, he went the freeze-brand route. I'm betting the horse stayed asymptomatic for a couple years, long enough for the doc to feel the horse wasn't a carrier. Then he gave the horse to Gail.

"That's why she never took him to a horse show. You can't show a horse anywhere—and I mean anywhere, without a

Coggins test. And now I know why she named him what she did."

"Allie?" Henry asked.

"Allie for short," I said. "His full name is All Dressed Up—"

Henry finished the sentence, ". . . and No Place to Go. That's quite clever."

"Clever didn't get her anything except this mess," I said. "And a horse she's so obsessed with, she may have killed a couple of people for. Some vets think a positive Coggins is just like being HIV positive. Of course, Doc Loc isn't one of those vets. He thinks the Coggins test is worthless."

Henry's fingers were tap-dancing across the keys. "Go on," he said.

"The Miss Clairol, sable brown? To cover the freeze brand. I'll bet Wally walked in on one of Allie's hair appointments. He must have been blackmailing her, too. Poor Gail, that horse is her life."

"What about Sully?" Henry said. "How does she fit in?"

"Sully worked for Doc Loc after Gail did. She was quite the gossip, so is Doc Loc. Maybe he said something about Allie to Sully and maybe Sully said something to Gail and maybe Gail got mad or scared enough to—"

"Kill her and Wally," Henry said. "Then she'd be rid of all her problems."

"Except I gave her a new one—Jeff."

"It certainly fits," Henry said.

"That's the problem. It fits too well. You know what they say, 'If it seems too good to be true, it probably is.' I don't know, maybe she did do it and maybe I'm not letting myself believe Gail could be behind all this."

Henry stopped typing. "Nattie, it's possible the only thing Gail is guilty of is harboring an illegal horse—and maybe not even that. I think you should go talk to that vet, find out what happened. We still have to interview Keith Rollings and the Mayfields, as well as ask Lucy a few more questions. Remember, Gail's not the only one with a good reason to kill Wally."

CHAPTER 28

Back when Jim and Tammy Bakker were in the amusement park business, I-77 used to be the highway to heaven, transporting thousands of vacationing Christians to their Mecca—Heritage USA. That all changed when Jim got thrown in the slammer and Tammy served up divorce papers and turned around to marry the guy who built their palace.

Now I-77 is just another interstate. Except for one thing. Around Charlotte, there's a stretch of green on both sides of the speeding cars that has the highest incidence of Rocky Mountain spotted fever in the world. I guess that means if you have a flat tire, you'd better tuck in your socks and put on a hat.

Luckily, I had no car trouble on my way to Doc Loc's, which involved a twenty-minute trip down tick alley to Fort Mill, South Carolina.

And luckily, Doc Loc had been home when I called from the office. He wasn't keen on my coming, not at first. I'd heard he's become a bit of a recluse since his license got yanked. When I told him I thought Gail might be in a bad way, he agreed to meet me.

I drove down his long, rutted driveway, not believing what I saw. Long in the tooth would be a kind way to describe his farm, though at one time it must have been a pretty snazzy spread. Now the fencing was half down, the barn battered to the point it looked unsafe, and his house, well, I'd have been right at home twenty years ago, when I lived in a dirt-floored basement. In my current state of good mental health, you couldn't have paid me to live there.

"Hello, hello, hello," he said to me as I got out of my Rabbit.

Doc Loc's got a voice that wouldn't need a loudspeaker anywhere. With his pink skin, fluffy white hair, and brushy mustache, he looks like an albino Captain Kangaroo who forgot his sun screen. I've never seen the man without a big smile on his face and something kind to say about someone.

"So what's wrong with our Gail?" he said. "I hope she and Rob didn't get into a spat again. I keep telling that girl she's got to be like a duck around him. 'Just let the water roll on off you. Roll on off.' "

"Easier said than done, with Rob," I said.

"You're right about that," Doc Loc said. "But that man knows horses. I've never seen anyone take as good a care of them as Rob. 'Course, that's what makes him so tough to work for. Now tell me about Gail. You know, she called me not too long after you did. Odd thing was, she was whispering and talking fast. Sounded like she didn't want anyone to know she was on the phone. I've got to say, she wasn't very happy to hear you were on your way down. I thought you two were joined at the hip. Is it you and Gail who've been fighting? If it is, the last thing I want to do is get between two women. No sir, I'd rather walk through a mares' field when they're all in season."

"I haven't been fighting with anyone, just working on a story," I said. "In fact, I've been trying to get in touch with Gail for days. Did she say where she was?"

"Didn't ask," Doc Loc said. "I assumed she was at the barn. That's where she always is. Is she in trouble? Whatever I can do to help . . . You know, I'd do anything for her."

"Well, that might be part of the problem," I started to say.

On the way over, I'd worked and reworked what I was going to say. If Doc Loc confirmed my suspicions about Allie, that would amount to confessing to yet another veterinary crime. I worried that he might deny everything to save his skin. What I hadn't counted on was the decency of this man—and how much he cared about Gail.

The whole story tumbled out, mostly the way I'd planned to say it. Mostly, I say, because something happened that I hadn't planned on, something I've never done during an interview. I cried.

"Gail's my best friend. I hope to hell there isn't a lick of truth to anything I've just said. I'm here hoping you'll tell me I'm a crazy woman with an overactive imagination."

Doc Loc wasn't smiling now. His brow was wrinkled and his lips were clenched.

"Wish I could do that." He sighed and shook his head. "I really do, but I can't. Tell those silly bastards at the paper to stop wasting you on the women's page. You should be doing this kind of work all the time because you're right about everything. The horse. The Coggins, the whole nine yards. As a yearling, that colt tested positive and the state vet's office was all over him, pulling blood, issuing quarantines, freeze-branding a two-inch-high A-56 down the left side of his neck.

"They 'strongly suggested' I destroy him. I 'strongly suggested' they get off my property before I destroyed something other than that colt. I've seen too many healthy horses killed for nothing because Leroy Coggins developed a test which may or may not work. That colt never showed a sign of anything or passed along anything to any one of my horses. He was the first and last to test positive at my farm. I kept him for five years to make sure he was healthy and not a carrier, and then I gave him to Gail. I thought I was doing her a favor. . . ."

"Who else knows?"

"No one. I may be a fool, but I'm not a damned fool. I'd be crazy to tell anyone—"

He paused for a few moments and was about to finish his sentence when I said, "Are you sure? What about Sully Cameron?"

Doc Loc looked at me as if he were examining something under a microscope. "What's in that brain of yours? Radio transistors? I was just wondering myself about Sully. When she worked for me, we went to a barn and a horse came up positive. The owner chose to have the mare destroyed and I was, well, angry doesn't even begin to describe it. In my truck, on the way to the next call, I was ranting about the stupidity of the Coggins test and I started to say something about Allie. I stopped myself, I thought in time. Maybe I said enough for her to piece it together. You know how Sully is, too damn smart for her own good."

That made me two for two. One more and Gail would be out.

"Was," I said.

"Excuse me?" Doc Loc said. "Was what?"

"Sully was."

"Do you mean to say Sully is dead?"

I nodded and told him about her winding up in a ditch and Gail getting in a huff about Sully on the phone with me.

"Could be coincidence, you know," Doc Loc said. "Unless there's something else you haven't told me. And I'm guessing there is, judging by the color of your face. Much whiter and you'll be lying here on this red clay."

Then I told him about Jeff. His pink skin blanched as pale as mine.

"No wonder you look like you lost your best friend," Doc Loc said. "Because I'm afraid you just might have."

CHAPTER 29

I went back up the interstate. The way I felt, a flat tire in the middle of tick alley would have been merciful. At least then I could think about something other than the possibility that my best friend might have murdered three people.

The same officious-looking guards greeted me in the lobby. I showed them my Harris Teeter card again. And again they weren't about to let me upstairs.

"Where were you guys when we needed you?" I muttered.

"What?"

"Forget it," I said. "Can I just use your phone to call upstairs?"

I didn't feel like seeing everyone in the newsroom, anyway. I called Henry. "Meet me in the cafeteria, okay? And would you mind telling these guards I'm the same person they let in here this morning."

I handed the phone to one of them and he grunted.

Henry was waiting for me at a table by the window. There were two large paper cups in front of him.

"Milk, right?" he said, and slid the coffee over my way.

I filled him in on my trip to Doc Loc's.

"Nattie, you were right on the money on this. Very impressive. Now, let's figure out what our next step is. If you can't find Gail, then I think you should . . . Nattie, are you all right? You look terrible. What's wrong?"

I always thought the difference between men and women was the Three Stooges. Men loved them as kids, women hated them. But the real difference between the sexes is best friends. Men just don't get what it means to have one.

"Henry, this is Gail, my best friend, we're talking about."

"No. We're talking about a story and an investigation. I'm sorry your friend is involved. However, she is and I can't change that. You have to divorce yourself from your feelings on this one. I know it's difficult, but if you don't, you'll get mired down by your emotions."

"What would you know about emotions?"

"You're right, I wouldn't, not at work. Think you can do the same? I'm sure it must be painful. If it's too painful, let's figure out something else. You can do sidebars, and I'll continue. Or I'll work the Gail angle. Something. Where to, Nattie? The choice is yours."

I looked at Henry sitting there. There wasn't a tense muscle in his face or a hint of anger anywhere.

"Where to?" I said. "The end. Let's go, wherever—and to whomever—it takes us."

I got out my reporter's pad and a Rolling Ball.

"Okay, Henry, here we go. Let's do Gail last. Let me get my footing back. Any luck nailing an interview with Rollings or the Mayfields?"

Henry flipped through his reporter's pad. "Rollings wasn't eager to talk. I left three messages with his wife, who was extremely pleasant but completely ineffectual. On the fourth try I told her to tell her husband I'd recently interviewed a Mrs. Annie Newson, which raised questions I thought he could help me clear up."

I must have had a blank look on my face.

"A little digging turned up the name. One Mrs. Annie Newson, employed by the Rollingses since 1971 as a domestic worker, mother of the little girl whom Keith molested."

"Whoo-ha, Henry, way to go. I bet that got Keith's fingers tapping out your number in no time."

"Twelve minutes," Henry said. "I timed him. He was very polite on the phone. 'How can I help you,' et cetera, et cetera. Never mentioned Annie Newson. He agreed to meet us Thursday at a place called the Hunt Box, in Camden."

"Thursday? Today's Monday."

"He claims to be a very busy man. As for the Mayfields. Edward Mayfield's secretary squeezed in a place for us on Friday. And I did get through to the daughter who said she would prefer to speak with you. She's expecting you to call her tomorrow around nine A.M."

"Okay," I said. "That leaves Lucy and Gail. Before I leave today, I'll call Lucy's. I want to talk to Dorothy anyway, tell her about Jeff. I don't know what to do about Gail. I haven't told the police about her. Think I should?"

"What about Tony? Does he know?"

"No," I said. "I was too upset to talk yesterday or last night."

"I wouldn't say anything, then. All you've got on Gail is a suspicion, and that's not enough to unleash the police on her. Give me her mother's name and approximate age, and I'll have the Raleigh bureau go over to the DMV and pull her driving record. That'll get us her address and then we can get her phone number. Maybe Gail's mother can help us find her. Give me Gail's address and I'll stop at her house, talk to neighbors, ask around and see what I can find."

We finished our coffee and headed upstairs. By the zing in my innards and the rumbling in my stomach, I could tell Henry hadn't gone the decaf route.

241

"I'll meet you at your desk," I said, and walked quickly to the women's room. Caffeine.

Henry's ear was planted in the phone and I did the same at the desk next to his. I hadn't been back to my desk since Saturday night and had no plans to do so anytime soon. Even Candace, the automaton, agreed that was a good idea.

I dialed Lucy's number. She answered, and before I could get my whole name out, she said, "I know who this is."

Nothing like cutting to the chase. I did the same and asked her right out if Henry and I could come back down to Camden this week. "A few more things about Wally have come up."

"Was that before or after you had your little talk with Dorothy?" Lucy said. "She told me you were here. If I were you, I wouldn't listen to one word that woman says. She thinks she's some kind of voodoo queen. She's crazy, that's what she is."

"She was right about Sully," I said.

"What? What are you talking about? What do you mean?"

"Sully's dead."

"Oh, my God." The phone slammed to the floor. Five minutes passed and I finally hung up.

So much for our interview.

I wrote Gail's address down on a piece of paper and slipped it to Henry, who was still talking on the phone and taking notes. I waved and mouthed the words "Off to the barn, I'll call you."

Old man Clarke's big taupe turbo-diesel was there, along with an assortment of Volvos and Beemers. I didn't see Gail's little red Tercel anywhere.

I saddled up Brenda and strapped on my hard hat reluctantly. It was hot, as usual, and I thought about skipping the helmet. Rob wasn't around to scream at me and old man Clarke was in the office, so he'd never know. I started to undo the buckle, when something spooked Brenda and she shied into me and knocked me down.

"Okay," I said. "I'll wear the hat."

I'm a great believer in signs, real or imagined.

I grabbed Brenda's reins and rushed out of the barn, breaking one of the big rules at February Farm. I didn't sign out on the blackboard. You're not supposed to go on trail without writing the time you left on the board. But I was in a hurry to relax.

It didn't take long for the magic to take hold. In fifteen minutes I barely knew my name was Nattie Gold, let alone that I was working on a murder story where my best friend was the main suspect. The summer smells were intoxicating, demanding my full attention with their boisterous assault on my senses. The honeysuckle and its jubilant sweetness felt like a crescendo of fuchsia swirling around me. Then a few steps farther, the soft, melancholy call of fallen leaves becoming earth again; their deep, musty smell a quiet, reedy circle of dark amber.

I was in glory land again.

The trail was wide enough to pick up an easy canter. I pressed my right leg into Brenda and she glided into the left lead, as asked. I reached down and patted her neck. "Good girl."

Brenda has what's called a rocking horse canter, smooth as a day that goes right. I felt as if I were riding a cloud. If I had to choose between this and anything else, and I mean *anything*, there'd be no choice.

I looped the reins to her and rose into a two-point, meaning my rear—the third point—was out of the saddle and off her back. She continued to canter quietly in a steady one-two-three rhythm. Ahead I saw the trail narrow, so I started to gather up the reins.

Before I knew what happened, her hind end scooted up and under her. She bolted to the side and then blasted in a flat-out gallop. Tree branches flew by and in my face before I could get the reins tight enough to hold her mouth and try to slow her down. I pulled. She galloped faster. I pulled and pulled. She grabbed hold of the bit and I had nothing but a runaway horse in my hands.

She bolted again to the side and I heard why. A loud pop. A gunshot grazed my head, and I could smell the sizzle of fake velvet. My hunt cap, I'd have been dead without it.

Brenda ran faster and faster. The shots kept coming.

She was tearing through woods, turning and twisting down a trail I'd ever only walked her on. I clamped my legs around her and grabbed her mane. The shots kept coming. And coming.

She galloped faster. The trail took a sharp turn to the left and so did Brenda, at a flat-out gallop. Her feet slipped out from under her. As she scrambled to get her footing, I heard a rustling in the woods. Before I had a chance to turn and look, a shot rang out. It hit Brenda. She leapt up and took off wildly, heading straight for a fallen tree blocking the path.

The trunk alone was at least four feet high. But that wasn't the worst part. On the other side of the trunk were five or six branches sticking straight up, making the whole thing one giant oxer fence. I hate oxers, and Brenda was going full barrel toward the biggest, ugliest oxer I'd ever seen.

I yanked up the reins, planted my right hand into her neck, and jerked as hard as I could with my left hand. It's called a pulley rein, and it's supposed to stop the most hard-mouthed runaway. I could have been riding her in a halter for all the good that did.

I tried to pull the reins again, but they slipped through my fingers. I looked down. My hands were covered in blood. I heard another shot.

I looked up and into the oxer. Brenda leapt into the air. She catapulted with such thrust, I flew over her left shoulder and across the tree. I watched in sickening slo-mo as the ground got closer and closer.

Wham.

I crashed back first and saw Brenda coming over the oxer and onto me. In midair she twisted her body hard to the right; three of her feet landed in the tree; the fourth on me.

Everything went black.

Then I saw Brenda. She was pushing a lump of something with her nose. I looked again. That lump of something was me. It was getting farther and farther away.

I was surrounded by the deepest and most complex blue I'd ever seen. It was all colors, shimmering together in a strange cerulean iridescence. At the very end of the horizon I could see a crescent of bright yellow. Like the blue, the yellow was filled with tiny vibrating pinpoints of all colors popping in and out, back and forth. I felt as if I were watching the molecules dance.

"Nattie."

That voice. So familiar. I didn't want to turn away from the yellow. I wanted to go to it. But that voice.

"Nattie, over here. Come back."

I made myself turn toward the voice. It took all my will. The bright yellow was where I wanted to be.

"David?"

"Nattie, for crying out loud, that horse stepped on your ankle, not on your head. You don't belong here. It's too soon. You always were a precocious kid. A great kid, but precocious."

"David?" It was David, my stepfather. In a brown tweed jacket and olive turtleneck. Thirty pounds thinner and twenty years younger. I ran to him, hugged him, and started babbling.

"I've missed you so much. I've never stopped thinking about you. I never did tell you I loved you, or how much you meant to me, that you were a godsend, that I would have turned out to be a mess if it hadn't have been for you. Mom is a basket case without you. Ever since you di—"

I stopped cold.

"Died," I said. "Died. What are you doing here, anyway?"

David squeezed me. He was like a big bear. I remember the first time he hugged me. I was a screwed-up ten-year-old who couldn't say much besides "Fuck you." He told me he was going to marry my mother and we were going to be a family. He hugged me then and I felt safe for the first time in a very long time. It felt good to feel that way again.

"No, it's not what am *I* doing here. It's what are *you* doing here? You've always rushed into things like a meshuggener, way before you or anything else was ready. You gave your mother and me conniptions. You gotta stop rushing, Nattie. Especially now, especially on this. And while I'm on the subject, I want you to tell your mother something. She won't listen to me, never has, so why should I expect any different now?

"Look at me, Nattie. Notice anything?"

What could I say to a ghost?

"My weight, my weight, I'm talking about my stomach. It's gone. Tell her that, and tell her I kept my end of the bargain and now it's her turn. She'll know what I'm talking about. I've got to go, dear. I love you."

He leaned forward and kissed me on my cheek. Then he whispered in my ear. "I can't say any more than this: Work on those lead changes. Now go. You've got two grandchildren to give me yet.

"Go, go back."

I came to, to a cloud of warm air puffing against my cheek and something soft pushing at my face. I opened my eyes. Brenda's nose was next to me, she was trying to get me to move.

"David?" I said.

No answer. Of course there was no answer. He was dead and I wasn't sure what just happened to me, where I was, or how I got there. Then I looked around. I was lying flat on my back. I raised myself on my elbows, leaned forward, and started to stand. I lifted my right leg in the air, to push myself up. I watched in horror as my right foot flopped over, completely to the left, as if it weren't connected to the rest of the leg. It wasn't.

That's when the pain hit. A screeching blast like I'd never felt before. I broke out into a sweat and started to shiver.

Then I remembered the gunshots and the fallen tree and how I got where I was—and that there might be someone on the other side of the maple aiming a Magnum my way.

I tried to crawl. The slightest movement sent spears of fire up my leg.

I wasn't going anywhere. I was stuck in the middle of a forest with a leg that wasn't connected to the rest of me and a maniac who'd just been playing target practice with me and my horse.

What's worse, no one expected me back at the barn because no one knew I was gone, unless . . .

I waved my arms. "Shoooo, Brenda, get, go back to the barn. . . ."

Brenda trotted, then galloped away. I listened to her hoofbeats moving farther and farther from me. Then I listened some more. No shots. No footsteps. Maybe my maniac called it a day or maybe I was being set up for the big kill.

I strained to listen for the slightest movement. A rustling leaf, a snapped branch. All I could hear was the incessant chirping of a forest full of horny crickets. If I'd had a watch, I could've figured out the temperature—Dolbear's formula. At least it would have been something to do, something other than lying in wait for a bullet between my eyes.

Instead, I lay my head back down on the ground and closed my eyes. Then I did something that doesn't come natural to me.

247

I prayed.

A few weeks back I'd read a story that came over the wires about a doctor, Larry Dossey, who scientifically documents the power of prayer. He's got studies up the wazoo that show heart patients heal faster and sprouts sprout faster—if they've been prayed over.

If it could work for a sprout . . .

CHAPTER 30

"Tony, Tony, over here. Quick."

I felt something clammy moving up and down my arm. I must have fallen asleep. I opened my eyes and saw Rin Tin Tin, his wet nose busily working my skin. I watched his bristly brown fur shimmering in the beam of a flashlight. My eyes traveled up the beam to Henry.

I was alive. My maniac had indeed called it quits.

"Henry, thank God," I said. I started to move and felt as if my leg were being used to roast marshmallows.

"Ahhh," I screamed.

"Don't move, Nattie. Just lie still. You're okay, you're going to be all right."

"Whew, boy, this sucker hurts," I said. "I thought you're supposed to have endorphins that kick in at times like this. Where are mine now? What am I, endorphin challenged? It feels like there's a hot poker inside my leg."

Henry looked as if he'd seen a ghost. I was about to tell him not to worry, that I just had.

He mumbled, ". . . being branded from the inside out."

Then I remembered what he'd just remembered. Dorothy and her strange leg pain when she shook my hand. She'd said just that, ". . . being branded from the inside out." That about summed up how I felt. Then I remembered what else she'd said.

"Yeah, well," I said, "just because she's right on that one

249

doesn't mean we're getting married or anything. Psychics can be wrong, too." I started to laugh, but that made me move and that made it hurt worse.

"Ahhh," I screamed again.

"Nattie, for once in your life, just be quiet. Lie still. Tony's calling the rescue squad."

"You've got to find Brenda. She's bleeding. I think that bastard landed a bullet in her someplace. Please, I'll be quiet, just go find her."

"She's fine, she's fine, Nattie. She's at the barn, the vet's on the way. Rob said the wound looks superficial, a graze to her shoulder. She's lucky, and so, may I add, are you. We would have never known you were lying here had it not been for Mr. Clarke."

"Old man Clarke? He hates my guts."

"Well, perhaps he was afraid of the bad press he'd get having a reporter die on his trails. He's the one who called Tony to tell him you were missing. Apparently, he noticed that Brenda's stall was empty, saw your car parked out front and no message as to your whereabouts on the blackboard. He's not very happy that you didn't sign out."

"Huh, so old man Clarke saved my life. And I thought what happened before you came was stranger than truth."

"What do you mean?"

"Another time. Just get me to a hospital. This pain isn't getting any better."

CHAPTER 31

I n the emergency room I did what you do in emergency rooms. I waited.

And waited.

And filled out forms.

Finally, they wheeled me up to X ray, where they laid me out on a steel table and covered my private parts with a lead apron.

The two X-ray techs slipped behind a shield.

And I waited some more.

Ten or fifteen minutes passed. I craned my neck to see where they'd gone and saw them standing behind the shield. One of them had Sunday's *Appeal* in her hand. "That's her," she whispered to the other tech. "The fashion editor."

What a time to be recognized. "Writer," I called out. "Not editor. This leg's killing me. Any chance of getting something for the pain?"

"Sorry, dear, not until the doctor sees you. Say, I've got a question for you: Do those New York designers expect women to wear all those see-through clothes?"

If I'd screamed "Get me some goddamned drugs," no doubt she'd report to Fred that I'd been rude. Rude to the reading public.

So, instead, I smiled as best I could. "No one expected the mini to come back . . ."

She wheeled me back down to emergency, talking the entire

way about her wardrobe and how her husband hates it. I didn't get a word in.

"Thanks for the advice, hon," she said as she parked my gurney.

I watched the clock's spindly second hand make its rounds thirteen and a half times before the doctor entered. Judging by his demeanor and his specialty—orthopedics—I'm sure he aced his way through the I-am-God classes in med school, that probably being his first and last A in any academic endeavor. The joke on orthopods, according to a doctor friend of mine, is they're strong as a bull and twice as smart.

"Riding accident, right?" he said.

He took a pair of scissors and sliced down the side seams of my jeans and lifted off the top half as if he were filleting a fish. I groaned, not in pain, but embarrassment. I was a living lesson in every mother's primer: Always wear nice underwear.

I was wearing my worst pair. Between the horse show and what happened at the office, I hadn't had time to wash. I was down to the dregs. The elastic was stretched beyond function, the color was unrecognizable, and they were ventilated in places never imagined by an underwear designer.

"Oh . . ." I moaned.

"I'll get you something for the pain in just a second," the doctor said.

"What, a new pair of underpants?"

"I've seen worse. This leg is another matter."

He turned toward the nurse, "Eight milligrams of Astramorph."

She poked a needle in my hand and pressed down the plunger, sending hot sparkles of deliverance through my veins.

Before I had a chance to complain how much the shot hurt, I was in la-la land. Blastoff complete, with the aptly named Astramorph.

The doctor put his hands around my foot and yanked it

toward my leg. My brain was saying, "Scream out in pain," but my body was singing, " 'Everything is beautiful, in its own way . . .' "

The next thing I knew, someone was wrapping my entire leg in warm, wet, soft plaster. Ooohh, baby, don't stop.

The doctor looked down at my eyes. "She's got too much on board. Point two milligrams of Narcan."

The nurse stuck me with another needle.

"No, no," I said. "I haven't felt this good since nineteen seventy . . ."

As fast as it came on, it went. I was back to reality, and the reality was both my fibula and tibia had been severed by the impact of Brenda's hoof. I looked down at an expanse of white and saw a cast that ran from the tip of my foot to the top of my thigh.

"How soon can I ride?"

"Very funny," the doctor said.

"I'm not joking. How long before the cast comes off?"

"Three months if you're lucky. As for riding again, I'd say no. You'll be lucky if you walk without a limp. This is a serious break, compounded by the fact it's in a joint. The synovial fluid slows down healing."

He could say whatever he wanted to. But as sure as my name is Nattie Gold, I'd be on a horse again.

The doctor turned toward the nurse. "ICU for one night."

And with that he bade me adieu in his own doctorly way, which is to say he walked out.

The nurse wheeled me into the hall and down to the elevator. Behind me, I heard the frantic clicking of high heels rushing toward me.

A voice called out: "If that's Natalie Gold on the stretcher, *stop*, stop right now."

Not just any voice. It was my mother, looking as bad as she'd looked the day David died.

Her eyes were puffy and red. Her face, not too many shades away from corpse gray.

She grabbed my hand. "Nattie, Nattie, you're all right. Those horses of yours. I can't stand it. All the time I worry. I worry that something exactly like this will happen. When are you going to stop with the horses?"

"Mom, calm down. I'm not dead. I just have a broken leg. Apparently a doozie of a one. And just for the record, it wasn't Brenda's fault."

The elevator door opened.

The nurse said, "I've got to take her to ICU. You can ride up with her. After that, you can see her fifteen minutes every hour."

My mother's face turned grayer.

"ICU," she said loudly. "What do you mean, ICU? That's intensive care. Intensive care, where you put dying people, people in critical condition. I thought she just had a broken leg. What aren't you telling me? Who's the doctor? What's his name? I want to talk to him right now."

The nurse, in her most nursely voice, said, "Mrs. Gold, your daughter is fine. It's just standard procedure to put someone with a break like this in ICU for the night. It has nothing to do with being in critical condition. She can go home tomorrow. She's fine, really."

My mother bought it. I didn't. I read *A Separate Peace*. I know what happens in the end. The kid dies after he breaks his leg and a blob of fat escapes from his bone marrow and zooms through his blood vessels straight to his brain. Boom, a fat embolism. An internal blowout.

"I'm fine, Mom." If we all said it enough, maybe it would come true. "But guess what, good news."

"Good news? Your leg is broken, what could be good about that?"

"I think I saw David."

My mother turned grayer. Any more and they'd have to wheel another gurney in for her.

"It might have been a dream. I don't know what it was exactly."

I told her most of it. I skipped the part about the bright yellow light and dancing molecules. I didn't want her to think I was still circling earth in the USS Astramorph.

"Then he said something about a bargain, he wanted you to know he lost weight. Which he did, he looked great. Tweed blazer, olive turtleneck, nice corduroys. Very dapper. He always was a handsome guy. He said, 'Tell her I kept my end of the bargain and now it's her turn. She'll know what I'm talking about.' What *was* he talking about?"

My mother sank to the floor. The nurse hit the alarm button on the elevator and within seconds someone official was waving a bottle of ammonia under her nose.

The nurse started to call for a wheelchair, and my mother wobbled back up to a stand. She leaned on the gurney with one hand, and with the other brushed the floor dirt from her black linen skirt. Expensive Donna Karan black linen skirt. My mother shops only the designer floor at Dillard's.

"No wheelchair," she said. "I'm all right now."

"Was there a bargain you guys made to each other?" I said.

Her eyes teared up. I don't think she's gone a day since his death without crying. "If I'd made him do it, he'd be alive today. He was going to lose weight if I stopped smoking."

"Well," I said. "I guess it's time to chuck your Chesterfield Lights."

CHAPTER 32

No floating pieces of fat did me in. Two days later I was hobbling up my steps on a new set of crutches. My father, Lou, was on one side, my mother, on the other, giving Lou instructions. Lou had turned off his hearing aid and was just nodding in agreement to whatever she said.

"When she goes out, go with her. I don't care if she gives you a hard time. Go with her. And call that sheriff friend of hers, let him know where you're going. . . ."

"Mom, I'm thirty-six years old. I can take care of myself."

She snapped back quicker than a slingshot. "Oh, really, is this what you call taking care of yourself?"

They guided me to the sofa.

"Sit," my mother said. "The doctor said to keep your leg propped up as much as possible. And remember, no going out today. He said not until tomorrow, after you've had a chance to rest."

"Mother, I'm fine, don't you have an estate to settle or custody battle to fight? Don't you have something else to worry about besides me?"

"How could I? Between the horses and the story you're working on, how could I have time to worry about anything else but you?" She started to light a cigarette.

"Mom, not in my apartment. If you want to kill yourself, do it where I can't see it or smell it. Okay?"

I didn't want to remind her about her deal with David again. Just the mention of his name set off the waterworks—for both of us.

"Nattie, I'm due in court this afternoon . . ."

"Go, go," I said. "Lou's here. He can help me if I need it."

She rolled her eyes. She hadn't trusted Lou with me since the day I was born. I can't say I blame her. On Sundays, visitation day when I was a kid, he often returned me broken and/or bloody. Not that he ever laid a hand on me; the problem was, he let me do whatever I wanted, which once meant jumping out of a moving car. Then, a few years later, he took me on my first driving lesson—and fell asleep while I tried to negotiate the Schuylkill Expressway, a nasty stretch of road in Philadelphia where everyone plays chicken at seventy miles an hour.

Before my mother left, she extracted a promise that I'd call her every night.

"If I don't hear from you by ten, I'm calling the police."

I knew she meant it. The police have looked for me many times in my life, the first being when I was eight and taking a nap in my bed. She wasn't even embarrassed when they found me burrowed beneath my covers.

"I'm a taxpayer," she'd said.

"I'll call, I swear," I said to her as she walked to the door. "Stop worrying. And you, remember, no more cigarettes."

The plan was for Lou to stay with me. My mother had a full caseload in her law practice and she needed the dough. David was a great guy, but no financial wizard.

The police posted a round-the-clock watch on my apartment, so I felt relatively safe. I still hadn't heard from Gail, and I'd left at least fifty-four messages on her machine.

Henry wanted to cancel our interviews: Keith and Lucy on Thursday, Melissa's father on Friday, Melissa and Mumsy late that afternoon. I told him no, that I'd be there even if I had to wheel myself there.

Which I didn't. Lou rented me a car with automatic transmission. That way, I could drive with my left foot and prop my right leg across the passenger's seat. The best part was, it had air-conditioning.

Now, if only my apartment did.

I heard Lou banging and whirring around in the kitchen. I grabbed the story notes I'd written in the hospital and read over them.

"Nat, drink this." Lou handed me a large glass of thick red-orange liquid.

I winced.

"It's carrot juice. Vitamin A. The more you drink, the faster your leg will get better."

"Lou, it's great you came to stay with me. But, look, this is going to work only if you lay off. And I mean it. No carrot juice, no vitamins, no anything unless I ask for it. Let's just say I'm taking a different path than you. Okay?"

He placed the glass on the table next to me.

"Sure, Nats. It's here if you want it. I'll be back in a minute. I'm going to bring some to Joan."

Mrs. Flock. They'd hit it off the first time they met six months ago.

I called Tony.

"No prints anywhere," he said. "None on Jeff's computer, your computer, the chair, nothing. It's too damn bad those boys can't run prints off of French fries and ketchup. You'd have your murderer if they could."

"Yeah, well, maybe next murder. But something's gotta break soon besides my leg. And speaking of, give that old dog of yours a big kiss for me. I'd have been stuck in the woods the whole night if it hadn't been for him."

"You betcha, I will. 'Course, I gotta tell you Henry looked at me a little peculiarly when I pulled out your camisole, or undershirt, whatever it is you call that thing, and pressed it to Rin's nose."

I must have left it there that night. I'd been in such a hurry to get my clothes off, I didn't know where I threw half of them.

"Where'd you find it?"

"Under Rin, he was sleeping on it. That dog loves you like his long-lost mother. We had ourselves a little argument about who was going to keep it. I was sure glad to have it when Mr. Clarke called and told me you were missing."

"How'd Henry get involved in the search?"

"I called him. It was the fair thing to do. The right thing and he was awfully appreciative of it. Then he saw me pull out your undershirt to give Rin the scent. He didn't say 'How come you've got yourself a piece of Nattie's underwear,' but I could just 'bout hear him thinking it."

"I don't know, Tony. Henry's got his emotions well trained. He puts a stay command on them when he walks through the door at work and they don't utter a peep until I don't know when. Maybe never. He's the most composed person I know. You never know what he's thinking, or feeling."

"I did that night. Right before we found you, Rin found some blood, I guess it was your mare's, but we didn't know that. We thought it might be yours. I knew exactly what he was feeling. The same as me. Scared something bad."

"Yeah, me, too. But then the weirdest thing happened. I stopped being scared. . . . I'm not sure what happened to me out there. . . . I can't go into it now. . . . Call me if you hear anything more from the lab. And thanks again. This time to you."

I hobbled over to Mrs. Flock's where she and my father were embedded in conversation about chakras.

"Lou, I'm going to lie down for a while, then Henry's picking me up. We're going to Melissa Mayfield's house to interview her. Here's her number, if you or anyone needs me."

I went back to my apartment. The message light was blinking on my answering machine.

It was Gail, whispering and talking fast: "Nattie, it's me. I know you know about Allie. Don't say anything to anyone." Click.

"Shit." I slammed my crutch against the wall. My father and Mrs. Flock came running.

CHAPTER 33

"How was Jeff's memorial?" I said to the back of Henry's head. He was driving, I was stretched across the backseat of my rental car.

"Filled to capacity. Everyone from the newsroom, the bureaus, anchors from all three television stations. WBTV covered it."

"Everyone but me . . ." I said. I didn't finish the sentence—"and it was my fault"—because I didn't want Henry to know I was wallowing in guilt.

"Nattie," Henry said, turning to look at me. "Should I remind you that you couldn't have been there? You were in the intensive care unit."

He turned back to the road. "What's the street number again?"

"Three twelve," I said.

"This is it, then." He pulled into a horseshoe driveway. Facing us was a redbrick mansion with a lot of shiny brass around. I reached down for my crutches and notepad.

"Let's go," I said.

Melissa and her mother had agreed to meet us at five. We were a few minutes early.

Henry took baby steps to keep pace with me. I rang the doorbell; I heard an electronic version of "Dixie."

No answer. I rang it again. . . . "land of cotton, long forgotten, look away . . ."

No answer.

I looked at my notepad. "She said it was 312 Queens Road."

"Queens Road what?" Henry said.

I slapped my palm against my forehead. "Jeez, how stupid could I be? It's probably East or West. This isn't it. Or maybe it is and she's decided she doesn't want to see us, which wouldn't surprise me. Just like that brat up near Iron Station who agreed to talk to me about a charity horse show coming to Charlotte. I drove an hour to her place and then she sent her groom to tell me she wasn't up to talking. Horse show people, what can I say? I'll try the bell once more, then let's work our way through the Queens Road maze."

No answer.

We wove around the oak-lined labyrinth for ten minutes before we found it: 312 Queens Road, this time 312 Queens Road East. Again it was three commanding stories of redbrick, but this one was tangled in enough white wrought iron trim to make it look like an outpost from Fort Lee, New Jersey.

I rang the bell. Chimes this time.

A woman with Melissa's face and wrinkles answered the door.

"Please come in," she said. Behind her stood Melissa, in matching everything.

"Goodness, Nattie, what happened to you?"

"A big, ugly oxer," I said.

I introduced Henry and we all walked into the living room, which confirmed my theory about old-line Wasps. No taste, but plenty of money they spend once a generational line, at the start. Between the highboys and lowboys and Louis the fifths through twenty-sevenths, there were enough serious antiques to keep Sotheby's in business for a year.

Try to make yourself comfortable on a satin brocade camelback bench masquerading as a sofa.

Melissa and her mother wore identical expressions—polite but cautious smiles.

Henry and I had decided to let me start, since Melissa had lied to me about her whereabouts the night of Wally's murder.

"You know, Melissa, I was going over my notes and I just wanted to check a few things. You said you and your mother were shopping. Montaldo's?"

She nodded. The smiles started to slip.

"Do you remember what department? Did you buy anything?"

Mrs. Mayfield looked at Melissa. The last time I saw that expression was when a deer ran in front of my car.

Then she turned toward me and said, "Why?" her accent stretching the one-syllable why to a three-syllabled *whaah*. "Is something wrong?"

"I hope not," I said. "I was just checking that I got it down right when Melissa told me you and she were shopping at Montaldo's."

Melissa touched her mother's arm and said quietly, "Mother, she's not stupid. Can't I just tell them?"

Mrs. Mayfield was silent. Just as I was about to say "Tell us what?" she said, "Mr. Goode, if you would please excuse us, I'd like to speak to Miss Gold privately. Would you mind terribly waiting in the foyer for just a few minutes?"

I was beginning to be able to read Henry, especially since his emotions had just disobeyed the stay command. He looked flustered and a little bit agitated.

"Mrs. Mayfield, Nattie and I are both working on this story. Whatever you say to her, you can say to me as well."

"Mr. Goode, I don't care to say to you what I will say to Miss Gold. So if you don't mind, Melissa will show you to the foyer."

Those steel magnolias, don't cross them.

Melissa took Henry's arm and marched him right out of there.

Mrs. Mayfield waited for her daughter to return before she started to speak.

"I'm terribly sorry that Melissa lied to you about where we were that night. We weren't shopping at Montie's. How could we be? It was closed for inventory. But surely you know that already, don't you?"

I nodded. "Yes, ma'am, I do."

A well-placed ma'am has its use, especially in the South, when you're trying to grease the wheels of a confession. Or whatever it was Mrs. Mayfield was about to do.

She continued, her voice soft and her accent thick. I felt as if I were listening to Melanie bear her soul to Scarlett.

"She lied because of me. I asked her to keep it secret."

Then she was silent again. And again Melissa touched her mother's arm.

"Mother, I'll tell her. I keep telling you it's nothing to be ashamed of. By now Nattie must be thinking you or I killed Wally."

Actually, I wasn't. I all but ruled them off the suspect list when I saw that look in Mrs. Mayfield's eyes. It was the look of the stalked, not the stalker.

"Mother and I were not at Montaldo's. I told you that only be-cause it was the first thing that came to my mind. We were in the basement of First Presbyterian, Room 10-B. We were there for a support group meeting."

"Support group?" I said. "As in 12-step? As in anonymity? Is that why you lied?"

Melissa shook her head. "No, I don't think that would be nearly as embarrassing for Mother. No, neither of us is an alco-holic. We both have Crohn's disease and last year Mother had a colostomy. It was a colostomy support group."

Mrs. Mayfield's face flushed. She looked away and smoothed her already-smooth skirt flat against her hips. "I know it's old-fashioned, but this is something I don't want anyone to know about. Have you any other questions?"

"Mrs. Mayfield, I'm sorry if this has been painful for you. I didn't mean to invade your privacy," I said, though some would argue that *is* the job description of a journalist. "And I do have just one more question. Melissa, have you heard from Gail?"

"Why, yes. Yes, I have," she said. "Gail called a couple of days ago and asked if I'd talked to you recently about Allie or Doc Loc. I told her that your partner had just scheduled an interview with Mother and me, but I didn't know what about. She sounded upset. Is Gail all right?"

"Oh, sure, everything's fine," I said. I wished I meant it.

I briefed Henry in the car, though I didn't tell him what kind of support group they'd attended. I owed Mrs. Mayfield that much.

"What about dinner?" Henry said. "How about a quick bite at Gus's Sir Beef. We can eat and write up a list of questions we want to ask Keith and Melissa's father."

"Hmmm, tempting. I love their vegetable plate and banana pudding. Sure, why not? I gotta call Lou and let him know. Mind if I invite him along?"

"No, I enjoy your father. He's quite a character. Just one request: Ask him to talk about something other than the Lemon Grass Institute."

Lou had cornered Henry at the hospital and told him in excruciating detail about his visits to that clinic and its regime of raw foods and colon integrity.

As it turned out, Lou had dinner plans with Mrs. Flock. Nature burgers on the grill. "I'll save you one, Nat," Lou said.

Henry and I got to Gus's and, as usual, there was a line. The place was crammed with families: little kids, smeary with mashed potatoes and chocolate milk, were laughing and crying and running around like banshees.

Henry looked as sad as a basset hound. "This is where I take Hank and Chet every Wednesday night after soccer. I've been talking to them on the phone every night before they go to bed and every morning before I go to work. . . ."

Is there anything sweeter than a man mooning over his kids? Not hardly.

"Henry, they'll be back as soon as we crack this thing. So let's get to work."

I pulled out my reporter's pad and started scribbling. Before we even sat down, we had four pages of notes, questions, and possible leads to follow.

The vegetables were big and delicious as usual, and the banana pudding was a religious experience.

By the time I got home, it was dark. Henry helped me up the steps.

It seemed as if he wanted to come in and talk some more.

"I'd ask you in, but I'm bushed and my leg is throbbing."

"Oh, no, no. That's all right. If I look a bit lost, it's because I am. I'm not used to not having to put the boys to bed. . . ."

"Henry, go home and call them. I'm sure they're up. It's not even close to midnight. That's their bedtime, isn't it?"

He laughed and it was good to see someone laugh. There'd been too many damn tears this week—and it wasn't even half over.

"See you tomorrow," he said. "I'll meet you at *The Appeal* around nine-thirty and we'll go to Mayfield's office from there."

CHAPTER 34

No one can snore like Lou. If I didn't know the whole story, I'd have said that's what went wrong in my parents' marriage. Six years of sleepless nights for my mother.

If only life were that simple. She could have gotten herself a good pair of earplugs and saved me thousands of dollars in therapy. Snoring, however, was the least of their marital problems. If someone tried to find the two most dissimilar people on the face of the earth and forced them to get married, that would have been my mother and father. The only thing they had in common was beauty and hormones. Back when they met, he looked like Robert Mitchum, she like Ava Gardner.

But like I said to Gail about my old beau, John: After the first night, what difference does it make how they look anyway?

I bent down over Lou and shouted into his good ear, good being a stretch in terms since he has only twenty percent hearing in that one. "Lou, Lou, I can't sleep with you snoring like that."

He rolled over on the futon spread out on my living room floor and the barrage stopped. For the moment.

I hobbled back to bed and tried to will myself asleep before he changed position and started snoring again. Unfortunately, sleeping is like enlightenment—you can't force either. I lay there counting imaginary strides between imaginary fences.

Somewhere after my fourteenth time around the same course of big oxers, I must have fallen asleep.

I was in the middle of a dream about little kids and banana pudding when I felt someone shaking my shoulder. It was Lou.

"Nat, do you have any bicarbonate of soda? I'm not used to spicy food."

"Spicy food? What's spicy in nature burgers?"

I got up and scrounged around my kitchen. "Here's some Alka-Seltzer. It's the best I can do."

Plop, plop, fizz, fizz. He was back asleep, and snoring, in ten minutes. I should have been so lucky.

I turned my fan to its highest setting to screen out the snoring. Still, I couldn't sleep.

I started counting strides again, and every time I began to drift off, something jarred me back to consciousness. My body was willing to take the nocturnal plunge, but my mind wasn't about to let go.

Something was eating at me.

I kept thinking about the barn and Brenda. I had that bad feeling again. Or did I? Things have a way of taking on an evil spin when it's dark and late and you're tired. I rolled around on my bed, trying to get comfortable, which is difficult when a quarter of your body is encased in plaster.

I sat up. Something *was* wrong.

"Lou, Lou, wake up."

He was sleeping on his good ear and snoring loud enough to wake everyone in all sixteen units of my apartment house.

"Lou, Lou, get up." I shook his shoulder.

"Huh? Nat, are you okay? What's wrong?"

"Come on, get dressed. I promised Mom I wouldn't go out late by myself. We're going to the barn. I think something's wrong. I got a bad feeling."

Anyone else would have told me to go back to sleep. But Lou loved this mumbo-jumbo stuff.

I threw a pair of shorts and a T-shirt on and then called

Tony. He lived only a few minutes from the barn. Plus, he carried a gun.

After two rings his message machine picked up: "Hello, as you can tell, I'm not here right now to answer the phone. But if it's an emergency or you just got yourself a bad hankering to talk to me, call me at 365-4424."

It didn't take a psychic to figure out whose number that was. I wasn't going to call him there, not at three in the morning—or, for that matter, anytime.

I didn't know if I should call Henry. I'd want him to call me. So I did. He picked up on the first ring.

"It's me, Nattie."

"Is anything wrong?" That being the normal response to a phone call at three in the morning.

"I think so. Maybe. At the barn. I'm going out there to make sure. You don't have to go. You probably think I'm crazy. . . ."

"Nattie, stop. I'll be there in fifteen minutes. After everything that's happened, I have to say, anything's possible. Don't go in if I'm not there. Promise? And call Tony."

"He's not home."

"Oh, that's interesting. Things must be going well with Sharon."

I guess I know what else they'd talked about that night in the woods.

I said, "I gotta go. I'll meet you there. Don't you go in either. I don't like this feeling."

Lou was waiting by the front door, slapping his hands all over his head. "It gets the Ki going," he said.

"Well, then," I said, "let's get your Ki and get going. I don't want to find a dead horse."

Mrs. Flock's porch light flicked on as we walked by.

"Lou, Nattie? It's three in the morning. Where are you going in such a rush?"

My father hadn't put in his hearing aid, so he didn't hear her. He smiled, "Joan, I loved those marinated onions."

I pulled at Lou's hand to speed him up. "We're going to check on my horse," I said.

Lou turned toward Mrs. Flock and said, "Joan, we're going to Nat's barn. She thinks there's something wrong with her horse."

"Lou," I said loudly and into his right ear. "Let's go. I already told her. I hope to hell you brought your hearing aid. I'm not screaming at you the whole way out there."

Lou rummaged around in his shorts pocket and pulled out what looked like a jumbo flesh-colored lima bean.

"Got it," he said. "I'm tuning you in."

He popped the thing in his ear and it started screeching, high-pitched and annoying to everyone but Lou, who hadn't heard the upper ranges of sound since 1943 in Salerno, Italy. He'd lost his hearing in World War II, after three and a half years of rifles and mortar exploding too close to his head.

I motioned to his ear. "Turn it down, you're gonna call all the dogs in the neighborhood.

"Mrs. Flock," I said, "go back to sleep. We'll see you tomorrow. Oh, and by the way, you don't have to call Tony this time. I already tried, he's not home. Henry's meeting us there."

Mrs. Flock wanted to go with us. And Lou was up for it, too. But I didn't have the time to wait for her to change, nor did I want to listen to their chakra talk in the car.

"All right, then," she said. "Stop by my apartment on your way back. I'll be up, and waiting."

There wasn't another car on the road. I was driving, Lou was in the backseat. I pressed my left foot into the accelerator and cranked the speedometer up. I didn't stop until the fluorescent green numbers hit eighty-five.

Lou didn't say a word. My mother was probably twitching in bed—maternal radar.

I made it to the entrance of February Farm in sixteen minutes. I sped halfway down the driveway, spraying shards of white stone everywhere. In the distance I saw Henry's silver Honda parked in front. I slowed down. I didn't want to announce my arrival.

As I swung around the driveway, I saw another vehicle parked in the tractor shed. Small and red. It was Gail's Tercel. Henry's car was dark and empty and I could see the aisle lights in the barn, through the crack in the door. Henry had gone in. Damn, I'd told him to wait for me.

My heart started pounding. Please, let this not be true.

"Lou, Henry's in there and I think he's in trouble. I'm going to sneak in the office and call the police. I can get in the back way without anyone seeing me. You stay here, and if I don't come out in five or ten minutes, walk up the back steps and wake up Rob. Call the police from his apartment."

"That's not a good idea, Nat. Let's go get the police first."

I was scared, and being scared makes me mad. "Now's not the time to start playing father. I'm going inside."

I would have slammed the car door, but even in my anger I knew that would be stupid. I grabbed my crutches and inched my way around to the back door of the barn office. I reached under the mounting block and found the spare key.

I unlocked the door and snuck in. Pretty damn quietly, I must say, for a person with a full leg cast and crutches. It was dark and I couldn't see the table from the floor. So I did what I always do when I get lost on course: I counted strides. I knew it was about five steps to the phone. By step four I was almost there. Just as I was about to make a reach for the phone I caught a glimpse of what was happening in the barn.

And I didn't like it one bit.

I slammed open the office door with my crutch and rushed down the aisle to Brenda's stall.

"Nattie, get back." It was Henry, pressed against the wall by

271

Brenda's flank and the back of somebody who was about to inject something into my horse.

"Gail, stop!!!!" I screamed.

"Guess again."

She spun around.

"Lucy. You?"

"Surprise. I guess the game's over. Not for me, I mean. For you and your mare. And let's not forget Robert Redford over here. Don't take another step. If you do, I won't give you a chance to say good-bye to this sweet horse of yours."

I stopped. Can't argue with a hypodermic needle in one hand and a Glock in the other.

Dammit, the story of my life. Act first, think later. I should've called the police before I charged in like a crippled Jean-Claude Van Damme.

Maybe Lou would make it to Rob's in time for the police to rescue us. But I'd been gone only a minute and I told him to wait five or ten. What to do . . . She loved to talk, I had to get her talking.

"I don't get it, Lucy. If you're such a big animal lover, how come you had your horse killed?"

"Shut up, Nattie. You don't know what you're talking about."

"Your house looks like a pigsty because of all your last-chance dogs. What gives, Lucy? How come you had your horse killed? Doesn't that count? Or does money make everything right, including having your beloved Lady shish-kebabbed."

It was like watching Melissa crumble that time I mentioned Waysie. Or, more accurately, seeing Superman turn into Bizaroman. She squinched her face up like she was having a heart attack or a bad case of gas. It wasn't a pretty sight, or site, for that matter. All those years of sun, and lines of coke, had imprinted enough cracks and crevices to make her uncrinkled face look rough enough. But squinched, she looked like a topo map of hell.

"Stupid fucking idiot. I didn't want *Lady* killed. That wasn't the plan. That wasn't what I told Wally to do. But that little asshole was meaner than you are stupid. He was supposed to wait until I got another horse that looked like Lady, then do that horse. Lady would be safe and on her way to Wisconsin to live with La Donna."

"Oh, I get it, you're a selective humanitarian. You're just Mother Teresa in riding britches. Sure. Did you think no one would recognize the horse you've carted to every show up and down the East Coast *and* the desert circuit?"

"You don't get anything, you idiot. The plan was, La Donna could ride her but not show her. No one would have known. In Wisconsin she'd be just another bay mare with no chrome. I thought reporters are supposed to be so damn smart."

Henry caught on to my game of buying time.

He said, "Not always. What gave you that idea?"

"Shut up, pretty boy. Just shut up and let me think what to do."

She was getting flustered. We had to keep her talking before her fingers started twitching.

"Why the insurance scam, Lucy? What's a quarter of a million dollars to the Bladstone fortune?"

"Ever hear the words prenuptial agreement? Is that too many syllables for you? I needed the money, because I have no money without him. And without him is what I want to be. Without him, without that little shitty house of his and without that stupid old nigger talking voodoo."

"Come on, Lucy, show a little more class than that. I don't think you'd hear Dorothy call you an ugly piece of PWT, though God knows she'd be right. So where did Sully figure in your big plan? What'd she do to deserve the Lucy treatment?"

"What are you talking about?"

"Sully. Your favorite braider. Dead in a ditch."

"Don't be ridiculous," Lucy hissed. "I didn't kill Sully. Why would I do that?"

"Who knows? Maybe you didn't like that lemon bread she made you, after all. You've got two murders under your belt, why not three. What's another corpse to a pro like you?"

"You're stupider than you look. Here, I'll spell it out for you so you don't have to die stupid. I didn't intend to kill your friend at the paper. He just showed up at the wrong time carrying the wrong thing. Christ, no ketchup. Who can eat fries without ketchup?"

Then it hit me. Gail. That's who. I should've remembered. No red food.

"And I sure as hell didn't kill Sully. Wally killed her. Which I'm sure he enjoyed doing. He knew how much I liked her. That's not why he did it, though. I'd told her to be at the barn at five to braid Lady for the show. She walked in on Wally killing Lady. Got it? Have I made it simple enough for the two of you? How about you, Miss Fashion Writer, understand what I'm talking about yet? Or is anything more than hemlines too complicated for you? Nattie, go back to the fashion beat. You're out of your league."

Like I said, if one more person made one more comment about fashion writing, I'd explode. My whole body pumped up, I could feel the anger pummeling through me. This was it, the last time *anyone* said *anything* about fashion writing. I was Mohammed Ali, I was Arnold Schwarzenegger, I was Linda Hamilton on crutches.

I pivoted on my good leg and swung twenty pounds of plaster into Lucy's gut. I felt the cast crack and my leg along with it. The gun scattered down the blacktop aisle. Brenda spooked and slammed into Henry.

"Grab the gun," I yelled.

Lucy made a dive for it.

So did I.

She got there first.

"Drop it, drop it now or this goes right through you."

I couldn't believe my ears. It was Gail. She was standing over Lucy with a pitchfork aimed at Lucy's back.

Lucy's fingers stayed wrapped around the gun.

"Lucy, I said let go and I mean it. I'll kill you if I have to."

Gail's fury splotches were a solid mass of red. She lowered the pitchfork and pressed it against Lucy. "Drop the fucking gun. Now."

Lucy unwrapped her fingers and I grabbed the gun. My endorphins finally made an appearance. I knew my leg should be hurting something awful, yet all I felt was a dull pounding.

I said, "Well, Jesus H. Christ, Gail, where did you come from and where the hell have you been?"

"In Allie's stall. I'll tell you all about it once we take care of this piece of scum."

I looked at Lucy, lying face-down on the macadam with a gun pointed toward her head and a pitchfork planted against her back.

"You know, Lucy," I said. "You might be right about fashion. Since I'm so good at it, as you graciously pointed out earlier, I think this is the time to tell you that that shade of green you're wearing is all wrong for your coloring. Especially now, your tone is a bit off. You're a Spring, and Springs should wear only warm tones. Say, for instance, orange. And guess what? It's your lucky day. That's the color of this season's prison garb."

Lucy wasn't laughing. Gail was. And so was Henry, who was walking toward us with a rope lead shank. "Let's tie her up. I've had enough of her for the night."

Henry wrapped the rope around Lucy's wrists and did some fancy Wasp boat knot he must have learned in sailing camp. Then he slipped his arm around Gail.

"You had us worried," he said.

"Us?" I said.

"What do you think I am, a robot? Yes, I was worried. Of course I was worried. She's your best friend. I know what Gail means to you."

"Next thing I know you'll be attending a séance. What is this, stretch-and-grow-night?"

Lucy tried to move and Gail pressed the pitchfork harder into her back. "God, Nattie, give the man a break, and what the hell happened to your leg?"

"Gail, where have you been, in a cave?"

"Close."

Now that Gail's color had returned to normal, I could see that she looked like she'd been through hell. Her eyes were dropped deep in her skull and she had a darker set of circles than Rocky Raccoon.

"I was a mess after Jeff told me to leave his apartment. I fell off the wagon big time. I went to the Bootpull and started downing hookers of tequila—in between calling Jeff. What really did me in was when a woman answered his phone at his desk. It was two or three in the morning and she says, 'Oh, he's busy. Very busy, if you get my drift.' I didn't know it was this piece of shit lying here."

She jabbed Lucy's back. I'd have liked her to finish the job. Instead, I said, "Easy, Gail. She's got to be in one piece to stand trial."

"Yeah, I guess you're right. Too bad. Anyway, I had a bottle in my car and kept drinking until I passed out. I woke up the next morning and started the whole thing over again. Again and again. I don't even remember driving myself to Tall Oaks. But I must have. I knew the place, because I've taken my mother there so many times. They've got a tough-love sobering-up program. No outside contact with anyone. No calls, no visits, nothing, until your head clears out. I kept sneaking to the phone and I kept getting caught."

I sidled my way next to Gail while I kept the gun pointed at

Lucy's head. I didn't know how well boat knots hold up on murderers, and I wasn't going to take any chances.

I balanced on one crutch and hugged Gail.

She started crying.

"I didn't want him dead. Even if he didn't love me, I didn't want him dead. . . . I thought it was the real thing. He's dead, Nat. . . ."

"I know, I know. It's all right. It's over now. We'll get through this. Everything's over. . . ."

"It's not for me, Nattie. I'm out on a pass only until tomorrow. I can't face anyone yet. That's why I came here after Rob closed up the barn. I hadn't seen Allie for so long, I thought I'd go crazy. I must have fallen asleep in his stall. It's not over, Nat. Nothing's over. I can't lose him, too, Nat. You know that."

I did. More than anyone, I did.

I leaned over and kissed her cheek.

"Gail," I said, "you've got yourself a great horse who's a jerk sometimes about his lead changes. What's the big deal? So you won't take him to any shows. I don't care if he never steps foot off this farm. He can stay here forever, as far as I'm concerned. What you do with him is your business, no one else's."

EPILOGUE

G ail dried out. I healed. Though it took a six-inch aluminum screw to bolt my leg back together the second time.

Henry and I wrote ourselves one hell of a blockbuster. Rack cards, television promos, even a full-page ad in *The Columbia Journalism Review*. I have to admit, the normally penurious big boys at chain central in Miami pulled out all the financial stops to promote our four-part series, "Murder on the A-Show Circuit."

To celebrate, Henry and I went to Country City USA, but we never even heard the twang of a guitar. He refused to park in the handicapped spot, even though I had a cast up to my crotch and would've had to hobble into the place on crutches. I got mad enough to tell him to take me home. Which he did. It took three days of cold stares across the newsroom before we started talking to each other again.

The Pulitzers don't come up for another few months. Already the buzz is that our series is the one to beat for local reporting.

Tony and his wife are still bouncing back and forth between marriage and separation. Though he did pay up on his bet to me. A couple of Sundays after the stories ran, he cooked the biggest, greasiest, and most delicious, southern breakfast I've ever had. We were four at the table: Tony and Sharon, and Henry and me, with Rin Tin Tin, a sleeping heap of fur on top of my feet. We would have been six at the table, but Henry sent the two little Goodes outside for making fart sounds with their mouths.

Lou and Mrs. Flock realized they were long-lost soulmates

who were Indian brothers during their last lives together. They're touring Stonehenge now and plan to spend the winter in Machu Picchu, looking for the Fourteenth Celestine prophecy.

My mother's still smoking, and crying for David.

Me? I still feel guilty about Jeff, and it hurts plenty to walk by his desk. I think about him a lot and wonder if maybe he and David are laughing up a storm somewhere. Candace reluctantly agreed to let me move to a different desk, away from the bloodstains in the carpet that no stain remover has yet to erase. I got a new desk mate, too. A young kid straight out of J school. She's a professional virgin who can't even say the word *sex* let alone do it. So much for a continuation of my Monday-morning-quarterback sessions with Jeff. Not that I'd have much to report these days.

But she's very polite to the readers and *I* use the computer whenever *I* want.

I'm still writing a Sunday fashion column and the powers that be are still saying "soon," as in soon the budget will open up so they can create a full-time feature writing job for me. As in soon we'll all be living on Mars.

Most important, Doctor Doom was wrong about my riding future. I was back in the saddle before the cast came off. As for the predicted limp, he was wrong on that score, too. Orthopods. I walk fine and other than the screw head he left sticking out beneath the skin of my ankle, you'd never know I broke my leg.

We all got through the summer somehow. Though it was hard. It was hot and sad. But it's over now, finally. Fall is the best time to ride. Cool days with just enough bite in the air. And the smells . . . a cacophony of sounds that make me giddy. I'm heading there now. I've got a date with a sweet-tempered mare. Brenda Starr.

We're going back to glory land.

ABOUT THE AUTHOR

JODY JAFFE has long experience in both the worlds of journalism and horse shows. For the past twenty-four years she has been riding and showing hunters. She spent ten years as a feature writer for *The Charlotte Observer*. She makes her home in Washington, D.C. *Horse of a Different Killer* is her first novel.